THE LIFE WE MAKE

Caroline Bath lives with her partner in West Yorkshire, near her son and grandchildren. She has a teaching and research background in early childhood education and also writes poetry. *The Life We Make* is her first novel.

The Life We Make

A NOVEL *by*
Caroline Bath

VP

Valley Press

First published in 2023 by Valley Press
Woodend, The Crescent, Scarborough, UK, YO11 2PW
www.valleypressuk.com

ISBN 978-1-915606-27-3
Cat. no. VP0228

Copyright © Caroline Bath 2023

The right of Caroline Bath to be identified as the
author of this work has been asserted in accordance with
the Copyright, Designs and Patents Act 1988.

All rights reserved. No part of this publication may be
reproduced, stored in or introduced into a retrieval system,
or transmitted in any form, by any means (electronic,
mechanical, photocopying, recording or otherwise) without
prior written permission from the rights holders.

A CIP record for this book is available from the British Library.

Cover and text design by Jamie McGarry.

Printed and bound in Great Britain by
Imprint Digital, Upton Pyne, Exeter.

For the next generation: Frazer, Bobby and Layla

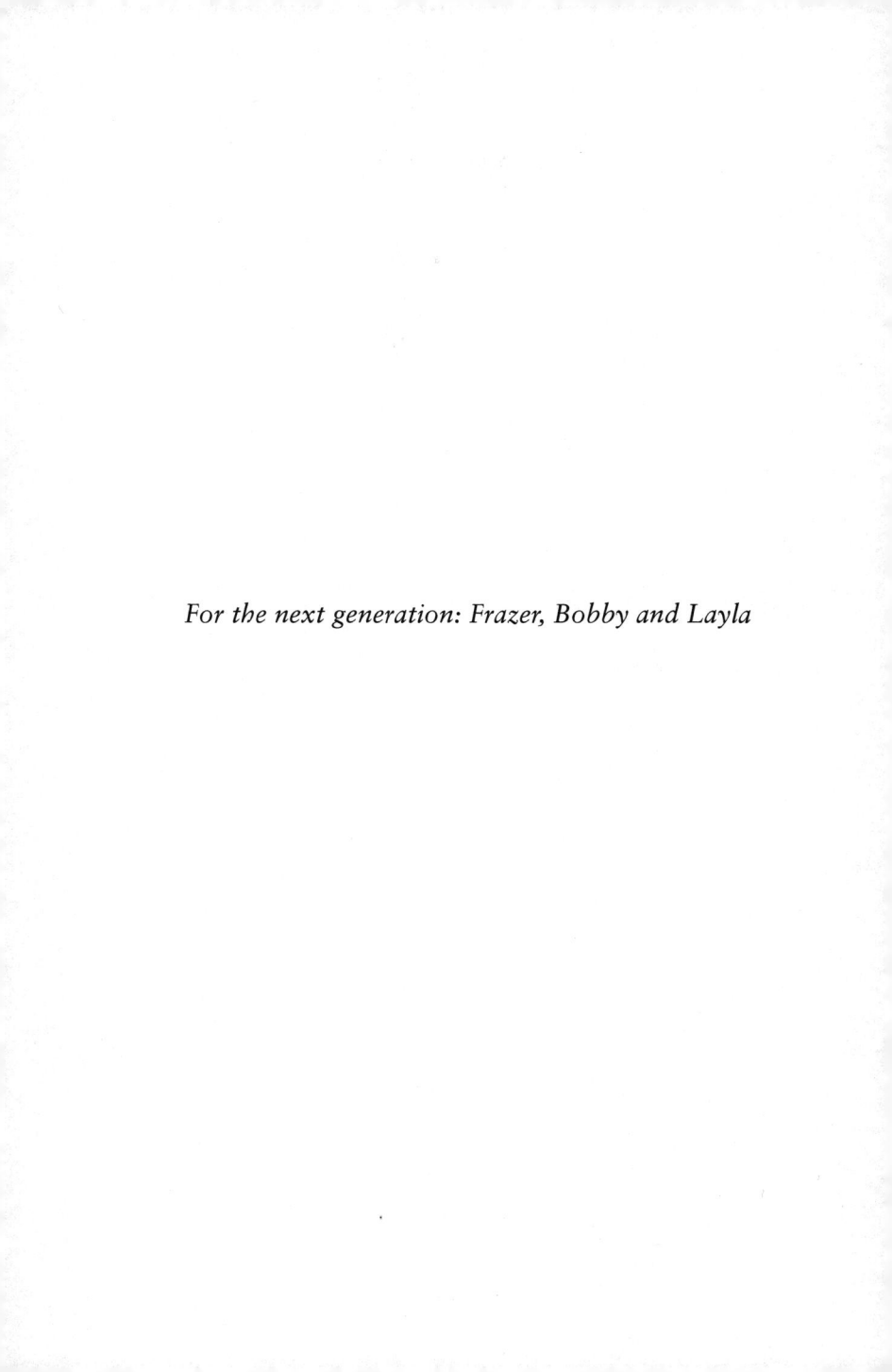

PART ONE

Your absence has gone through me
Like thread through a needle.
Everything I do is stitched with its colour.

W.S. Merwin, 'Separation'

Prologue: December 1931

EVA

Whenever I feel worried like this, I make a cave with my covers and stay there for a few minutes. The air is warm, sounds are muffled, and the dark keeps me safe. People don't realise that nine-year-olds get worried, but I've been worried for as long as I can remember – and I remember a lot – not quite being a baby, but I remember being small and seeing grown-up legs coming and going, then, suddenly, strange faces looming at me when I was picked up. It was scary at first, but Daddy was there, holding me and I knew his face. It had creases going in different directions which gathered around his wide mouth when he smiled at me. Most of his front teeth were white, but I could always see a blackened tooth at the back when he opened his mouth, pretending that he was surprised to see me. *Bunny, where have you been hiding?* he would say, his whole face a smile, and his mouth open – I always giggled which made him clutch me tighter. Then it was good to see faces, not legs – and giggling at the right time meant that other faces crowded in behind his, and I would bathe in a sea of smiles. I could bring happiness to the world, so long as he was there to lift me up.

I'm too big for him to pick me up now, he tells me, but at least he's here again. There have been times when he wasn't here, and Mummy wouldn't say his name. Helen would tell me that he was coming back when his job finished, so I learnt to wait. Then, after I waited, he would come back and make me happy again, and I'd go with him to buy cigarettes, as if he'd never been away. Mummy was furious, but I was relieved that he'd found us because I wasn't sure that he knew where we lived after we left the flat with the hiss of the sea. I wondered if I'd made up that place, but when he came back, he told me about it, and it became real again – as he did. His face had a few more creases and his hair started further back than I expected, but his teeth were the same.

When Daddy came back that last time, that was when I started to grow fast, and my worries got bigger. Everyone kept saying how much I'd grown, which was embarrassing. So I would sink into my knees and avoid people's eyes – at least the eyes of the people I didn't want to meet which was, at that point, most people. Now, I'm better at looking them in the eye. He taught me that people back off if you look straight back at them. It doesn't make sense, but he was right – you look up, and they leave you alone. It's like magic.

This evening, Mummy is downstairs, probably sewing because that's what she always does, unless she's cooking or shopping. Helen is at the church youth group. When she went out, the sky was closing in and Mummy told her to button up her coat and make sure that she didn't walk back on her own. Before she went, Helen handed me a book and told me I'd like it. It was really a boy's book which was why she thought I'd like it. *Let Mummy get on with her jobs and tell me about it when I get home*, she said, and I nodded and brought it up here to read, in the warmth of my bed.

That was over an hour ago. At first, the words joined up and made sentences. I could see the boy in the story – his shorts and socks and jersey with its ragged sleeves – but then I was just staring at the words and the boy, Tom he's called, was getting thinner and paler, so I put down the book and got under the covers and he faded away.

I know what's happening in real life – Daddy should be home by now and I can't read because I'm waiting. Instead of Tom, I'm seeing *him*. Perhaps he's in The Buck, but if he doesn't set off across the common soon, Mummy won't speak to him, and he'll smile at me with his teeth slightly bared which means that he's worried.

Last time I looked out from under the covers, my little bedside clock said it was eight o'clock which means it won't be long before Helen is back. He's always back before her so if I listen carefully, I might hear Mummy say his name – *Art* – then I'll know, just from the tone of her voice, if he's in trouble. She's the one to fear, not him.

I swing my legs off the bed and my feet hit the icy lino. I count to five, like Helen taught me to do when it's cold, then run through all the places he might be. Why is he so difficult to keep track of? I pull on my slippers and put my dressing gown on over my clothes – Mummy can make a fuss if she wants, but I'm going to ask her where he is.

The stairs creak in the usual places as I head downstairs. The radio is playing softly in the sitting room – she's listening to the Light Programme. I open the door, half hoping that Daddy has crept in without me hearing. Her needle glints in the firelight. The coal smoke makes my nose itch.

'Yes, Eva? I thought you might be getting ready for bed by now. Why aren't you in your pyjamas?' She sounds funny. It's like I've done something wrong but it's not that.

'Daddy's a bit late tonight,' I say, but she doesn't even look up. 'Will he be back soon?' The words come out in a rush.

She puts her sewing down and looks at me. There's pink around her eyes. 'That's not for you to wonder about. It's bed you should be thinking about.' Her mouth is tight – she won't tell me anything, when she's like this, so I turn to go back upstairs and wait. My stomach is hurting, and I'm starting to feel sick. 'Are you all right, Eva?' Her voice is wavery, but she carries on. 'Helen will be back soon, and she will come and say goodnight'. I look at her and want to say, *Why Helen? Why not Daddy?* I knead my stomach with my fist, so she can't see. She never talks when he goes missing – silence is a bad sign.

There's a rush of cold air on the stairs as I climb back up to my bedroom. I change into my pyjamas, numb to the cold. The windows are beginning to frost over, so I scrape off a patch with my fingernails to see if I can spy anyone outside. Straight away, there's Helen's dark blue mac, followed by the sound of the back door. Then she appears under the window again and hands something over the gate, but I can't see who's on the other side. The back door goes once more, and I hear her footsteps on the kitchen tiles. She's humming 'Good King Wenceslas' and I can tell from the clunk of the door handle that she's going into the sitting room. Her voice mingles with Mummy's – there's no sharp words like when Daddy comes back late. Everything is calm, but I want an argument and to know he's safe.

I'm not always scared when he's late. Sometimes I get into bed, pick up whichever book is on my bedside table and read it until I fall asleep. Then, when he finally gets in and peeks in at me, I half wake, as a crack of light falls across my bed, and his face shines in the doorway. I'm shaking now. If only Helen would look in on me and tell me what's happening and who was on the other side of the gate. Was it him? But if so, why hasn't he come inside with her? I slump into bed and pull the covers over my head – then everything goes from grey to black then stops.

*

'Eva, what's the matter? Are you all right?' It's Helen's voice. 'Did you make yourself faint? We mustn't worry Mummy.' I roll back the covers, see her outline against the white ceiling. The bedside table comes into focus, and I realise I'm still in bed. I look over to the window and see the patch I scraped off.

'Is Daddy back?' I say. My head throbs.

'Don't worry about him,' Helen says. She turns away and shuts the door. I want to believe her – that he's all right, I really do. Her kind, round face is pink from the frosty walk home. But it's always Mummy she's worried about, and *she's* always fine. She manages things. It's Daddy who needs help.

'I'm fine. Don't tell Mummy I had another funny turn, will you? I'm as right as rain now.'

'Good girl. How was the book, by the way?' Helen knows I'm pretending.

'I haven't read much of it yet. I'm saving it for when Daddy's back.'

'Can I get you a glass of water for that head?' her mouth twitches – I've crossed a line.

'I'll be fine. It was just that I was shaking. I don't know why…' She has her concerned look but I'm pretending. I *do* know why I was shaking. I always know when big things are going to happen. I just do.

'I'm overexcited.' She smiles and goes back downstairs. I hug my knees and rock, head down. I forgot to ask her who was on the other side of the gate.

Chapter One

ARTHUR

He'd wanted to go with his family at first, but also wanted to stay and carry on with the job he was doing very well at, thank you very much. It was an impossible decision to make, so he'd not made it – and now they were leaving without him. He felt a mixture of guilt and fear that they'd have to manage without him – after all, he was the eldest. But *he'd* have to manage without them and that didn't seem right, either. Was the chance of a new life in Canada worth it?

'Will you come to Liverpool to see us off, Art?' Dennis interrupted his inner turmoil.

'I might come with you all the way, Den.' He pushed back the kitchen chair and got up.

It was two days till they set sail, and too late for Arthur to go with them – he knew that. Over to his left, the tickets for the ship were clamped to the dresser under a glass paperweight. His father had gone to London to buy them, which was already further than anyone they knew had ever been. His mother and sister were upstairs packing but he didn't have anything pressing to do, so he grabbed his coat and slammed the door behind him. He needed to walk, put one foot in front of the other and circle his territory. These streets in Caversham had been there all his life. He knew every crooked paving stone, every weed poking up by the walls on Queens Road. He could look into anyone's parlour and know their names. He waved at Annie Orchard, crouching to light the fire in number twenty-two.

Canada. It sounded good, but had his parents thought carefully about it enough? And why did they have to take his brothers and sister with them as well? *What do you know about farming and prairies?* he'd levelled at Harold, whose bright idea it had been.

I know enough, Harold had said. Too confident. Why did his parents always listen to *him*?

The tackety noise of his hobnails on the pavestones calmed him. He was walking in the direction of Christchurch Meadows where he would be able to think clearly. He headed for the streetlamps around the edge of the green expanse. The river moaned in the distance, and he could see slivers of light reflecting on its surface. He inhaled the moist river air and felt better. The path was covered with a coating of frost. It didn't feel as though spring was around the corner.

He forced himself to think about what was now inevitable. His parents and siblings were heading for a place called Halifax and would be at sea for at least ten days. His mother had been comforted by the name of their destination. *My aunt's second cousin went to Halifax,* she'd said over Sunday dinner. *This is a different Halifax,* Arthur had reminded her, frustrated by her attempt at cheerfulness. Why was it that only he could see the dangers ahead? She accepted that he wasn't going with them but kept going on about him joining them later – *You'll come and visit next summer, and maybe then…* she'd said. But his grocery job suited him – and it was here, not there. He liked paved streets, he even liked rain – and he didn't like snow. So why would he head for a country that had bears and mountains, and where people didn't see grass for half the year? It was too risky altogether. But as much as he didn't want to go, he couldn't imagine life without them. Dennis was a good lad and even Harold made Arthur laugh sometimes.

He loved the muddle in the kitchen on late afternoons after work and his sister showing him her new dresses. It was ridiculous that they were prepared to go hundreds of miles with only vague offers of work. His father said they had nothing to lose – except him, Arthur could have said – but why on earth did his mother have to agree to it so easily?

He did a loop around the shadowy paths of the Meadows and was nearly at the riverside. Closer to, the water bellowed back at him and made him think of the expanse of sea that would soon be between him and his parents. His pace quickened as the wasted attempts to get his parents to change their minds ran through his mind. *Let Harold and Dennis go ahead while you and Mother stay here,* he'd said, as a last-ditch attempt to stop his father from taking all his money out of the bank and heading off for London. But his father had just looked through him and said it'd been decided.

Arthur hunched his shoulders against the cold and turned homewards. Despite what he'd said to Dennis, he was staying here in Caversham. Sometimes life was like that – no middle ground – so you had to face things head on. He walked briskly back up the road. The lighted squares of the front windows sharpened up ahead as he slowed his pace for a minute and made sure that his breathing was under control. They were all pulling away from him, but he had two more days as part of the family, so he'd better try and make the most of it.

*

By the end of the next day, Arthur was surrounded by boxes. He squeezed his things into two carpet bags and watched as his brothers hauled the huge trunk down the stairs. The house had been let out to clear all his father's outstanding debts, including, most recently, the cost of buying the five tickets. *You do see that, son, don't you?* his father had said. *Anyway, you're too young to live here on your own so it's lucky you've got an uncle and aunt to board with. Then, who knows? Perhaps a wife and house of your own.* His father was never normally this cheery and Arthur wanted back the glum man who had disappeared.

He was determined to stay with his family right until the sea parted them from him. He squeezed into the carriage as they made their way north, then heaved the trunk off the train and onto the crowded platform at Liverpool Lime Street. Then it was onto a rattling tram bound for the docks. Once there, the shipping office told them that the tides were wrong and that they would have to board a ferry to a place called Birkenhead where their ship was moored. Crowds of other passengers were pushing towards the boat so Arthur said he'd stay on the dock to wave them off, but as his mother scrambled onto the ferry, their trunk fell over, and she had to strain to get it upright, so couldn't wave back. He tried to see where Harold was to help her out, but he'd disappeared.

Mesmerised by muddy spume, Arthur was overwhelmed with anger and panic. His mother had melted into the throng of passengers and was beyond his reach; his father had evaporated; his siblings were lost in the crowd. It had all happened so fast – it was as if he'd lost a limb. He stood for a while then limped off to find the wretched hotel room his father had said was *his treat*. The Liverpool streets were confusingly similar, and he felt small and fragile. When he found the hotel, his room looked out onto a shabby side street. He sat on the bed and shivered, counting the hours until he could head home. It was the eleventh of February 1911; he was seventeen; his family had deserted him, and his life was wafer-thin.

Chapter Two

Late May had white clouds of blossom, and by early June the days were baking hot. It was five months since his parents and siblings had departed and Arthur was still getting used to his new situation. Sometimes he awoke and wondered why it was so quiet. Then he remembered and felt bereft all over again. The job helped and Mr Wood was always giving him new responsibilities – the latest was doing deliveries. On the first Wednesday in June, he stood on the kerb outside the shop and took a deep breath of fragranced air, then loaded a large box into the delivery bicycle basket. He was heading for a new customer at the milliner's shop on Prospect Street. As he swung his leg over the crossbar and set off, the blood rushed to his head. It was good to be outside.

He leant his bicycle against the milliner's shop front and took a minute to admire the colourful window display. Then he rolled up his sleeves, heaved up the box, and made his way to the elaborate door. The bell tinkled as he pushed it open. Inside was more fine again, with an elaborate dark polished wood counter and heavily decorated walls.

'Would you mind waiting a minute?' said a young lady from behind the counter. She was showing samples of patterned fabrics to a tall lady. He could only see the back of the customer but guessed from her dress that she was from one of the big houses – too grand to be one of his customers. The assistant was smoothing out different strips on the counter and stroking them with her long fingers. He eased the heavy box down by the far wall and stood waiting, staring at the lavish furnishings.

'No, not there!' The young lady appeared from behind the counter. Her skirts were gathered into the narrowest waist that he had ever seen, sweeping around her stately yet petite figure. She pointed to a spot further along the wall. He pushed the box along as directed.

'I'll be off then, Miss.' He tipped his cap and tripped over a chair behind him as he turned to go.

'If you could wait a minute, Mrs Buttershaw will be down to settle up with you.' She went back behind the counter, and he could see that she was smiling.

He waited, entranced by the small white teeth behind the smile. She picked up the samples again. It was refreshing to see an assistant like him who seemed to know her job. He watched her carefully, hoping she didn't notice. After a few minutes, footsteps descended the stairs behind him, and a large lady appeared, blocking his view. He backed further into the wall.

'I'll have the same order next week, if you please,' she said. 'Tell Miss Lyford when you'll be calling.' She counted out some notes into his hand, and he tucked them into the pocket of his apron, as she started back up the steps.

The customer had gone, and the young lady was polishing the counter. He glanced at her. Strands of curls framed her perfectly symmetrical face. She was a picture.

'Some customers are hard to please, don't you find?' her voice rang out.

Arthur jumped, surprised that she was addressing him. 'You must be Miss Lyford.' He doffed his cap and she laughed. 'Mrs Buttershaw says to tell you when I'll be calling by.'

'And when would that be?' Her voice thrilled him

with its playfulness. They were behaving like schoolchildren, but it was fun.

'Same time, if that suits, but always Wednesday.' He had to stop himself from grinning directly at her. She mustn't think he was being forward.

'I'm forgetting my manners. I'm Agnes.' She offered him her hand. 'But,' she paused and frowned at him, '*Please* don't call me Aggie.' He shook her hand and felt a shock of delight at its warmth.

'I'm Arthur, but don't call me Art!' She laughed so he searched for something else to say. 'Your window displays are marvellous. I don't suppose that's anything to do with you, is it?'

'Well, yes, actually – it is. Most people don't know a good display when they see one – even the ladies on Park Avenue in Caversham.'

Encouraged, he carried on. 'The hats are very cleverly tilted, and the colour combinations work well too.' He noticed that she also tilted her head as he spoke. 'You might be surprised to know that cans and packets need to be displayed carefully too. Some customers say they notice it, so maybe your customers *do* like your displays but just don't say.' He was pleased with the impression he was making.

Her face lit up and her pale blue eyes widened in pleasure. 'I hope you're right. In fact, you're the first person to say *anything*. Mrs Buttershaw always says when I'm doing something wrong…' She looked down, then stared right up into his eyes. 'It really is very kind of you.'

Arthur's day seemed lighter and airier – she was not only beautiful but also seemed to like him.

The rest of the week dragged. He had the weekend to get through and two whole days before he could deliver groceries to the milliners again. When Wednesday finally came around, she turned her gaze on him again and looked even prettier than he'd remembered. He searched his mind for anything shop-related that he thought would interest her. She seemed to really *listen* to him, and they talked for ages before he realised he had to get back to help Mr Wood. From then on, Wednesdays always boosted his spirits.

*

Even though Arthur made the most of his job, he hated lodging at his uncle's house. His uncle was expecting payment that Arthur's father hadn't promised, and, as if to remind him, his aunt sniffed loudly whenever he came into the parlour. Arthur tried bringing home groceries to placate her, but he still had to share a room with a cousin half his age. Occasionally, he would take a long route to work and walk past his old house on Queens Street to catch a glimpse of the new family there, but it only deepened his feelings of loneliness, so he started to avoid it. Only the thought of meeting Agnes cheered him up.

His employer, Mr Wood, was a steady man with a Yorkshire accent who was well liked by his customers. He didn't pester them with bills and slipped in extra items when he saw people struggling to make ends meet. He liked Arthur's flair for mental arithmetic and reliability. In turn, Arthur had a deep respect for him. Four weeks after first meeting Agnes, as Mr Wood was about to leave, he braced himself to speak to him.

He'd thought long and hard about what to say all day. 'Since my parents left, I haven't quite been myself. I'm grateful to you for my job and all your help, but I need somewhere else to stay, somewhere where I'm not in the way ... and I wondered ... I don't suppose that there's room over the shop with you and Mrs Wood?'

Mr Wood's face creased with sympathy. 'Well, Art. It might be possible. I can see that things haven't worked out so well with you, what with – well, you being left on your own. Let me ask Mrs Wood when I get home.'

Arthur's request worked and a spare room was made available to him the next day. *Don't be eating us out of house, home and shop, mind*, Mr Wood said when he told Arthur the good news. It was a much-repeated joke of his. Arthur went straight back to his uncle's, trimmed down his belongings to one carpet bag and was installed in the new room in time for supper. Mrs Wood was a good cook like his mother, and kind, too, so she made sure that he had an extra-large helping of stew, and then showed him to his room. He felt better straight away. The best thing about his new lodgings was that he was above his work – and work was familiar. He knew where every can and packet should go, and understood which shelves had extra capacity and which had crooked niches for displaying items. He could make a shelf full of groceries sell itself. Work was now his home, and home his work – it suited him well.

Feeling more settled and buoyed up by his flirtation with Agnes, he started to flatter the female customers. *You'll be a good cook, then, Mrs Hall, I know my mother used to say that your cakes were the pride of the neighbourhood*. Talking like this during the day also made his mother feel closer, even though in the evenings, it was still hard not to let worries about her and the others crowd his thoughts. He lay on his bed and smoked one cigarette after another, always inhaling slowly and evenly, marking time until he was back in the shop again. The main thing that lightened his mood was seeing Agnes, but he was scared of asking her to walk out with him in case she said no, and he decided he'd rather see just a little of her than lose her altogether.

Mr Wood had noticed Arthur's interest in the female customers. 'The thing is, Art, of course the ladies like it that you're noticing them, but they don't always want to hear about your mother. I'm not even sure anyone round here knew her that well...' Arthur opened his mouth to say something, but Mr Wood carried on. 'Stop me if I'm wrong, but Mrs Wood and I think that perhaps you're still missing them all. Do you know how they're getting on?'

Arthur felt his throat tighten and coughed so that he wouldn't cry. He took a deep breath. 'I don't think things have worked out as they expected. That's all I know.' He knew a bit more than that from his mother's last letter but couldn't trust himself to stay composed in the face of such kindness and concern.

'Well, lad. I'll help you in any way I can – you've got a lot to offer the grocery business. But I can see it's difficult for you. I know what it's like to miss family, too.' Mr Wood had several brothers and sisters back in Yorkshire but also several who owned shops nearby.

Arthur couldn't see how it was the same for him, but it was kind of him to say so. 'Thank you, sir. I'm very grateful to you and Mrs Wood.'

'Aye, lad, and we like having you here. A bit like a son to us.'

At that, Arthur had to make an excuse to leave quickly as his eyes were filling up. He thought he heard Mr Wood's voice wobble, too.

Later that day, in the storeroom and well out of Mr Wood's gaze, he got out the latest letter from his mother and re-read it. They had changed their plans and not bought land. Instead, Harold was working on a farm with board, but no wage, and his father was trying to get work on the new railroad. The family had crossed Canada and were now in a place called Winnipeg, but from what he could gather, they weren't much better off than they had been in Caversham. Reading between the lines, they were a lot worse off. There was little satisfaction in feeling he'd been right about Canada. His eyes scanned the neat sloping handwriting one more time as his fury at Harold reignited. A feeling of profound loneliness hit him, as he gripped the letter and sat down on a stool. He had nothing left to lose – next Wednesday, he would ask Agnes to walk out with him.

*

He needn't have worried. Agnes said a clear yes, and for the next few weeks, he met her after work for a walk in the park. She had told him about her two sisters and one brother which inversely matched his two brothers and one sister. She was the youngest, whilst he was the eldest, so there was a symmetry which pleased him. She seemed to like him, and he more than liked her and couldn't help but smile at the way she bit her lip when she listened to him.

Walking out with Agnes changed Arthur's outlook on his life. Late at night, when he imagined her lying alone, just like he was, the anticipation of seeing her again propelled him into the next day. He now spent the evenings with Mr and Mrs Wood talking about how *his young milliner's assistant* was doing. Mrs Wood approved of Agnes and gave him tips about the sort of things that she would enjoy talking about. With her help, he soon became more successful at conversing and felt more relaxed when he walked beside Agnes and asked about her day at work. His confidence increased even more when, after the fourth week of walking out with her, she suggested that he meet her family.

Her home was on the other side of Caversham. It was

comfortable but respectable, and strikingly similar to his own family home. Mr Lyford was welcoming but simply couldn't believe that a whole family would leave a son behind. 'What, all of them? They *all* went and left you behind?'

His bluntness made Arthur feel uncomfortable. He told him what a fair employer Mr Wood was, and how, because of his job, his family had had to go without him. He even said that Canada was a 'land of opportunity' for his younger brothers.

Mr Lyford was having none of it. 'I wouldn't do that to my eldest, and she's married and has a husband of her own. It's criminal. I take my hat off to you, I really do. It can't have been easy.' Arthur clamped his mouth shut. He wasn't sure if he felt proud, sad, embarrassed or angry. All he did know was that his situation now singled him out for pity.

Mr Lyford carried on talking. 'Anyway, Aggie likes you, so that's good enough for me. Believe me, she's not an easy young lady to please, that one.' He smiled. Agnes was out of the room, helping her mother with the tea tray. 'Perhaps in time, there might be more to this "friendship", then?'

Arthur was impelled to nod. At last, he'd stopped talking about Arthur's family and got onto his own. 'I hope so, sir. I'm very fond of Agnes.'

'Oh, so she's got you calling her "Agnes", has she?' Mr Lyford laughed. 'Don't fall for her airs and graces. She can be impetuous and difficult when she wants to be.'

Arthur tried to laugh back, as if he knew exactly what Mr Lyford meant, but he hadn't seen that side of Agnes. Indeed, he couldn't imagine it, but he supposed that she might get frustrated by her father at times. He remembered his sister Maudie slamming the door in his father's face once.

'Ah, here she is – the girl in question!' Mr Lyford turned as Agnes came through the door with a loaded tray.

'I hope you've not been rude about me to Arthur. He doesn't understand families,' Agnes said, smiling at Arthur as she placed the tray on the table.

'Don't you worry, my girl. This one is a gentleman. He wouldn't listen to me.' Mr Lyford shook his head, playfully.

Arthur was glad that Mr Lyford approved of him but Agnes's words about families cut him to the quick. He made a mental note to say more to her about his brothers and sister. But whatever he said to her, they were gone, and Agnes's two sisters and a brother – Lou, Kate and Alfie – were here, and, in time, they could become family to him. As he sipped the tea from the cup Agnes handed him, he reasoned, that if he couldn't go back, he might as well go forward. He would ask her to marry him – not straight away but very, very soon.

That evening, he wrote to his mother and told her about the Lyford family. He described the hats in Agnes's window display and passed on her tips about double looping thread. Leaning forward with pride pulsing through him, he promised his mother that, one day, she would wear a hat that Agnes had made. When he sealed the envelope, he closed his eyes and imagined himself on the deck of an enormous boat with Agnes on one side and a large oval hat box on the other.

Chapter Three

The golden haze of autumn sun mixed with a slight chill gave everything in the Meadows a keen edge. Agnes was talking, but the relentless hum of the river in the background kept taking Arthur back to eighteen months ago when he'd charged round here alone in the dark, half-mad with worry about what to do – whether to go with his family or stay. If he *had* gone with them, he wouldn't be a few days away from marrying the young lady on his arm. Indeed, he would never have met her. It was a sobering thought.

'What did your mother think of the invitation?' She tugged at his arm impatiently. 'Are you listening to me?'

'Yes. She liked it, of course.'

'It's going to be odd without them at the wedding. Odder still that I've never even met them.' He had no answer. He was triumphant when she'd accepted his proposal, one Sunday afternoon in June. The way she'd rushed off to tell her sister the news had released a lid on his emotions, and he'd wanted to tell her everything that had troubled him in the last year. At last, there was someone who was going to stick around. He hadn't thought much about the next steps, but she was quick to design a wedding invitation, seeking out the best stationer and impressing upon him all the design skills she'd learnt from millinery. The cover had two gold embossed *A*'s and inside their full names sat on opposite sides of the page with a fine silver arrow shot between the *f* and the *o* of *Lyford*.

He thought the invitation was beautiful but secretly wondered if his mother would find the decoration fussy. Might she also feel hurt that he was building a life of his own, rather than joining them in Canada? When her reply finally arrived, it confirmed only what he already knew: *Your father and I are sad not to be at your wedding, but we know you understand our situation.* He threw the letter down in frustration – and what exactly *was* their situation? Didn't she realise he worried about how they would make a living out there? He felt let down that his parents wouldn't be at his wedding but was determined not to let Agnes know that his family were struggling.

'She loved the engagement photo you sent her. I think her words were *she's a beauty*,' he placated her – her quest for the perfect wedding had made her irritable lately. He knew his side of the church would be empty compared to hers but there was nothing he could do about it – his uncle and aunt had snubbed him since he'd moved out, so they weren't coming. Thankfully, Mr and Mrs Wood would be there, and kept saying how much they were looking forward to it.

'Arthur! I'm sure your mother didn't say that,' Agnes tugged at his arm again and smiled, much to his relief. 'Really, I'm just an ordinary girl, even if I do like nice things. It's important to have nice things around you, don't you think?'

'Yes,' Arthur replied without thinking. A young man was staring at her, as they walked alongside the river. Other men should keep their eyes to themselves, he thought, especially as she was clearly a respectable woman.

'You agree, then? That we won't put up with second best?' she persisted.

'You shall have what your heart desires, madam.' His mock formality made her smile again. The young man was behind them now, and Agnes all his own again. That's the way he would keep it. She'd come into his life when he was deserted – there was no way he'd let her go. If it took nice things to keep her, then nice things she would have.

The Meadows were behind them, as they passed terraced houses, making their way back to her home.

'Last minute things,' she said, sounding animated. They were now in sight of the end of her street. 'Elsie and Maude have made a fuss about coming, but I'm running out of space on my side. Do you think they could sit with Mrs Buttershaw on your side? It'd even things up a bit.' He winced at the name Maude – his sister's, who was working night and day as a milkmaid.

'Yes, the more the merrier on my side ... I can't wait to see the dress,' he remembered to add. Agnes had been furious when he'd quibbled over the cost, but now she squeezed his arm.

'Well, we're nearly there – man and wife!' She released her arm from his as they approached her front door, then turned to him. 'Who would have thought that I'd become Mrs Borton on the tenth of September 1912!' He frowned in confusion. 'Mrs *Agnes* Borton, that is,' she clarified.

'Ah, that'll take some getting used to.' He felt unsettled again – his mother, as well as his sister, crowded back into Arthur's thoughts.

'Make sure you're there on time, won't you?' There was a catch in her voice and just for the slightest moment, he forgot what she was referring to. Then she grabbed his arm again and laughed.

'Oh, yes. I'll be there,' he said, feeling much better to see her so happy. 'You can rely on me.' However many seats were unfilled at his wedding, Agnes Lyford was going to be his wife.

*

'Living with my family gives us no privacy – I need a household.' Agnes hung her head. They were on their own in the Lyford's parlour, sitting at either end of a horsehair sofa that had seen better days. Their wedding photo beamed down from the sideboard – Agnes frequently examined it and commented on the way the detail on her lacy sleeves and gown had reflected the autumn light. The day had been magnificent, Arthur thought. Even his parents' absence hadn't spoiled things and here he was living with her family, now his own, he dared to think. Today, all the siblings were at home for Agnes's mother's birthday, so the house was full of activity.

'Household' was a grand word for home, but he loved how, with her eye for detail, she made every room she inhabited into a palace. Even a vase placed, just so, by her made an ordinary table seem grand.

'We knew we'd have to wait a bit for our own place. But it'll be worth it – being married is the main thing for now.' Arthur folded his arms over his chest.

'It is, and it *is* wonderful, but I'm a married woman and don't expect to share a privy with my sister and brother. It's a miracle they're not sitting here with us right now!' Agnes sighed with a theatrical force. Arthur thought she even looked pretty when she was annoyed.

'Mr Wood said he would only help us if we were prepared to move, so of course I said it was impossible.' He waited for another loud sigh from Agnes.

'What do you mean he would "help us"? Help us how?' she said, leaning forward.

'I told him I couldn't move to another shop, even if it did mean we would get a flat to ourselves.' Arthur wasn't sure why he suddenly felt awkward.

'Why on earth did you say that?' she grabbed his hand.

'Because it'd be a long way from Caversham and your parents.' He moved sideways on the sofa as if to make his point. Agnes stared at him with eyes widened.

'Whereabouts? Arthur, for goodness sake, I can't believe you haven't mentioned this before now! The intensity of her stare made him feel unsure about everything. Why was she being like this over something that he'd already dealt with?

'It was West Ealing. Mr Wood's brother, Stanley, told him that we could have the flat above his shop if I agreed to manage things for him...' His voice petered out.

'And what's this flat like?' Her voice was rising higher and higher. Her stare still fixed on him.

'Small, and it'd be such a long way to go – '

'Nonsense. Lou's not far from there and it can't be any smaller than our room here! This could be the new start we need – *and* a step up from you being a delivery boy! Why didn't you tell me?'

'I – '

A crashing sound like breaking glass rang out from the direction of the kitchen and Agnes sprang up.

'You see – it's impossible here!' She rushed out past him. Arthur stayed sitting for a moment. He'd thought she was pleased that he wanted to live with her family. Domestic clatter only added to the intimacy, as far as he was concerned. He liked living with the Lyfords and they seemed to like him. Plus, he wasn't just a delivery boy. He followed her into the kitchen where Lou was bent down, picking up shards of blue and green glass off the kitchen floor. Her husband worked in a glassworks, a few miles north of West Ealing, which meant that every possible shape, size and colour of glass container decorated the Lyford's kitchen. A knock to the dresser often sent one flying. Agnes had the broom in her hands and was sweeping when he arrived.

'Lou – tell Arthur about West Ealing. It's nice, isn't it?' she said, looking directly at him.

'But this is your home,' Arthur protested, 'I honestly didn't think you'd want to leave.'

Lou stood up. 'Mind where you stand, Arthur. Eddie knocked these off and it's a real mess. What on earth are you arguing about and what has West Ealing got to do with anything?'

'I'm sorry but it's so exciting – we're going to live near you and Fred, and I'll have a flat of my own. Arthur's got a new job!'

'Well, that's marvellous, Ag. Tell me all about it.'

Arthur leant against the open door as they searched for stray shards and talked. Agnes was like a force of nature when she decided something, and it made him feel uneasy. His mother had always done what his father told her – rightly or wrongly it was the way of things – but Agnes had turned marriage on its head and seemed to want to tell *him* what to do. Now she was talking to Lou about whether they should have the blue or red settee in their future flat! He couldn't stop Agnes when she was like this, but it made him feel useless. He hadn't even agreed to the move! His heart was racing, and he felt a kernel of annoyance – he would have to find a way to stop her deciding everything in the future.

'See, Arthur? I know you like it when I decide things!' Agnes said as she tipped the last of the glass shards into the bin. He nodded, tight-lipped. Next time, he told himself, I will keep things to myself.

By the end of the following week, Mr Wood had made the necessary arrangements. The new shop was a bit bigger, but Arthur was getting paid quite a bit less because of the flat they going to live in. It bothered him, but he could see that it was fair – and he was going to be a 'manager' after all. Agnes was so excited, he had to admit that it made the move seem easy. A few bits of furniture and heavier personal items would be sent on later in Mr Wood's trap, so they only had their immediate clothes to take with them.

In the last week of November, they were ready to say their goodbyes. Arthur was dreading this moment with Mr and Mrs Wood, but they didn't seem too upset to see him go.

'She's a lovely girl, Arthur. You do what you can to make her happy. And call us Ernest and Ida from now on,' Mr Wood said, as they waved them off. Arthur shook his hand vigorously and mumbled his thanks as they boarded the bus into Reading. He was scared of saying any more, in case he started to cry. He grabbed some bags, so he wouldn't catch Mrs Wood's eye.

Once they were on the train going towards London, Arthur counted ten stations, including a change to another line, before they got off at Ealing Broadway. It's a long way from Caversham, he thought, as they alighted, but Agnes still looked happy. She would have her household so maybe she would settle down and be a little less forceful. Marriage involves some compromise, he told himself. He was sure his mother had once said something like that. He would try and bear that in mind.

*

The shop was freezing when he first stepped inside, and the piles of dust in the corners suggested neglect. He released the shutters to let in some light and then ran his finger over one of the shelves – not just dusty but dirty. Still, that could be fixed, Arthur told himself. There had been several managers before him which might explain why things were as they were, and the shelves badly stocked. He reasoned that no one had taken proper charge of things, so he steeled himself to change things for the better.

The younger Mr Wood met him on the first morning and explained the basics. 'The stockroom is small, so we have to run a tight ship.' Arthur bit his tongue. It looked anything but a tight ship to him. 'I order and pay for what we need, so the takings go directly to me. Your job is to keep the customers happy, and I'll call in at the end of every week. I'm sure you'll get the hang of things quickly, from what Ernest tells me.' Arthur nodded. This Mr Wood had none of the obvious warmth of his elder brother and clearly didn't expect to be called 'Stanley'. But at least he seemed to have a good opinion of him.

Arthur quickly learnt the layout of the new shop but couldn't understand why all the cans were stacked down one long wall. It made everything seem lopsided, so he moved a few of them onto the shelf along the opposite wall – it was a start, he thought. On the second day, a young assistant called Jack showed up for a couple of hours to do some lifting and carrying. He set about shifting sacks from the storeroom without asking for instruction and worked quickly and quietly, but apart from him, Arthur was on his own. The customers seemed to hardly notice his presence – they weren't regulars in the same way the customers were in the Caversham shop. After Jack had left and Arthur had had several churlish encounters with customers, he wondered if even Canada might feel less alien. At least he would *know* that he was in a foreign country then.

'The stock is low,' he muttered to Agnes one Sunday evening in early December.

'He's well dressed for a shopkeeper, though,' she said, as she straightened a cushion.

Arthur felt frustrated – she clearly didn't understand what he was up against. 'Perhaps he should take as much interest in his business as he does in his clothes, then. *This* Mr Wood only seems interested in book-keeping and invoices. He doesn't seem to care about the stock like his brother did.'

'Just give him a chance, Arthur. After all, he's given you one and made you a manager which is a step up from where you were and means that you can change things.' She sounded annoyed, so he didn't say any more. The minute they'd arrived in Ealing, Agnes had measured the windows for new curtains and found a fabric shop on the high street. Then she'd spent two days sewing on her sister's sewing machine. The bright floral curtains had made the tiny flat feel like home and the old armchair looked stately with the velvet cushion she'd made. She didn't seem to be missing her parents – in fact, she'd been more cheerful than ever since they'd arrived. But he could see she was losing patience with him now, so he sat down and started to think about what more changes he could make.

The next morning, while Mr Wood was making his fleeting visit to check the books, Arthur decided he would follow Agnes's example and forge ahead with plans.

'I can see you're busy, sir, so, if you'd let me, I can buy the Christmas stock. One of the customers has told me where we can get a decent supply of vegetables and turkeys.'

Mr Wood stopped, raised his eyebrows and tucked his pencil behind his ear. 'All right then, but I can't pay you more. My brother did you a favour and you've got the flat, so that's that.'

Arthur was frustrated that his idea wasn't received with more enthusiasm. The flat was hardly a great reward for his efforts, and it was Agnes who had improved it. Still, at least he had taken charge of something. When Mr Wood had gone, he surveyed the shelves for gaps in the stock. As he started to the storeroom, he heard Agnes's steps on the stairs, and her head appeared round the door.

'Not too busy this afternoon?' she smiled at him.

'No, but things are looking up. You'll be pleased to hear Mr Wood has let me do the order for the Christmas stock.' He paused. 'Perhaps you'd like to come with me to pick it up?'

Her smile faded. She gripped the door and arched her eyebrow in mock surprise. 'You *know* that groceries aren't for me, Arthur. Hats are my business.'

'Well, I thought you might want to help me in the shop but perhaps there's a milliner in West Ealing that would take you on,' he said. Her brow then creased in real surprise. She had what he thought of as her 'dark look' – the one that he'd first seen when their wedding plans were going awry.

'That's not what I meant at all. Married ladies don't work, Arthur. You don't seem to realise. Lou doesn't work, and Fred doesn't expect her to. My mother *certainly* didn't work, well, except for bringing children into the world...' She stopped abruptly and looked down. 'Anyway, my work is making this flat a suitable place for us to live in comfortably.' She finished off with a flourish of the duster she was holding.

Arthur thought of Lou running after her two little ones – she was hardly a lady of leisure, but whenever children came into the conversation Agnes seemed to falter. Was she embarrassed? When he climbed on top of her and lifted her nightgown up, he did what married men were meant to do. But she always got straight up, washed herself, then turned away from him. Did she mind what he did? Didn't she realise it was part of being a wife? He tried to be a good husband – surely she could give him some credit for his efforts?

Arthur shook his head in irritation as she disappeared upstairs to make dinner. He finished his list and put it in the till for safekeeping. Agnes was spending all her time with Lou, who was probably getting her two little ones ready for bed right now, so why *was* she so reticent about having a child of their own? He'd made the move to West Ealing for her and in the back of his mind, he'd expected children to come next. The more he thought about it, the more he thought that a child of their own would bring them together and was exactly what he wanted.

*

He consulted the list of departments and headed for Ladies Fashion on the first floor. It was the Friday before Christmas and he'd seen an advertisement for French kid gloves that would be a perfect present for Agnes. Eldred and Sayers' department store was just the place to get them, its grand frontage dominating the sweep of Ealing Broadway.

'Excuse me miss, I'm looking for some gloves for my wife,' he asked. He could imagine Agnes working here – she had the same demeanour as the young lady in front of him. 'I saw this advertisement.' Arthur unfolded the paper he'd torn out of the paper and held it out for her to see.

The assistant looked at him from behind her spectacles. 'We sell a very large number of types of gloves. What exactly was sir after?'

'The best quality French kid gloves.' He stood to his full height to try and assert some authority. He didn't have much time, and he needed to get on with making a purchase.

She peered up at him. 'They're two shillings and eleven pence if you want the *finest* quality, sir.' It was more than he was expecting but he nodded. She returned with a pair of gloves resting on a piece of white tissue, then reached out her arms so he could inspect them.

'They do look very fine.' He wasn't sure what else to say. 'Can you wrap them?' He looked at the large department store clock, as the assistant disappeared again. She returned with a parcel of green tissue and red ribbon.

'It'll match the Christmas tree. Madam will love them.'

He fleetingly wondered if he should also buy some decorations for the tree, but time was short, so he paid and left, nearly running into the path of a tram on The Broadway. Fingering the empty wallet in his pocket, he thought of his mother preparing for a snowbound Christmas Day. His father had gone to a place called Medicine Hat to work and the water had made him ill, so she was having to manage the house on her own. He'd wired her some money and hoped she'd get it in time to buy a decent turkey. But he'd *also* promised Agnes that he would supply the Lyfords with a turkey and had just spent the last of his cash. The only answer to his dilemma had been to add an extra turkey to the stock list that Mr Wood paid for. With all the extra responsibility he was taking on at the shop, he reckoned it was a Christmas bonus that he could pay back in January. Walking down The Broadway, he felt satisfied with himself for the first time since they'd moved to West Ealing. With a bit more perseverance, he would make his new job into something to be proud of, after all being a manager meant he could change things to suit him. Perhaps Agnes had been right.

*

The following Monday, the twenty-third of December, was freezing. Agnes was getting ready to go to her parents' house and her father had come to collect the turkey and carry her bags. Arthur was going to join them on Christmas Eve after the shop closed.

'Right, young man. What is it that I owe you for all this finery?' Mr Lyford waved his wallet at him.

'It's all sorted out, Alfred. My treat,' Arthur assured him.

'Mrs Lyford and I appreciate that, son. We've a lot of mouths to feed this year. Kate's beau is coming. Then you and Agnes; and Lou and Fred and their little ones. Aggie is lucky to have a man of means to look after her. This new shop has certainly moved you up in the world.' He swept his arm round as if it was an empire.

'Not really. But the younger Mr Wood does let me do more than his older brother did.'

'You seem to have a bit more cash now.' Mr Lyford seemed more curious than respectful, and Arthur wasn't sure quite what he was getting at.

'I promised to look after your daughter and that's what I'm doing, Alfred.' Arthur hoped that Mr Lyford would leave him to get back to work. It was almost as if he could see through him to the debt he'd run up. He decided to change the subject.

'Are there wedding bells in the air for Kate and Jack?' He knew Mr Lyford saw Kate as the 'difficult' one.

'I'll let you know as soon as I do!' Mr Lyford chuckled. 'Don't have daughters, Arthur. They're too much trouble and they cost too much when they marry!'

He'd changed the subject, but not entirely. At last, Mr Lyford took out his watch and checked the time. 'Right, where's that youngest daughter of mine? We need to be off to the station now.' On cue, Agnes appeared, bundled up and with two suitcases.

'I'll see you tomorrow when the customers have all gone,' Arthur said to her.

'I'm not sure where we're all going to sleep, but the dinner will be good!' Agnes replied, following her father who had grabbed the box and one of her bags on his way to the door.

At five o'clock the next day, Arthur picked up his carpet bag and started to run to the station. He placed Agnes's present inside his jacket pocket, safely tucked beside his wallet.

As he approached the ticket office, he could hear the hiss of the engine building up steam. He yanked his wallet out and a flash of green and red tumbled out onto the wet floor. Yelping with annoyance, he bent down to rescue it, but the tissue had turned soggy, and the colour of the ribbon had started to run, so he paid for his ticket, quickly discarded both paper and ribbon and stuffed the gloves into his bag. He boarded the train just before the screech of the whistle signalled its departure.

Once safely aboard, he opened his bag again, took the gloves out and checked them over. Thankfully, they looked undamaged. On top of his clothes was a large brown envelope that a bill had arrived in that morning, so he took out the bill and stuffed the gloves into the envelope. Agnes needn't know he'd ruined the wrapping – after all, he'd gone to a lot of trouble and Christmas wrapping paper only ends up on the fire. The gloves were the main thing, he thought.

He sat back as the train headed due west. For a minute, the darkness disorientated him. Lights speckled the dark horizon and he felt that he could be anywhere. He imagined where he might get to if he kept going in this same direction for a week without stopping.

Canada perhaps? His heart quickened at the thought, and a vision of his mother's face on that wretched boat came to him. He doubled his coat over his chest and pictured her trying to shovel a path through the snowdrifts. He'd got a wife and a new job – but what was *her* life like? Harold and his father were fools to up sticks and go to the other side of the world like that. He knew now, as he'd always suspected, that once you leave home, there's no going back – everything changes. Even West Ealing was too far from Caversham, as far as he was concerned. He would do all he could, to make sure he never moved again.

Chapter Four

AGNES

She put on a brave face over the Christmas dinner table. Opening the brown paper envelope in front of her sisters and brother was embarrassing, even if the gloves *were* French. Jack had given Kate a box tied with a large red bow, so Arthur's envelope only made her feel worse. Maybe, now they were married, he thought he didn't need to make things special.

When they first met, she'd loved how attentive he was to her. True, they'd mostly talked 'shop', but it was their link – their respective trades. Of course, she'd leapt at the chance to have an admirer again, especially when Tom had announced he was marrying someone else and said that she'd only been *a bit of fun*. Walking out with Arthur showed that she was worth more than that. Agnes wished Tom could see her looking radiant with Arthur, and then regret what he'd done. His betrayal was disastrous and even though she'd pretended to her sisters that she didn't care, she knew that they'd seen the depth of her devastation. Thankfully, Arthur was altogether a more serious person, and his dark hair and eyes were nice – more than nice. Looked at in a certain way, he was really very handsome, as well as reliable. He might just be a grocer, but his manners made up for that and she'd needed at least the *hope* of marriage after Tom's humiliation of her.

When Arthur told her he'd just had his eighteenth birthday, she immediately changed her age, so he wouldn't realise she was two years older than him. Age was a small deception and thinking they were the same age had brought them closer. Now, less than a year after meeting, here they were – a married couple spending their first Christmas together. She'd had a narrow escape from spinsterhood.

All in all, she should forget the envelope and concentrate on more important things. Her mother had gone to a lot of trouble. The table was decorated, and the napkins carefully rolled into shiny red napkin rings which looked new, but she was slightly alarmed by the changes in the home that had been a second skin to her only a few months ago.

'Make sure you sit next to Arthur, Aggie,' Lou shouted back from the kitchen as they hovered over the chairs not sure which one to claim. Her mother had been swallowed up by the clatter and smells in the small kitchen.

'This is the biggest bird she's ever stuffed into her oven.' Her father looked at Arthur as they shuffled their seats under the table. She felt a pang of irritation at the attention he was getting from her family. Nobody seemed interested in her angle on things anymore. They used to ask her about which millinery fabrics were popular, but since she married, they only seemed interested in Arthur's groceries. From being the special one in the family, she now felt as ordinary as Kate or Lou.

'It's a wonderful spread.' Arthur said, as her mother and sister paraded in from the kitchen with the turkey and plates of steaming vegetables. Agnes joined in the applause and resolved to cheer herself up. After all, this *was* their first Christmas together and everyone was pleased to be there.

What's wrong with me? she thought. Her father grabbed the carving knife and made a pantomime action of sharpening it.

Her name rose over the din. Alfie was grinning across the table at her.

'Will we have to fit an extra little one around the table next year? Have you and Art settled into family life yet?' Everybody looked towards her. Lou's two carried on making a racket.

Her throat tightened. 'Oh, we won't be having little ones just yet – we need a bigger place first... Children aren't for everyone, you know, Alfie.' Arthur shifted in his chair next to her.

'Where have all these strange ideas come from, Aggie?' Her father poised mid-carve. 'Lou and Fred started straight away.' Lou blushed and the others laughed.

Agnes blushed as well, but more with annoyance than embarrassment. 'I was a professional woman not so long back, you know, Father. You and Mother were determined that I shouldn't go into service, or marry for that matter, so I'm taking being a wife a step at a time and I'm certainly not rushing into having a family just yet.'

Everyone's attention switched from her to Arthur, a few inches to her right. 'Children will come along when the time is right,' he added, barely skipping a beat.

Mary Lyford's head nodded slightly, but it was Agnes's father who broke the tension. 'I'm not sure what you mean by that, lad, but if it keeps Agnes in the life she's become accustomed to, so be it! She's always made out that she's better than the rest of us.'

'That was because Lou and Kate dressed her up like a doll all the time.' Her mother had spoken, and they all looked at her.

'Well, she was *like* a doll – absolutely sweet with blonde curls, too. Pity that didn't last!' Kate said, and everyone laughed again.

Agnes was unsettled. Her sisters had a habit of putting

her in her place and she wasn't sure whether Arthur was on her side or not – she wasn't even sure exactly where she stood. She had tackled marriage in the same vein that their relationship started: by adopting a self-assured air which captivated Arthur. But did it make her seem haughty? She remembered when she and Kate had argued over a dress her mother had made. *It'll fit one of you*, her mother had said, *and whoever it fits can have it*. Agnes thought the colour and material were right for her and was sure her mother had her in mind, but then Kate had turned on her, *You always think the good things in this family are for you – but there are three of us, you know.* Then, before slamming the living room door in her face, Kate had shouted, *Why do you always have to be so haughty?*

Was being haughty an obstacle to a successful marriage? Perhaps she should soften. They were still stuck in their shopkeeper roles – she the superior one and Arthur the steadfast one – but her millinery days were over. She thought about her future as a married woman; without a position which made well-to-do ladies ask your opinion about things like materials and colours. She'd learnt so much as a milliner. Not just about customers, but also about making hats; how to bend the felt to exactly the right angle and hold it in position; how to make joins in material that nobody could see. She'd achieved a good level in her craft, yet she'd chosen Arthur over all that, mainly because she didn't want to miss the chance to marry.

Agnes took small mouthfuls of the turkey and vegetables piled on her plate and looked at her mother. There were grease marks on her cuffs, and she was smiling at Alfie who was larking about as usual. It was her mother who had led Agnes to expect more from life, so perhaps that was why marriage, far from being the start of a fairy-tale, now seemed more like the end of one. Even though she was drawn to Arthur's lean figure, she couldn't help but feel scared by what he did in bed might lead to. Why was she like this? He was a good man, so she must try harder to be a good wife. After all, there was no going back to her old life now.

Pudding was served. 'There's a silver sixpence in there somewhere. Whoever finds it has to sing a song!' Alfie was his usual excitable self and everyone's spoons started to clatter against their bowls.

'You seem subdued,' Arthur turned and whispered to her. 'Don't bother about Kate – she's probably jealous of you.'

Agnes felt relieved that he'd seen her side of things without her explaining it to him. She squeezed his hand. 'The gloves were lovely, Art,' she whispered back. 'I'm sorry if I seemed ungrateful.' He looked taken aback. 'I'm going to try harder to be a good wife to you. I'm going to try...'

Before he could reply, there was a shriek from the other side of the table, 'Arthur's got it – I can see it!' Alfie was pointing. She looked down at his plate and poking out of the pudding was the glint of a silver sixpence.

'All my Christmases have come in one.' Arthur squeezed her hand back so hard she was relieved when he let go, to stop Alfie grabbing the sixpence.

*

During the first months of the new year, Agnes resolved to try different ways to be a good wife. As well as sewing him new shirts, she practised tips from her sisters about how to improve her cooking. Every evening when Arthur finished work, she showed him the buttonholes she'd done or the cake she'd baked that day.

But as the spring days stretched out into summer, she started to run out of ideas. There was only one more way for her to be *really* useful and she was determined to prove herself.

On the first Monday in June, she went downstairs, put on a large brown apron and set to work stacking shelves in the shop.

Arthur watched her, as she bent to unpack boxes. 'Don't exert yourself too hard and remember that shifting the sacks is my job. Come and get me if there's anything heavy that needs doing.'

'Of course. You're in charge.'

That day, she cut cheese, sliced a ham and measured endless bags of sugar from the large sack at the back of the shop. Her apron was heavy, the loop scratched the back of her neck and her back ached, but despite all the discomfort, she was pleasant to the customers, and they started to tell her about themselves. She was surprised by how much she enjoyed it.

By the third day, Agnes was starting to get the hang of the grocery business, but Arthur didn't seem to notice her hard work. Not only that but she was also getting frustrated by his approach to shop work and terseness with the customers. She decided that she would talk to him about it, so as they closed up for the day, she turned to him.

'Millinery was my first love but it's not so different from grocery. You've got to be interested in your customers. They like to get to know you.'

'Not really the same as selling hats, though, is it?' Arthur replied, not even bothering to look at her.

She remembered the heavy oak milliner's counter and the way she'd presented swatches to dozens of ladies, commenting on their discerning eye or their tiny waist. Flattery alone had sold several hats and, in only a week in grocery, she had also found that when she admired a customer's hair, shoes, or even children – and, best of all, as far as she was concerned, their hat – they stayed a little longer in the shop and bought more items. But Arthur was so wrapped up in stocking the shelves, he didn't see the human side of things. Before she could explain further to him, the hubbub of a noisy crowd drifted into the shop. She looked out of the window and saw that several people had gathered over the road by a news billboard.

'Why don't you go and see what the fuss is about?' She grabbed the brush to sweep up while Arthur went over to get a paper. In a few minutes, he came back with the paper tightly rolled in his fist.

'Well?' she said.

'Everyone's saying that a suffragette has thrown herself in front of the King's horse and been killed,' Arthur replied, waving the paper at her.

Agnes looked at him in horror. 'The poor King. The woman must be mad!'

He put the newspaper down and started to adjust some cans. 'Maybe. But I expect the *poor King* has enough rubies to make up for his horse losing a race. I'm more worried about the steelworker chaps near Birmingham who are on strike because they're not getting paid right.'

'But why would anyone throw themselves under a horse *or* go on strike on a lovely day like this? The world's gone mad!' She was upset that he still hadn't commented on her own day's work, never mind the steelworkers near Birmingham.

Arthur didn't answer, so she swivelled round decisively, picked up the newspaper, and set off upstairs. In the kitchen, she grabbed a large steel knife and started to saw the beef into cubes like Kate had shown her. Did suffragettes make dinner like she was doing? She hadn't paid much attention to them before, except to laugh when her father made fun of them.

When the meat and vegetables were safely simmering in the pot, she sat on one of the wooden chairs and read the newspaper. It seemed the woman had come from a good family and been to university – Oxford, at that – so she ought to know what she was doing. She didn't have a husband or children. She thought back to her work that day – she *was* proud of what she was doing but maybe she was going too far to prove a point. Was she behaving in a strange way? Perhaps Arthur didn't want her help after all and that was why he'd not said anything. Even worse, supposing the customers thought that she was working in the shop because she was a suffragette? That wasn't it at all – she just wanted to be a good wife and for her husband to be proud of her.

After dinner, they tackled the washing up together.

'I've been thinking.' Agnes looked down into the sink. 'I'm not sure it's right for me to work with you in the shop. It's not what we got married for, is it?' Arthur wiped the knife slowly and said nothing, so she set about scrubbing the pan with extra fervour, staring down at its chipped edges.

'Perhaps you're not cut out for grocery,' he said at last. He sounded relieved which irritated her. *That* wasn't why she had changed her mind.

'I just think that I should stick to homemaking.' She paused. 'And maybe, if I do that, we'll be *lucky*.' That got his attention – he knew what she meant.

As she turned back to the dishes, she imagined the thundering of hooves that had knocked the suffragette down. Maybe this was a sign to her that she should settle down and start a family before it was too late. Maybe it wasn't enough just to be a wife and it was time for her to be a mother as well. Best of all, now she had made the decision to give him a child, Arthur would be even more glad that he'd married her.

Chapter Five

She said nothing when Arthur referred to the unborn baby as a *he* who would help him in the shop. It was wonderful to finally be expecting – two years of disappointment had replaced a fear of childbirth with the huge fear that she might never conceive at all. The first time she felt the baby move, she was overcome with a sense of awe and then something else which she decided was joy, there was no other word for it. Both she and Arthur were happy at the same time. At last, they had a joint venture, just as she'd planned.

Their baby daughter was born on a bitingly cold January morning in 1916, and despite the searing pain, Agnes was completely floored by the miracle of her arrival. When the midwife left, they were together for the first time as a family.

'I can't believe she's ours.' She gazed at the baby's tiny feet and hands, then looked up at Arthur. He was pale.

'If only my mother could see her,' he said.

He was always talking about his mother, but Agnes had never actually met the woman. 'Well, at least she has one grandmother,' she eventually replied. 'But what will happen if you have to go? It's not going to be easy for me to manage here on my own,' she added.

'Women do, though.' Arthur stared at the wall above her head, then turned and left the bedroom. She heard him pacing round the sitting room as she nursed the baby. Perhaps she'd been a bit harsh about his mother – after all, she wasn't dead, just a long way away. She winced a little as the baby latched on. It was hard to relax when their happiness was tempered not only by absent family but also by the war in Europe which had stepped up with more men leaving home to fight. When the baby had finished suckling, Arthur reappeared.

'Let's concentrate on the baby for now,' he said, looking down at them both. 'And if I have to go, so be it.' She couldn't argue with that.

The following week, Agnes asked Kate to move in to help out – *just in case*. Kate agreed, glad to have something to take her mind off Jack leaving. She was desperate to make a fuss of the latest member of the family and soon took charge of the morning routine.

'She's so alert, Ag. Have you thought of a name yet? Lou and I think that 'Helen' would be nice – with an H, not plain old 'Ellen'.' She folded some clean nappies while Agnes fed the baby.

Agnes' brow furrowed as she looked up at Kate. Her mind was occupied with other things, and she hadn't settled on a name yet. 'I wonder if Arthur's disappointed she's not a boy – I'm sure he is. Most men want sons, don't they? He's always so difficult to work out…' Her voice faded away.

Kate shrugged. 'You should know him by now – you've been married nearly four years! Anyway, his baby needs a name.'

'*My* baby, you mean!' They both laughed and Agnes held her closer. Thank goodness, Kate was so reliable. She'd felt much closer to her lately and was ashamed that she hadn't appreciated her more before. 'I like Helen. It sounds so much better than Ellen. It was clever of you and Lou to think of it.' The baby gurgled. 'She's going to be a good baby.' Agnes smiled at the red face of tiny Helen. 'I couldn't believe it when she arrived so perfect.'

'You were lucky, Ag. Think of Lou and her second.' The trauma of Lou's second child's birth was partly what had scared Agnes about having a child in the first place. The only good side she could see was that Lou was now unable to bear another child, so spared the trauma of it happening again.

'How's Jack doing?' Agnes asked, turning to her sister. Despite several breakups and reconciliations, he and Kate still hadn't married before he left for the front. Arthur always said it was the longest engagement in history.

'I don't hear much. But Father thinks it's marvellous. Before he joined up, he always said he was a ne'er do well and now he's a hero.' Kate bent closer to Agnes. 'Has Arthur heard anything yet?'

'He hates seeing the other men going off and hides from customers, so he won't have to ask after their sons or husbands. It'd be awful if he had to go when we've a newborn, and he's needed in the shop.'

'Well, I don't want to worry you, Ag, but he might not have a choice. I've heard that married men will soon be called up. You'll have to be prepared like the rest of us were.' Agnes bit her lip and instantly pushed away a sense of uneasiness. Things were so much better between her and Arthur now they had the baby, and she didn't want anything to spoil things. She wanted to escape the war and for everything in their own little world to be perfect.

*

The letter came when Helen was four months old. Agnes watched as Arthur inserted the knife and sliced open the envelope.

'Well? Where will you be sent to?' she said, as he

pulled out a single sheet and read it. They'd just finished their lunch, but she hadn't managed to eat much because Arthur had put the letter on one side and insisted that they wait to open it.

'Let's hope not France or Belgium. Anyway, I have to report to a training camp first. Then they'll decide where to send me.' He sounded grim. The baby was crying, and the commotion was drifting down into the shop, but she didn't care if anyone heard. She thought they'd be lucky, so how could this be happening to them?

'You don't need to worry. I'll probably be looking after the stores. I won't be at the front line. I'll be much safer than men like Kate's Jack.' He sounded too calm, she thought.

'But what will become of *us*?' She knew she was being dramatic, but it *was* dramatic. 'What will she do without a father?' She thrust Helen at him. Perhaps her warm body would make him realise what was happening to them.

Arthur took her clumsily in his arms. 'I'm sure we'll all be fine.' Why was he always reasonable when he should be furious? 'Mr Wood will take over the shop and you can stay right here with Helen. We knew this might happen.' Nothing she could say made any difference, so she gave him one of her long hard looks while he jiggled Helen up and down on his knee. He might not see things from her point of view, but at least she could make him feel uncomfortable when she fixed her eyes on him like that.

'Your family will help out,' he said. This was not what she wanted to hear.

'Only a bus and two train rides away! My family aren't exactly on our doorstep.' She didn't know if she was angry or upset now.

'But you like Ealing. It was what you wanted.'

'Yes, I like Ealing as a *married* woman – not as a deserted one. It should be Mr Wood who's going, not you, so I won't be helping him in the shop.'

Her eyes were filling up with tears, but she hated him seeing her cry, so she put on her coat and swept out the door, leaving him with the baby and the shop to manage. If she was going to live on her own, she needed a moment or two on her own to get used to the idea. Arthur was wrong, she was sure. She had a feeling in her gut, and no idea why it had suddenly taken hold of her, that they were *not* going to be fine at all, but yet there was nothing she could do about it – nothing at all.

*

When the baby cried at night, she always woke up immediately, as if she'd never been asleep at all. A cool spring had turned into a humid summer and Arthur had been in Salonika for just over a month. In many ways, it was better now than when he'd been training, and she'd had to wait to find out where he was going to be sent. Despite her initial fuss, she accepted life without him there – even liked the calm steady routines of daily life that she had created for Helen. She especially liked having lunchtimes whenever they wanted to, with no one running up and down the steps to see to the shop below. She had found some loyal friends amongst the customers and had more in common with them since she'd told Alfie she disapproved of his support for the demonstrators in Trafalgar Square.

It was unusual for Helen to cry for so long. Agnes got up; pulled a woollen shawl around her shoulders and went through a possible list of problems: nappy, feeding, colic. She felt the nappy. It was dry but the baby's hands had escaped from the covers and were rubbing her face. Could she be teething? Should she leave her to cry? Her sisters' voices rattled in her head. *Think about our mother with lots of children to look after – she couldn't fuss over just one of us, we had to learn to fit in.* But they had been the ones fussing over her, the last in a line of children, several of whom had died in infancy. She shuddered at the thought of a tiny dead body.

Supposing Arthur never comes back, like so many of the other husbands and fathers, the black-edged cards in the windows sealing their fate? In the daytime, she refused to consider it could happen, but in the early hours she would lie in bed and imagine opening the black-edged telegram. Then? She was never sure what would follow that, though she'd seen plenty of wives and mothers dumbfounded and blank-faced going about their shopping downstairs.

Helen's wailing and frantic movements got louder, so she was forced back into the present. She might not always be a wife, but she would always be a mother. There was no way out.

'There, there.' She worked through the list of possible problems again and remembered the silver-handled teething ring that her mother had passed on to her. She opened a drawer and felt for it. It was still there – slightly indented by her own baby teeth. She warmed it in her palm, picked the baby up and eased the ring into her eager mouth. Her tiny eyes shone back with warmth. Hugging her closer, a shock of heat radiated right through to her bones. This was absolute love. It felt new and wonderful. She had seen signs of it in her own mother – the long look and half-smile when she watched them playing. Thinking back, there were even traces of it in her father, when he'd lifted her onto his shoulders with a laugh. It gave her an odd ache that Arthur might never hold his daughter again.

But, if this was real love, then what did she feel for Arthur? At the beginning, she wanted him to love her, and she wanted to feel for him like she had felt for Tom. But somehow, even though she knew he *was* nice looking, the spark had never fully ignited. She was the centre of his world – she was sure of that because she knew what being the centre felt like. But did she love him back? There were moments when she thought *maybe* she did – when his reliability and devotion were enough to make her think so. After all, look at what Tom had done to her – Arthur would never let her down like that.

But this baby – her daughter – she didn't even have to think whether she loved her. She just *did*. The moments they shared linked up and made a rope of love between them which felt unbreakable. It was a reason to live. Still holding Helen, she eased herself back into bed and tucked her feet under the covers. They could rest together until the morning light pressed against the window. Helen would fill the space that Arthur had left. If he didn't come back, God forbid, she would be more than enough for her to carry on.

*

Despite Agnes's worries about the distance, her parents visited regularly to help out. One Sunday morning, along with her brother, they all trouped in. An hour later she'd had enough of them all and the atmosphere in the room was fractious.

'I think of Arthur as my own son.' Her father looked squarely at his real own son, then carried on, 'Is he keeping his spirits up, Ag?' Alfie shuffled in his seat, scraped it back without a word and left the room.

Her mother sighed. 'I wish you wouldn't go on like that. He's got his reasons, not to mention, an infirmity.'

'His reasons to be a coward, you mean. That's his only infirmity! We need our young men out there – like Arthur is.' Her father stared at the chair where Alfie had been sitting a few minutes ago.

'Arthur's lucky he's got a safe posting. He wouldn't want to be fighting at the front.' She felt uncomfortable when her brother was criticised, and Arthur unduly valourised.

'You're doing a grand job with Helen. Being a mother must be a bit different from millinery.' Her mother wanted to change the subject. Their home had become a battleground all of its own and her mother's voice was frequently breaking and on the brink of tears.

'And from having a husband to wait on you!' Her father just couldn't let it rest.

'I manage pretty well without him, actually,' Agnes said. She couldn't remember a moment recently where she'd needed Arthur there to help out. At last, her father had the sense to shut up and she started to clear the table, unsure what else to tell them. It sounded as if Arthur was shopkeeping rather than fighting. Salonika was out of the firing line, so there wasn't much to tell. She was tired of writing letters saying the same things – the shop was fine, the baby was fine, everybody was fine. She had little news because her life was comparatively easy. She still went over to see Lou's family – Fred was saved from conscription by his job, so all was well there – and Kate came over to look after Helen so that Agnes could go out. In fact, she had a freedom that she'd never had before, even though it didn't seem right to enjoy it – not while she felt guilty that so many men were dying for their country and living in muddy holes on the front line. And not while her family fought over it.

Her mother helped her to wash up. 'I do wish your father would let up on Alfie. He gets so upset. I was wondering if perhaps he could come and stay with you?'

This was unexpected. Agnes stopped with her dishmop in the air. 'What about his job? I'm not sure Mr Wood would allow it – I mean, he's let us stay, but...'

'The brewery let him go, so I wondered if he could help out in the shop.' Her mother had obviously been thinking about this for a while.

'I could ask, I suppose, but Mr Wood – well, Stanley, he says I should call him – thinks that *I* should move in with *you* while Arthur's away. He might not like it if I move my family in here, instead.' She was playing for time. She loved Alfie but she wasn't sure she wanted him around all the time. He could be demanding of her time and his views were misguided. Then she would have to explain to people why he was here and not at the front. It would be embarrassing.

Her mother bent down to the dresser cupboard and sighed. 'I suppose it's a liberty, what with Arthur away and so on. I just thought that Alfie could help Mr Wood out, that's all.'

'I'll ask.'

She wouldn't. She loved the flat more and more with every cushion and curtain she sewed for it and wanted to keep it for herself and Helen. Who knows? Arthur might come back and the war end. Then Alfie could get on with his life without his father hounding him. She decided that instead of asking Mr Wood if Alfie could stay with her, she would visit home more regularly to see if she could help ease the tension.

The next Friday, Agnes packed a bag and placed it on the rack under Helen's pram, then set off for the station to take the train to Reading. It was an awkward journey, but the station guard helped her onto the train with the pram. The station entrance was flooded with young men in khaki uniforms, and she scanned the faces to see if she knew any of them. They reminded her of Arthur's departure and, uncomfortably, of her refusal to see him off properly.

A fresh blast of steam wetted her hair and face, as she headed onto the platform towards the carriages for Reading. As it cleared, she looked about for help with the pram. A young guard made his way towards her, just as Helen started to cry.

'You keep her with you, Mrs. Them Huns, they're murdering babies now, and in broad daylight.' He manoeuvred the empty pram with one hand while another blast of steam made Helen wail even louder. 'Bombed a school in the East End, that's what they've gone and done – men and women carrying out the bodies of their little ones, just like that in the middle of a London street. You're doing the right thing getting out, Mrs. Your husband would want you to be safe.' He hoisted the pram up into the carriage.

What was the man talking about? Agnes wondered. She clutched Helen a bit tighter and was reassured that the train, at least, was running normally. She struggled with the carriage door as the other passengers turned to look at her. The journey was slower than usual and once Helen had settled, Agnes started to imagine what it would be like to be leaving for France or Italy or Belgium. She shouldn't have been so selfish about Arthur going – it wasn't his choice after all. But if London was bombed, she might end up under more fire than he was. Suddenly, the war seemed more real to her.

The minute she opened the door to her parents' home, she could sense the turmoil. Nobody was where they usually were – the sitting room was empty, so she shouted out to see where everyone was. Finally, her mother appeared from the kitchen with a red face and looking as if she'd been crying.

'Alfie says he's going to join up, after all.' Her hands were tightly clenched. Kate came in behind her.

'We thought he might change his mind again, Ag – that's why we didn't tell you,' she said.

Her mother turned to face her father who had just come down from upstairs. 'If you hadn't made him feel like a coward, he might have stayed with us. He's not strong like Arthur – he won't last a minute. See if he'll listen to you, Agnes.'

'He's come to his senses at last. His bad lungs didn't stop him from working in the brewery, did they?' Her father's voice had an ugly edge to it.

She put her bag down. 'Kate, keep hold of Helen.' She started upstairs. War might be something that Arthur would cope with, but not Alfie – he was too young and, she agreed with her mother, too weak.

Alfie was packing. 'Hello, Ag. You've obviously heard Father's delighted that my 'infirmity' has been re-classified, so I can join up. At last, I can be a son that he can be proud of.' He sounded bitter. She heard her mother weeping downstairs.

'There's nothing here for me. Father doesn't speak to me, and Mother treats me as if I'm a child. I might as well go.' Alfie looked at her, his face flushed with anger.

Agnes doubted she could stop him. 'They need you here, though…' It sounded false. 'Mother loves you the best.' This received a snort of laughter.

'And Father disowns me. *You're* the one they're proud of.' She saw herself through Alfie's eyes – the clever daughter and the waiting wife, with a hero for a husband.

'Nothing is as it seems, you know. Go, if you have to, but I don't want you to go, Mother doesn't want you to go, and if Arthur was here, he wouldn't want you to go, either.' She had no idea whether he would or not, but it was worth a try.

Alfie carried on throwing things into a bag, tears starting to stream down his face. The war was slowly but surely eating up the men in her life. Only her father still believed in it – and he was too old to be called up. She shrugged her shoulders and left Alfie to pack. She was sick of it – it had taken away her husband and now it had broken her only brother. Thank goodness, at least, that women like her could cope, she thought, as she pounded back down the stairs to her sister and daughter.

Chapter Six

EVA

The school uniform looks new, even though it isn't. It's arranged on my bed perfectly. Everything's ready for the big day that everyone keeps talking about.

'Try it on, dear,' Mummy says. Helen is behind her. They've led me up here as part of an elaborate pantomime.

'You mean now?' I don't want to try, just to look.

'Go on, Eva. Mummy needs to know that it fits. It'll be too late to alter it tomorrow morning.' Helen is always on her side.

They want a dress rehearsal, so I struggle out of my polo neck, then undo the top button of the new shirt and slip it over my head. It's freezing. I twirl for my audience.

'Ah, a bit of room for growth – good.' Mummy is as practical as ever.

Next comes the tunic, so I wriggle out of my old skirt. The tunic goes over my head, and I tie the woollen girdle round my waist.

'Is it a bit long?' I turn to ask her.

'You're so *willowy*, dear, you need that length. You're only just twelve and you'll shoot up even more when you're in your teens. Anyway, it's stylish. Now, Helen will show you how to do the tie, then come downstairs and let me see the final effect.

Helen sits on the bed, smiling. 'You always look good – *even* in school uniform.'

'Not with these stick legs.' I go and sit at the dressing table, ready to start the tie tying.

Helen's face sits on my shoulder in the mirror. 'Bunny, you're a beauty, you really are,' she says. It's *his* voice and she's trying to be kind. She looks stricken. I think she's surprised herself. 'Don't tell Mummy.'

'Don't tell Mummy what?' I'm exasperated. Helen always thinks about her first, but I'm glad she used his name for me.

'Come on, then – let's get this tie knotted,' Helen grabs the tie off the bed and pretends to strangle me, so we start giggling. The sound of Mummy washing up downstairs drifts up the stairs. In a few minutes, she expects to see her second Wellesley High School girl perfectly turned out.

Mummy was determined that I'd be a scholarship girl, just like Helen. Margaret Evans and I both passed the exam, but her father said the uniform would be too expensive. When Mummy saw him in the grocers, she had said, *whatever it takes, Mr Evans, it's worth it*, holding her head in that arched way of hers. He turned his back on her, but she didn't care. She said to me later, *he's short-sighted, dear. You'll get a good job and earn well, if you work hard at Wellesley*. She wanted to say, *like Helen*, but we all know that I'm not like Helen. Helen is sensible, but no one says that about me. It doesn't matter, because Helen will soon leave school and get a good job to help make ends meet, and then I won't have to. So I'm glad she's sensible.

Helen pats my knotted tie in place and goes downstairs. I brush my hair and grip it back. My face looms in the mirror, larger than usual. The cheekbones are Mummy's, but the nose? I feel for the button on my shirt cuff and a thought slips into my head – the morning after Daddy left, my cuff had a button hanging off and I remember thinking it odd that Mummy hadn't scooped it up and sewed it on the night before. Could she already have known that he was leaving? Was that why she wouldn't tell me where he was?

Quite early on, I thought he might have gone to Canada to see Grandma and Grandpa – the Grandma and Pa we've never seen. Even Mummy has never met them, and when Daddy went, their letters and presents stopped, which made me think that maybe he was with them and saving up presents to bring back himself.

I'll dedicate tomorrow to him. He'd smile at the tangle I got into doing the tie up. Things keep going, even though he's not here, but when I try to imagine where he is and what he's doing, everything freezes. The thought of him trying out snowshoes in Canada cheers me up when it's cold like the day he left.

*

On the station platform, we jostle with men in well-worn suits. My perfect uniform is covered by an old gaberdine which Helen has just grown out of. Mummy says altering it is her next job.

'Keep close, Eva. And let the men get on first,' says Helen. 'Don't forget, if you see any other new girls, tell them they can walk to school with us. Not everyone has an older sister.'

Indeed, I think.

Puffing Billy lumbers to a halt and we push our way on. The carriages are packed, so we stand in the corridor. Helen looks nervously at me, but the sharp smell of grown men is exciting and doesn't worry me at all. All I have to do is follow her.

Before we reach school, Helen pulls me close. 'Remember, Eva – we're train girls, so we're allowed to come in late. It's because we've got scholarships and some girls will ignore you for that same reason. You must be tactful because their fathers pay for them to go to Wellesley.' A mention of fathers. 'You can see why they might be jealous.' I nod but think I might be jealous of *them* – with their fathers and their money.

We shuffle into the main hall, the steam clinging to our hair. It's vast. Heads turn to look at us, then turn back. There's a sea of serge tunics and I wonder if I can take my coat off without anyone noticing. Voices reach to the top of the ceiling and back down again. We stand quietly whilst everyone finishes singing the hymn. I shake off the wretched coat and shove it under my seat as we sit down.

When I'm shown to my classroom with the other new girls, I find a desk by the window. I don't recognise a single soul, but the lawns I look out at are a comfort and from my vantage point, I can almost pretend that I'm not in a classroom at all. Suddenly, I hear my name and look up.

'Eva Borton is the scholarship girl in our class this year, so I hope you'll make friends with her.' Miss Beauvoir, my class teacher, peers over and thirty more pairs of eyes examine me. I can barely breathe. The walls lean inward – every fibre of me wants to be somewhere – anywhere else than here. I quietly exhale as the hubbub of handing out books takes over and the lesson settles to a steady hum. There's a chill when the door is wedged back for break time – I look at the floor and follow the line of girls out.

'Suppose you think you're clever, being a scholarship girl,' a girl says under her breath, as we squeeze into the corridor. She's got long straight hair tied back and the whitest knee-length socks I've ever seen. There's an identical girl with her. I pretend I haven't heard her and make a beeline for the door to the playing field, gasping with relief when I'm outside and can blend into a throng. The grass is spongey, and I feel myself literally sinking into the ground. Shrinking from view will soon be my personal art form.

'Hello. I saw you on the train with your sister this morning.' My head flips round. The girl speaking to me – and actually *smiling* – is shorter than me but not as thin, and her hair is the reddest I've ever seen. She's on her own which is even better.

'Hello, I'm Eva.' I shuffle from one foot to another, trying to warm up. The girl looks nice.

'I went to St James's Elementary. That's why we haven't met before but I'm a county scholarship girl, like you. My name's Gwen.' I feel immensely grateful to her. 'This is a big step isn't it?' She sweeps her arms around the playing field as we stand there jointly shivering.

'My sister says I'll get used to it,' I say, 'Do you have a sister here?'

'No, but I've got a baby brother, so I shouldn't really be here. I'm not sure that my mother will cope without me, but she insisted I took the place when the county wrote to us.'

'So did my mother, but luckily there's nobody for me to look after at home because *I'm* the baby!' We laugh, but I can already picture Gwen grown up and me as her child beside her. I wish my hair would go into a neat plait like hers – it's tangling up in this wind. 'We need to get moving around to keep warm. Shall we see how many girls there are with white socks and how many with grey, like us?' I say.

'Have you noticed how the white sock girls go round in twos or threes and the grey sock girls are either on their own or in big groups?' Gwen gets straight to the heart of the matter. No wonder she won a scholarship!

'Shall we be the two grey sock girls who change things?' I reply, laughing. She has emboldened me, so we spend the rest of the break and dinner time sorting out who are friends and who are enemies.

Back on the train later that afternoon, I tell Helen about the mean white sock girls.

'Ignore them, like I told you. They're probably scared that you're clever and that they won't keep up with you.' The train rattles along at a steady pace and I sink into the carriage seat. Scholarship girls might be clever, like Helen says, but we're outcasts. I'm going to need Gwen.

*

Helen's right in some ways that the white socks girls fear us, but when I see the London tailor labels in their tunics, I'm hot with embarrassment over my second-hand uniform.

'Watch out that you don't trip over your hem!' One of them shouts after me during break time, and I find myself hitching my tunic up over the girdle.

'Don't rise to it. You're unlucky with your class – I've got a few nice girls in mine. Try not to give them anything to bother you about.' Gwen says, pulling a face which makes me laugh. She's always kind.

'I wish I could change classes, but they want to spread the scholarship girls out. Helen says that they want our *attitude* to rub off on the others, but it feels like the other way round to me. Honestly, Gwen. I do everything I can to try and make them like me. I even deliberately miss the goal in netball so they can call me butterfingers.'

'But you said that Miss Beauvoir chose your English essay twice to read out. That'll have annoyed them.'

'But I didn't brag about it. Who would I brag to, anyway? They just don't like me.'

'Well, they can't all be mean. How does your sister manage things?' Even Gwen's voice has an edge to it, now.

'Oh, Helen's completely different from me. No one dares to be mean to her. Even her enemies love her!' I know I sound peevish, but I need Gwen to feel what I'm feeling.

'It's bad luck, Eva. But maybe they're jealous because you're clever *and* pretty. I mean some of those girls aren't either of those things, are they?' Gwen sounds serious, but I laugh anyway.

Gwen's words resonate for the rest of the day. Maybe she wasn't just being kind. Maybe she was making a point. When I get home I sit at my dressing table, line up my brush and comb, and stare for a few minutes at my reflection. Am I *too* pretty? Is that the problem? Pretty is boring, anyway. I'd rather be attractive, than pretty. Perhaps I should move my parting to the side – that might make me look serious – maybe even stylish, like our art teacher. Perhaps the other girls would leave me alone if I changed the way I look. I pick up the comb and make a side parting.

There's a soft knock and Helen peeks round the door. 'What on earth are you doing, Eva – you look like a scarecrow!' Her face looms in the mirror behind me.

'Aunt Kate is always saying I've got good cheekbones, so I thought I'd try something different.'

Helen pulls a face. 'Isn't clever and well-groomed good enough for you?'

'I just thought I could get more of a *look*.'

'What sort of look?' She sounds truly baffled.

'You know Miss Dessin, the art teacher?'

'Yes – and everyone thinks she's a bit odd.' That's uncharitable for Helen.

'Well, I don't. She's kind to me, and she's different

from the other teachers – those scarves she wears. I still can't see quite how she ties and layers them. Anyway, she has a side parting.' I tilt my head for effect.

'Oh, I see. Well, yes – she's got a certain something, but she's a teacher. I'd be very careful about looking different from the other girls.' Helen sits on the bed.

I turn to face her. 'But we *are* different, aren't we? We can't afford the same things. I mean last week Miss Dessin showed us pictures of the European art treasures which we're supposed to go and see on the school trip. Then she quickly changed the subject because she knows I won't be going.'

Helen sits straight up suddenly, as if I've blasphemed. 'You haven't *said* that though, have you? We don't want people thinking we're poor. Mummy would hate it.'

'No, of course not, but everyone knows it, without us telling them. I mean look at us. We don't exactly have tailor-made uniforms, do we?' I can't believe I'm being this bold with her.

Helen looks annoyed. 'I keep telling you, Eva – it doesn't matter. You need to be strong and hold your head up. Mummy has done her absolute best for us, and she'd be upset if she thought you were ashamed of her. We're not the only ones in this situation, either. What about your friend, Gwen? *She* seems to manage.'

'I'm sorry, Helen. Yes, she does. It's just, I don't know – so *difficult*.' I draw the comb back through my hair and find the centre parting again.

She shrugs her shoulders. 'Well, don't over dramatise – we're the lucky ones, Eva.'

I wonder whether Helen's remembered that Daddy used to call me his *lucky girl*. He'd be really interested in the pictures of the European art treasures Miss Dessin showed us. *And* he'd have found a way for me to go on the trip – I just know he would.

Chapter Seven

ARTHUR

He had forgotten what England was like. After several days and nights, and several card games across Europe, he was overcome by the greenness of the fields emerging from the dawn light of Kent. He walked slowly from Ealing station with his kit bag slung over his shoulder, mesmerised by slashes of watery blue sky crystallising through the mist after an early morning shower. The buildings looked grander than he remembered, yet nothing felt solid. People waved and smiled. A few looked away with vacant eyes.

The shop had just opened. He stood for a few minutes outside the door, scared to go in.

'Art, lad – what a day this is! A rare treat to see you safely back at long last. It's been a long three years without you.' It was a familiar voice, and its owner came up behind him and clapped him on the back.

'What are you doing out here when you should be inside? She's waiting for you – I heard her upstairs early this morning getting everything ready.' Mr Wood's smile was too broad, and his teeth looked dangerous.

Arthur tried to smile back but fear gripped him.

'I might just... Perhaps I should ... get my bearings, before... How's Mrs Wood?' He shifted uneasily from one foot to the other.

'Never mind Mrs Wood – it's Mrs *Borton* you need to think about! In you go. I'll be back when you've had some time together.' Mr Wood pushed him through the shop door, then disappeared up the street. The jangle of the doorbell announced Arthur's arrival in the empty shop.

The shop was still and cold. He glanced at the shelves and saw that things had been moved – well, of course they would have been – it wasn't his shop anymore. He bent down and unlaced his boots, breathing in the dusty cool air, then he lined up his boots by the shop window. It was too early for customers, but he couldn't hear Agnes upstairs. Perhaps she'd gone out? He padded over to the stairs, put down his kitbag, looked up, then nearly fell backwards. Her unmistakable figure was starting down the stairs. His heart jolted at the sight of her – just as he remembered, stately and slim.

'Arthur!' She froze, clutching the newel post. He could hear a strangled quaver in her voice, as she came down the steps to him. He fell forward to hug her, but she only rested in his arms for a few seconds.

'Come up and have some tea.' She grabbed his hand.

'But the shop…'

'Turn the sign over – we'll close until Stanley gets back. Helen's waiting.'

He did as she suggested, surprised at her confident familiarity with Mr Wood. Then he picked up his bag and climbed the steps slowly. They were steeper than he remembered. He looked ahead into the small sitting room. It was also different – smaller, but neater and brighter somehow.

'I see you've kept yourself busy. It's so – so tidy.'

'This young lady has been my little helper.' She stood aside to show a little girl with a headful of golden curls that had come up behind her. She clung to her mother's skirts and regarded him shyly.

'Helen – it's your Daddy come back. You remember the stories I told you about him being a long way away, and how you said you couldn't wait to see him again?

Well, *here he is.*' She added a flourish with her arm, 'And he can't wait to tell you about his adventures!' The little girl shrank back even further into the skirts.

He went to pick her up, but she leapt away.

'It might take a while. It's to be expected,' Agnes said firmly. Helen remained still and quiet. 'She'll come round. Now, you need to unpack.' She looked round uncertainly, as if she expected a suitcase as well as his kitbag. 'I'll leave you be, while we go and make some breakfast.' She headed for the tiny kitchen with Helen still hanging onto her. He could hear Agnes trying to reassure her as pans clattered.

The reunion had lasted less than five minutes. Even if Helen did 'come round', he wondered when he would. The journey from Salonika was perilous, so Agnes had insisted that he should only come back when the war was over. Consequently, they had been apart for the full three years. And what was there to pick up? Helen had been a tiny baby when he'd left, and her reaction was evidence of the estrangement that had grown between them. He started to unpack his meagre items onto the settee.

That evening, he and Helen both sat mutely at the kitchen table while Agnes talked. 'She's bright, she is, Arthur. I've been showing her letters and Kate's sure that she's following the words when she reads to her. Helen's kept me going. Without her, it would have been much worse.' He could see her mouth moving and hear some words coming out, but they didn't mean anything and all the while, the little girl – his daughter – sat barely moving at all, with her eyes glued to her mother.

Agnes kept on. 'She's been sleeping in my, I mean, *our*, room. Just while you're away. I'll move her back, of course, but perhaps for now... The settee's not much different to the bunks you've been used to, I expect.'

Her cheer was wearing thin, and it hadn't cheered him up. Everything still seemed foreign – he was relieved that soon he'd be on his own again. Perhaps tomorrow, he'd find his way round the new stock downstairs and start to settle in.

After Agnes had gone to bed, he made himself comfortable under blankets on the settee, but it felt all wrong – almost like being in a foreign country all over again. He was back home, in a fashion, but what had it all been for? People here didn't understand that Macedonia hadn't been like France or Belgium. The men he'd been with had died from malaria – not shot wounds or trench foot. But malaria was tough, too, and the fever had sometimes made them beg to be shot. To add insult to injury – people back home called them 'Gardeners', as if they'd had nothing to do!

Dealing with the supplies had kept him from the front line, but he wouldn't apologise for that. What would have been the point of him changing places with a chap on the front line who didn't know about grocery? The other thing nobody here understood was the boredom; especially during the long evenings in the camp. That was why he and some of the other chaps had played cards, bartering with tobacco. Card games had made the time pass much quicker and had stopped them thinking about other things – bad things. He pulled the blanket over his shoulder and felt a deep tiredness sink into his bones. He'd survived. What more could he expect? Perhaps in time, he'd settle back into this life again.

*

Mr Wood wouldn't hear of him working in the shop for the next few days, so Arthur paced the small rooms upstairs, trying to familiarise himself with the new furnishings. Helen kept her distance, and Agnes seemed nervous. Whenever he tried to talk to her about the camp, her eyes followed Helen round the room. Eventually, he stopped trying to tell her about his time in Greece and concentrated on fitting in with her household routines.

From the first difficult encounter, he'd kept away from Helen and was as scared of frightening the child as the child was of him. But after a week back, he thought he should say something. 'Do you think that Helen would let me put her to bed tomorrow?' Agnes was setting about the dishes, so he had to shout.

After a few minutes, she leant round the door. 'Why don't you worry about the shop and leave Helen to me? Kate and Lou will be here on Sunday, so she'll see then that you're a member of *our* family and start to trust you.'

He thought it was a strange way to put it. Was he a member of *their* family? Who's family was his? He decided to let it rest for now, but in truth, whilst he was away, his thoughts had strayed more to his family in Canada, than to Agnes and the baby. Mother, Father, Dennis, Maude, and even Harold, had felt strangely real, yet it still niggled him that Helen rejected him now. Frustration at the situation was starting to get the better of him.

'She needs to trust me – I am her father, after all!' His voice was still loud, and Agnes had turned back to the dishes.

'She will. Give her more time.' She sounded tired. Perhaps he'd said enough for one night.

The next evening, after the dishes had been dried and cleared away, Agnes beckoned to him to join her in the kitchen. 'Leave her be,' she gestured to Helen playing quietly in the corner of the sitting room. Squashed in the small kitchen with her, he started to panic. He had no idea what was on her mind.

'I think you should move Helen's bed back into the box room, tonight, Arthur. She needs to know that you're here to stay.' Agnes's face reddened. 'And perhaps we should try sharing a bed again.'

He was surprised but pleased. 'It would be wonderful to be properly reunited.' He moved forwards, as if he might hug her but she flinched and gave him a curious look.

'What do you mean?'

'I mean for us to be a married couple again. I know I've been away for a long time, but I never stopped thinking of you as my wife.' She took a step back and rested her back against the sink.

'But I *am* your wife.'

'Yes, I know – of course you are – but being apart makes it difficult to be...' He was stumbling over words. The word *wife* felt alien. 'A husband.' He finished his sentence but felt lost as to what he was trying to say.

She stayed leaning back, head down and arms crossed. 'We're married and we should share a bed again. That's all – just share a bed.'

'That'll be wonderful. I'll move Helen's bed out and move my things in and we can be a proper ... family.' He wanted to say 'couple' but didn't dare to. He wasn't certain of what she meant, or even of what he meant. But he *was* glad – he had begun to desire her more keenly in the last few days.

The new daily – and nightly – routines comforted him. Agnes sometimes allowed him to put his arms around her in bed and hold her close. At first, she stayed tense but soon he thought she might want more from him. It was slow steps, but he could wait, even though he was as human as the next man and couldn't wait forever. He built bridges with Helen, too. She would sit at the other side of the rosewood table at dinner time and listen to him talk about the changes in the shop. Sometimes she smiled when he spoke to her. But when he tried to pick her up, Agnes still got between them, almost as if she didn't want him to get to know his daughter.

Perhaps these were problems to be expected – and in time Agnes would soften, and Helen would accept him. Lying in bed each night, he imagined the way it would be when Salonika was a distant memory and he and Agnes got used to each other again. Some evenings, he would look at her long slim back while she was cooking and want to wind his arms round her and rest his head on her shoulder, but he never did. It was true that he had missed her during the lonely nights when he'd first left England. Then, he supposed, he had got used to her absence. Now, for the sake of their marriage and child, he must be patient while they got to know each other for a second time.

Chapter Eight

One late afternoon, nearly a year after his return, Mr Wood – or 'Stanley', as Agnes now insisted on calling him – had left him to manage the shop alone. He kept hearing about servicemen who were unemployed and left high and dry, so every day he was grateful for his job and glad for the accommodation that went with it. He stood deep in thought, can in hand, dimly aware of the sound of footsteps behind him.

'Art, old chap!' He lurched forward – it was a voice from another world – the one he'd nearly managed to forget.

'What on earth are *you* doing here?' Arthur swivelled round, not just surprised but also a bit scared. He automatically checked that the door to the flat was closed. Charlie had been one of the fellows in the camp he'd avoided because of his knack for knowing everything that men wanted to keep quiet.

'Found you at last and what a backwater it is! I'd heard this was where you'd gone back to. I bet this establishment is glad to have you back.' Charlie looked around as if he was judging the shop's worth. Arthur remembered how everything about Charlie was double-edged – how he'd reel chaps in with flattery, then leave them dangling. You'd had to be really careful of him – once he'd even caught him reading one of his letters from Agnes.

'I'm lucky to have a job to come back to.' Arthur felt defensive already.

'Very humble of you, Art, but what else are you up to? Still at the cards? You were the best of the bunch, as I recall.' Charlie sounded the same – after something. But it was true – he *had* been the best card player – he could remain completely impassive with a good hand, yet also put on a convincing show when his hand was disastrous. He'd had a way of getting bigger bets out of desperate men. Agnes would be amazed if she knew.

'Different times now I've got my job and family back. What else does a man need? You still play?' He felt an edge of excitement.

'I most certainly do and that's why I'm here, old man. I want you to help me out – teach me a thing or two – from your experience, and all.'

'How so?' Arthur's heart thudded in his chest.

'Come down to the King's Arms next Thursday and see what I'm after. I'll introduce you to some players. You need to spread your talents about. You don't want to be stuck in with the wife every evening.' Charlie looked up as if he could see Agnes cooking and cleaning upstairs. 'I keep my dearest guessing where I am – keeps her keen, if you know what I mean! Us chaps need time together.'

Arthur could picture the camp and the clear cool evenings in the mess. It had been a comradeship that didn't compare with anything since. But it was a lifetime away.

'It's not easy to get away. I'll think about it.'

'You know where to find me then, old chap. But don't waste your talents.' Charlie's eyes bored right through him as he pumped his hand up and down, then turned and left.

*

Charlie's visit marked a change in Arthur's quest to regain family life and he started to feel restless again. He enjoyed a husband's sexual privileges every few weeks but was still unsure how to make Agnes desire him. Was Charlie right that he needed more male company?

One Sunday in the middle of summer, Kate arrived for dinner. She tramped up the steps and swooped on Helen. After a while, they all sat down to eat, and Agnes took command of the dinner table talk.

'I'm teaching her to read properly now' She gestured to Helen. 'She's always looking at labels in the shop.' Kate made an admiring noise, but Arthur couldn't respond at all. To make it worse, he wasn't sure why he was being so moody. 'She's very clever, you know, Arthur – we're lucky she likes to learn.' Agnes seemed determined to get something out of him but all he could do was look up and nod. There was a heavy silence as Agnes sprang up to get the dessert. 'It's your favourite!' A trifle jelly wobbled in front of him. He couldn't stand it any longer – his head was throbbing with frustration or pain – he didn't know what or why.

'I've got a job to do.' The words stuck to his throat as he got up. He grabbed his coat from the hallway and headed for the stairs.

'Well!' he heard Kate say but was soon out of the door and in the street. He wasn't sure where he was going but he needed to feel air on his face and have time to think.

The summer was tailing off and there was a brisk wind blowing a few leaves about. He lengthened his stride. If only his wife and her sister realised he had *lived* a bit – Salonika had changed him, and then Ealing had changed while he was away. How could a man be expected to just settle back in? Come to that, Agnes had changed, too. It was as if she ruled everything now and he was in the way. He strode along deeper and deeper in thought. A few other people were taking the air and he tipped his hat to two ladies. He was surprised to see their attention to him, and he smiled his best smile so that they laughed and smiled back at him. When he was in the shop, covered by his rough brown apron, women usually only wanted his attention to reach onto a high shelf for a packet or tin, but out and about like this, ladies seemed to appreciate him as a man. This was how it should be with *her*, he thought – appreciation rather than instruction. What could he do to get her to like him again?

The walking calmed him, and he started to feel embarrassed about his exit from the flat. He hadn't done himself any favours and if he was going to win Agnes over again, he needed to see things from her angle. Her sister had helped her when he was away, so he should be grateful, rather than rude. His stride shortened and he started back home feeling reinvigorated. Charlie's bravado had been at the edge of his mind, but he must forget it if he was going to concentrate on his marriage.

Kate had gone by the time he returned home, and Agnes was subdued. After finishing the clearing up, she sank into the armchair with a big sigh. Arthur sat beside her for a few minutes then he reached across and grasped her small nimble fingers.

'I'm sorry it's taking me so long to settle back down. I missed you so much when I was away.'

She shrank back and became tearful. 'I wanted you to see what Helen was doing when you were away – she's such a wonderful daughter – and it was hard on my own. But I suppose you had your work and I had mine.' He wasn't sure what she meant, especially since conscription wasn't work he'd chosen, but he decided to focus on Helen instead.

'She's a grand young thing. You did wonders with her.' Arthur stood up deliberately, offered Agnes his hand and pulled her to her feet. Then he gently folded his arms around her. For a moment they were quiet, wrapped in the embrace and, miraculously, he was relaxed – for the first time in years.

After a blissful few moments, she pulled apart slightly and looked up at him. 'I'm glad you're feeling better – there's something I've been wanting to say. I wanted to find the right time – you've still got so much to get used to – but we need a sister for Helen.' She looked down at her feet. He felt his soul flutter then plummet slightly, but still, he held her close.

'Yes, of course we do.' He was wrongfooted for a moment but also glad she wanted him, even if it was for another child. It made him feel like a properly married man for the first time in ages.

*

Arthur convinced himself that another baby would signal a change of fortune for them, but nothing happened as they hoped it would. He made love to Agnes every month, and he waited to see if it had 'worked'. Meanwhile, in January 1922, Helen reached her sixth birthday and Lou brought her children over. When Agnes and Helen led the children off to the kitchen to help with the dishes, Lou faced Arthur squarely over the dinner table.

'Helen seems so grown up now. She'd be so good with a little one.'

'Hmm,' Arthur looked at his watch and stood up. 'I'd better get back to work.' He definitely didn't want to talk to Lou about how hard they'd been trying for another baby, neither did he want Agnes to feel under any more pressure, but Lou's words made him wonder if something *was* wrong. His throat tightened with the familiar feeling of failure as he opened the shop door a few minutes later.

During the next few weeks, he decided to adjust to the idea of having a small family. He told Agnes about how tired his mother had been with her three boys and only girl. If Agnes could see the benefits of having just the one child, then he'd be happy with his only daughter too, and he made sure to say on two separate occasions how blessed they were by her clever and sensible nature.

Agnes seemed hardly to notice his efforts to make her feel better about things and Arthur feared that she might blame him for their situation. Then one cold evening she stood up from lighting the fire and turned to him with a grave expression.

'I think that we've been blessed with another child, after all.' She stood very still, half smiling at him until the penny dropped.

He grasped her hands, lost for words and surprised at how tearful he felt. 'Are you sure?' he eventually managed to utter.

Agnes laughed at his confusion. 'Three months now, I think,' she said. 'We'll be a proper family again, Art. We've come through our difficulties.' Arthur held his arms out to her and shook his head. His knees sagged with both relief and shock, still unable to take in what he was hearing.

A couple of months later, Arthur had adjusted to the idea of another baby, but the pregnancy was proving to be a difficulty all of its own – Agnes was anxious about the unborn child and couldn't or wouldn't sleep. Whatever Arthur said reduced her to tears and she shut him out to such a degree that the moroseness he'd fought off, returned even stronger than before. He knew he shouldn't crave her attention when she was struggling to manage a child and housekeeping, but in the evenings while she paced the flat, he sat mute, feeling even lonelier than he had on the battlefield of Salonika. It made no sense, just when they should feel happy, that they were both sinking fast.

Mr Wood usually dropped in once a month to see how things were going. The Wednesday before Easter, he thrust through the door first thing, bringing the spring air in with him. As usual, he went straight to the ledger that was kept in the stockroom and stood there tapping the page as if he was trying to catch Arthur out. Arthur stood in the doorway, trying to contain his frustration – if there was one thing he *was* sure of, it was his arithmetic.

'You've been busy by the looks of things. You must be working hard, Art.' Eventually, Mr Wood looked up, slapped the ledger shut and looked him up and down. 'You should be looking more cheerful, my lad. Business doing well and another young'un on the way. Think about how lucky you've been.' Arthur tried to smile but the corners of his mouth felt weighted down.

'How's the young lady doing? I expect you're hoping for a lad this time – not that my three aren't the death of me.'

Mr Wood's smile looked more like a sneer to Arthur. 'I can't think why anyone would want to have a boy when he could be sent off to fight at the drop of a hat,' he replied snappily.

Mr Wood took a step away from him. 'Well, true, I suppose. As you know, I couldn't fight because of my back and my boys, thank God, were too young. Mind you, we had to stop the eldest from pretending he was a year or two older and running off to join up. There's a lot of sadness for missing sons, that's for sure... But Art, *try* and look forward. You – having a boy, *or* a girl – will be a cause for celebration. I expect your Helen would love a little sister. And don't forget – daughters will look after you when you get too old to look after yourself!'

Arthur felt tearful at such encouragement and kindness in the face of his own meanness, but he found it difficult to think about getting older. War had taken that hope away from men. Sometimes it seemed as if he was suspended on an ever-present battlefield. He knew that other places – terrible places – existed with as hard-edged a reality as the shop he stood in, yet he wasn't joyful to be back home – war had taken that joy away. He envied Harold's impulse to emigrate and find a new home without having to see his friends die for it *and* he had his brother and sister nearby. Arthur, on the other hand, was permanently cut off. Agnes didn't seem to want him and even his mother had stopped pleading with him to join them. Her latest letter rested unread in his top pocket.

Mr Wood left, and Arthur cashed up, sat on the wooden till stool and thought about his time in Salonika. He thought about the card games in the mess and the pile of cigarettes – his winnings – which he used to hand out afterwards. They played to the sound of gunfire, sometimes distant, sometimes not, and he always carried on playing through it, so the other chaps would know he had nerve. Really, Agnes had no idea what he'd been through! Nor was she interested – she would be making dinner now and Helen would be playing with her dolls while his world felt like a million miles away.

He sighed and breathed in the musty air, feeling in his top pocket for his mother's letter. The stamp was the same King's head as they had on their stamps but this one was framed by maple leaves. He opened the seal carefully. *Dennis has a job*! Dennis had always been a worry to her, though Arthur had always known he would prove himself. Maude would be alright too – Helen had a look of her. He scanned the pages and decided he would read it through slowly after dinner while Agnes was seeing to Helen. It would give him something to look forward to. He wanted to anticipate their news for as long as possible and then savour it.

He tucked the stool neatly under the counter. Mr Wood was right, he did work hard, and the shop was doing well, so why did he feel no sense of pride or achievement? What was wrong with him?

'Dinner's ready!' Agnes's voice rolled down the stairs. He gripped the letter tightly and started to calculate how much he would need to save up to visit Canada. What would his mother make of his new family? Even as excitement rushed through him, he knew that Agnes would never agree to go on the long voyage, much less take a new baby, so he stuffed the letter back in his pocket.

'I'm on my way up, dear.' His limbs felt heavy. Mr Wood was right – he should look forwards to the new arrival and stop looking backwards to war and to those who had gone away. He should start to live like a lucky one.

Chapter Nine

AGNES

The baby was born early on a Wednesday morning, as autumn leaves fell, and post-war life took on more madness. Lying in bed after the midwife had left, Agnes felt heady with good fortune. She'd survived a nightmare of a pregnancy; had an uncomplicated delivery, and the baby was perfect. She was also glad that Helen had a sister – Arthur was so gloomy when sons were mentioned, it seemed that a daughter suited them both.

At last, her sisters would stop making comments about Helen being an 'only one'. At one point, Kate had actually said that people would think it abnormal to only have one child. Arthur had come back, after all – *unlike Jack*, she hadn't said. What Kate didn't realise, Agnes reflected, was how difficult it was to carry on a marriage *after* coming back. She prayed the baby would help Arthur to settle down.

There was a gentle knock on the door, and Arthur looked round the door. 'Are you ready for me to see her? Kate's with Helen.'

'Yes, come in. She's beautiful, Art – she really is.' He peered into the crib.

'She is.' He looked close to tears. 'Well done. You're a marvel.' Agnes fleetingly wondered if he was disappointed not to have a son, after all.

'She needs a special name, doesn't she? A special name for a special baby.'

'What about Maude – or Rose, even?' He still sounded choked.

'No, it's got to be lucky – like we are to have her. And this baby *is* lucky – being born in 1922, after the horrible war. You are happy, aren't you, Arthur? Another girl will be company for Helen.'

'What man wouldn't want two beautiful daughters?' He sounded as if he meant it.

'I want people to notice her, Art. Can we find an unusual name? Not an odd name. Just unusual.'

'I don't mind what you choose, dear.' He smiled and kissed her on the forehead. 'Would you like to show Helen her sister now?'

She was irked he didn't realise the importance of the right name. He'd once complained that Helen was named without consulting him, but now when he had the chance to name the new baby, all he could think of was his sister's or his mother's name! At the signal to approach, Kate ushered Helen in, and he slipped out. Helen stood away from the crib.

'It's your sister, darling. She needs you to look after her.' Agnes held out her arms to the six-year-old. 'It's lucky you're so sensible and helpful, isn't it?' Her words had the desired effect and Helen moved forward, reached into the crib and stroked the baby's head.

'Sister,' she said.

'And well done to *my* little sister.' Kate came forward, too, and hugged her. 'Thanks to you, I've two beautiful nieces.'

'And they're lucky to have a wonderful aunt. Does she look like a Maude or a Rose to you? Arthur's suggestions.'

Kate laughed. 'Absolutely not – you'll have to do better than that!'

'That's what I thought.' She looked at the baby's downy head and racked her brains.

'Whatever you call her, let's hope, being born on a

Wednesday, that she's not full of woe.'

'Like her father, you mean?' The words were out of Agnes's mouth without thinking.

Kate raised her eyebrows. 'Well, if this little one doesn't make him happy, I'm not sure what will. She's going to be the making of this family – I just know she is.'

*

The next few days passed by with the infant still unnamed. Agnes started to call her 'baby', despite Arthur's insistence on calling her 'she', as if no other females lived in the flat. More and more worried about finding the right name, a week after her birth, Agnes decided to take the baby to visit the bakery next door where a Polish woman worked who claimed to be psychic. Even though Arthur dismissed such claims as silly, she was curious. Perhaps a psychic would intuitively know what her baby should be called? She wrapped the baby in a shawl, left Helen with Arthur, and said she was going to pick up some fresh bread. The baker was a wiry man with thinning hair who'd skipped the war but had a reputation for being discreet, so Agnes hoped he wouldn't tell anyone about her request. She felt embarrassed, but excited too.

'It's not easy naming a child, Bill. If you choose one grandma's name, the other might get upset, and then there's sisters who think they know best!' She tried to make light of her dilemma.

'Wanda will tell you the baby's name.' Bill replied, 'But will you like a Polish name, because that's what she might choose?' Agnes wondered if she knew of any Polish names. Maybe this wasn't such a good idea, after all. The short, dark-haired woman who was listening to their conversation came out from behind the counter and moved towards her and the baby. She held her hand over the baby's head.

'I know it's a bit silly, but if you...' Agnes clasped the baby a bit tighter.

'Shhh,' said the woman. She lowered her hand down very slowly, as if a magnetic force was emanating from the baby's head. Agnes was too stunned to move away so she stood there until the woman looked up. 'Your baby is called *Eva*.' The woman's eyes were a steely grey.

'Oh.' Agnes looked over to the baker who had stopped chuckling and now had a serious expression on his face. He shrugged and turned away to serve a customer who had just walked in. She stood there for a minute, unsure what to do or say next.

'Eva, you think? As in E-V-A. Isn't that a bit – short?'

'Eeevaaaa.' The woman repeated back with utter certainty.

'Oh, I see – thank you.'

She returned next door and met Arthur at the counter.

'I've been thinking... What do you think about *Eva* as a name? It's English and it's simple but is it *too* unusual?'

Arthur looked down at the baby. 'No, not at all – it suits her. And how about 'Mary' after your mother?' He sounded as decisive as the woman had been.

It was kind of him to think of her mother. She looked at the baby and then over to Helen, who was standing by Arthur. 'Helen and Eva – the names do go together, I think. You know Arthur, I can see you in Helen. I hadn't noticed it before. But Eva – I think she's going to look more like me. Do you see it?'

'She's certainly a beauty.' He smiled broadly and the baby yawned. He looks happy for a change, Agnes thought. What a relief! For the first time, it felt like they could forget the war. Eva had given them all a new start.

Chapter Ten

By the time Eva was eight months old, she had a head of reddish-brown hair which was widely admired.

'What a lovely age this is!' Agnes said, as she ran her fingers through each baby curl and let it spring back. Eva was on her lap and Arthur was leafing through the local paper. The sitting room without Eva in it would be drab, Agnes thought, glancing at the worn arms of the settee.

'Take a look at this.' Arthur waved the paper in her direction, and she stopped arranging the curls. 'It says here that they're running a Bonny Baby Competition. You have to send in a photograph, and he or she can be up to nine months old.'

'Well, I'm not sure...' The curls bounced and bobbed. 'Then again, she *is* bonny.' Agnes lifted Eva and turned her to face the mirror which hung above the fireplace. Her own face was reflected alongside Eva's.

'We look well together, don't we?' She could see Arthur behind them. 'Is it open to anyone? I suppose we'd need to pay to have a photograph taken.' She was still looking at the mother and daughter tableau in the looking glass.

'It says that the photos are free if you go to that studio above the tailor's in the High Street,' Arthur replied.'

Agnes remembered the time her sisters had dressed her up for a photograph. The visit to the studio had been a day out, even better than a Sunday. She, Alfie and Kate were taken together – Alfie in the middle with his polished boots stretched out in front. There had been a rug under their feet – some sort of animal fur – and the photographer had made her hold a doll. It wasn't her own doll, and she'd had to sit for ages without moving which was hard. The photo still sat on her parents' mantlepiece.

'We've never had a really good portrait taken have we, Arthur?' She could see streaks of grey and wondered if she'd left it too late. 'Is there a prize for this competition?'

'The paper will publish the winning photos in a special supplement, it says,' She could still see Arthur in the mirror, scanning the pages.

'Like a film star, then. Let's make Eva into a film star!' She swung round to face him.

'Is Eva going to be a film star, Mummy?' Helen ran into the room, sensing the joyous atmosphere.

'She is. You're so clever, Helen, but Eva – well, Eva is beautiful!'

Arthur tousled Helen's hair. 'Brains earn more money than beauty, though. I have high hopes for this daughter,' he said, as she leaned into him.

'So do I – you *know* how proud I am of her, as well. But you have to use what talents you have in this life, so I think we *should* enter Eva into this competition.' Agnes looked over at Arthur with his arm now around Helen. Helen trusted him now, thank goodness, even though she herself couldn't always tell what mood he was going to be in each day. She sometimes wondered if they'd been close before he'd gone to war, but it was hard to remember because people were like shadows in her memory back then. Take her: she was little more than a girl when he'd left for Salonika, and the war had made her into a woman with views and opinions of her own. But now he was back, she wanted her daughters to have a father they could rely on – Eva mustn't go through what Helen had.

'Eva's beauty will speak for itself.' Arthur said, interrupting her thoughts. He held out his arms for her to give to Eva to him.

'What a beautiful picture!' She watched with pride as he embraced both daughters.

*

The studio was above a man's outfitters that she admired but had never entered. She parked the pram outside, careful not to obscure the window, and holding Eva firmly, nudged the door open with her shoulder.

It was a beautiful May morning. It had started damp with beads of moisture clinging on from the previous night's shower, but now the sun was poking through the residual clouds, and it was warmer than she'd expected. She was wearing her green wool coat and a hat that she'd made herself. It always attracted notes of approval from female customers. Eva was carefully bathed and dressed, and her mood was sunny to match the emerging day. In a final flourish, Agnes had dabbed some of her Eau de Cologne behind Eva's ears, as well as her own.

The stairs up to the studio were steep with a wooden handrail. It was like ascending a mountain and as she got near to the top step she looked up and saw a young man.

'Are you here for the baby photo? You'll have to join the queue in the waiting room.'

She pulled Eva closer, as the young man pointed her to the right. When she opened a door, she saw two other women, each with a baby in their arms. They eyed her, as she arranged herself on a rickety chair and set about trying to unpin her hat whilst keeping an eye on Eva to see that she didn't fall off her lap.

'Here, dear.' The woman nearest her offered a free arm.

'Thank you very much but I think I can manage.' Agnes recoiled from the arm. Why had she come? What was she thinking of?

'As you like, dear. Lovely hat – and she's a beauty.' The woman nodded towards Eva.

'Thank you – as is your son.' Agnes replied, though she thought that Eva was much the bonnier of the two. Luckily, at that point, the young man reappeared.

'Who's next?' He looked at each of them in turn. The woman next to Agnes got to her feet as her baby started to wail.

'Oh no, you've set him off.' She laughed and followed the young man through the door.

Agnes could still hear the commotion as she busied herself with Eva's shawl. Glancing further along the seats, she could see that the baby on her other side was asleep. She quickly looked away as the sun slanted through the window and lit up a patch of floor by her feet. The attic ceiling reflected it back and the effect was a shaft of light which enveloped her and Eva. As the sun warmed them, she relaxed and started to feel excited.

The young man came back, and the woman with her screaming baby hurried to the door out to the stairs. She heard the thump of her feet on the stairs as the wails of the baby started to recede.

'I think you'd better come in next. I can see how to use the light on her.' The young man was speaking to her.

She entered the studio. Straight ahead were two wooden chairs and over each was a large lamp fixed onto an elaborate frame. Umbrellas directed the glow from the lamps onto the chairs. She shielded her eyes, feeling temporarily blinded.

'Don't worry, Mrs... I'm going to try something different here.' The young man indicated for her to sit on a faded couch to the right of the chairs.

'Borton... Mrs Borton and Eva.' She held Eva out to him.

'Right, Mrs Borton, you'll need to hold Eva till I'm ready.' Agnes took in the large mural on the wall behind the couch. She felt as if she'd been transported into an entirely different, but not unpleasant, world of palm trees and elephants.

'I'm ready now. If you want to put Eva over there.' The young man pointed to a second couch under a small window in the end wall. The window faced the same way as the window in the waiting room and a similar shaft of light was filtering through. He turned off the lamps and the darkened room startled her as much as the lamplight had done a few minutes earlier. Adjusting to the new lighting, she lowered Eva onto the shawl which was draped over the couch and set about propping her up and adjusting her legs to make her secure. Finally, she twisted one of Eva's curls away from her face.

'There now – how's that?' Agnes stood back and scrutinised the scene, almost as if she was the photographer herself.

'Lovely, just lovely. No tears from this one then – she's a natural.'

Agnes watched how he used his hands to measure the distance, then how he ducked under the black curtain. The flash made her jump and Eva looked alarmed.

'It's alright, it's alright, Evie,' Agnes said, waving at her.

'That's just lovely – just like her mother,' came a muffled voice from under the cloth. 'And once again – a bright light.'

Eva barely blinked this time and Agnes felt the flash illuminate them both.

'That's it, then.' The man's head popped out from under the black curtain and smiled at her. It was over and she was being asked to leave. She took one last look at the different backdrops in the studio and decided to come back to have her own portrait taken. This was her sort of place – hers and Eva's.

*

'Auburn hair is far more *interesting*,' Kate said, as she stroked Eva's head. It was early in the morning on the first Monday in June. The result of the photo competition had been announced and a baby with blond curls had won the first prize. Eva's photo was highly commended.

'She was good in that studio, Kate. Really, *so* good. I'm going to make sure she always looks her best.' Agnes had her hands on her hips.

'Hmm.' Kate was still looking down at Eva who was sitting on her lap. 'Do you remember the time we had our portrait taken?'

'I was thinking about that when we were in the studio and how you dressed me up. You should see Helen dressing Eva up, just like you used to dress me – choosing a cardigan to match each outfit. She's like a second mother to her.'

'Like I was to you... Perhaps I realised then that I'd never have my own.' Kate said quietly.

Agnes winced and thought again how hard Jack's death had been for her. 'You're still young enough you know – and till the right man comes along, you can help with Eva. Take her out this morning, if you like.'

'Little Eva has us all circling around her – mother, aunts, sister, as well as a doting father!' Kate looked around as Arthur appeared at the top of the stairs.

'How's our little film star this morning, then?' He held out his arms to Eva.

Agnes stood up so she was between Arthur and Eva. 'She's fine, but we're getting her ready to go out. She's settled with Kate. Why don't you get things ready downstairs?'

Arthur let his arms fall to his sides. 'The shop is sorted out, so I thought I could spend a few minutes with my girls. Is Helen ready for school yet? I can walk her there before we open up.' He put his hands in his pockets and leant back on the sideboard.

Agnes thought about the boxes he'd thrown in a corner yesterday. The shop seemed far from sorted out to her. What was wrong with him? They'd lose business if he carried on like this. He was making her nervous. 'Helen's finding a cardigan for Eva to wear, and Kate can take her to school. She's taking Eva for a walk anyway,' she said.

Arthur looked over at Kate. 'You'd never think they were my daughters, would you?' His voice sounded thin and childish.

Agnes felt embarrassed. 'Kate's a great help to me, Arthur – you should be pleased. You've got your own work in the shop to do! This is how families are – fathers providing, and women looking after the children. Isn't that right, Kate?'

Kate shrugged. 'What would I know about families? But I won't take Helen if you'd rather I didn't, Arthur.' She handed Eva back to Agnes.

'I think you should apologise to Kate, Arthur.' Agnes pursed her lips.

He looked away and raked a hand through his hair. 'Thank you for your help,' he muttered, looking at the wall behind Kate.

It didn't sound like him at all. Agnes could see a vein on his forehead standing out. What was she supposed to do? Of course she wanted him to spend time with his daughters but recently when he tried to help out, he messed up their routines. More than once he'd roused Eva just as she was dropping off. He was starting to get in her way – that was the truth of it – and it was hard to be patient when he was miserable, too.

Kate picked up her knitting from the table and started clicking the needles.

'I'll tell Helen her father's taking her to school, then.' Agnes sighed.

Arthur started to say something then stopped and set off down the stairs instead. 'I'll do the boxes while I'm waiting. Tell her not to be too long,' he shouted back.

'I will.' Agnes looked over at Kate and shrugged.

Chapter Eleven

EVA

I'm waiting for the wireless to be switched on. Mummy and Helen are talking about money, whilst everyone else in the country only has one thing on their minds – the abdication. The coals in the grate start to crumble, as I stand over the fireplace trying to warm my legs. When I look down, my knees have reddened but I'm not sure if that's with the heat or the cold. At last, Helen reaches over and twists the knob. She's timed it just right – he's about to speak. I sit on one of the dining chairs.

Every evening this week, Mummy has muttered *that brassy American woman* under her breath. Tonight, she just shakes her head – we know what she thinks. We sit in silence and listen. I imagine he's talking directly to me but it's a lot to take in – history right here by our fading coals. He sounds so sad that we're crying – even Mummy. It ends, and Helen turns the wireless off. We sit.

'Well!' Mummy brushes her eyes with her hanky. We sit for a few minutes more. It's getting colder and she pushes her arms into her cardigan and hugs it round her.

'I think it's romantic – giving up the country for love.' I'm nervous saying it, but someone's got to say something. They look at me, then look away again.

'He wasn't up to the job,' Helen says, after a few seconds.

'He's thinking of the country,' I say.

'He's thinking of himself!' she says.

I wonder what Daddy thinks of the King. The King is giving up the country for a woman and he also gave up his family. Perhaps, he gave us up for another woman, too. The idea hits me hard. I think about it. It doesn't seem likely – Daddy didn't like *brassy women*. He always said Mummy was a natural beauty. But men do leave wives for other women and not all other women are brassy. Gwen has a stepmother somewhere, she says.

'Bed.' Mummy chips into my thoughts. 'We all need to go to bed. We can read the paper in the morning. Thank goodness for the Duke of York. Someone has to keep their head when others can't.'

I'm still thinking about the King and Daddy, and Gwen's stepmother. 'It'll be hard to sleep. Imagine how he's feeling tonight. He sounded so lost.'

'I hope she's worth it,' says Helen. 'It's probably her idea, all this.'

'But he loves her. Isn't that what matters most?' My question hangs in the air for a moment.

'Goodness knows what they'll live on!' Mummy has an answer of sorts. 'And his poor brother, thrown into the limelight. It just seems so ... *selfish*.'

I suddenly have a memory of Daddy getting in from work and her asking him where he'd been all day. It wasn't long before he disappeared. *Work, of course*, he said, and she turned to him and said, *what work would that be, Arthur?* I didn't catch the rest. Why didn't she know about his work? It didn't make any sense. There must be something about his work that I didn't know about. He didn't answer but turned and winked at me instead. He had a wild look and what he said next didn't make much sense. Drawing his feet together, he stood, as if to attention. *She's a real beauty, Mrs Agnes Borton, a real beauty.* I looked at Mummy, but her face was pinched and furious. She thought he was mocking her. But he meant it – I know he did.

*

The cornflakes are stale this morning and the kitchen is freezing.

'Why did you say Miss Beauvoir wanted to see you on Friday?' Helen's voice drifts over me. I'm still thinking about the King, and don't want to think about school, but she's looking at me with her question mark face. We're supposed to be eating breakfast, not talking.

'Oh, nothing really. She said something along the lines of, *how can you be Helen's sister…*' I've put on Miss Beauvoir's voice so well; I can see the corners of Helen's mouth twitching. She wants to laugh.

'It's not my fault that they compare you to me. You must have done something wrong.'

'Is Eva in trouble?' Mummy is taking an interest. I pull a face that she can't see. 'Why does this Miss whatever-her-name-is want her to be like you?' She sounds bewildered. I wait for Helen to come up with an answer.

'It's probably the way she looks… And the way she dresses.' That's mean for Helen. Anyone would think that it was her that was in trouble. I could say something back, but I don't. The truth is that last week, Miss Beauvoir had a word with me about looking smart. She said I mustn't let Helen down. That hurt, I admit.

I wait to see what Mummy will make of it all. She hasn't a clue about school, of course, so whatever she thinks, it'll probably be wrong.

'When she leaves the house every morning, she looks perfectly respectable,' Mummy says to Helen. Then, as I feared, she turns to me. 'What is Helen talking about and why are you getting into trouble at school?'

'I'm not in trouble. I'm just *not* Helen, that's all – I'm not as neat and tidy as she was when she was at school.' Mummy looks back at Helen who is looking at me.

'Eva, you *know* you're breaking rules – socks down, collar up. That's the point of a uniform – everyone's supposed to look the same!' Helen is het up and sounds it.

'Well, I don't want to look like everyone else!' I give as good as I get.

'You can't expect *everyone else* to like you then! First you wanted to look like Miss Dessin and now you're just plain unkempt. What's the matter with you? You'll get on with the town girls by taking care of the way you look.' My eyes are smarting. Helen's never normally this hard on me. She's practising being a teacher. 'And your hair is a mess, too. No wonder you don't fit in!'

Mummy looks from Helen to me and back again, as if she can't decide something. 'Eva, you're such a pretty girl. Why would you want to spoil the way you look?'

I stand head down. She doesn't know those town girls mock, whatever I look like and whatever I wear.

She goes to the pine dresser and starts rummaging in the drawer. 'You won't remember this, of course, but I was proud of you that day.' She pulls out an old photo and hands it to me.

'Is that me?' A baby looks up with trusting eyes. Heart-shaped face and a strap of her vest falling off her shoulder. And the light is just right.

'The photographer said you were a natural. He thought you might be a film star one day.' She's smiling.

'I love it when we read plays at school, so you never know.' The argument with Helen recedes into the distance. I see my name in lights.

'You didn't win – the competition, that is.' Helen's voice cuts in. She can't stop being mean.

'No, but she made us all very proud – and you, too, Helen.' Mummy takes the photo back and takes a final look before putting it away. Suddenly, I feel for Helen

– it isn't her fault that the teachers compare us – or that Mummy is proud of the way I look. Helen gets up to wash her bowl.

I plead with her back. 'The town girls leave me alone if I look scary – that's why I do it. I can't be neat and tidy like you were. I have to do things my way.'

She turns to face me again. 'Well, don't be surprised if Miss Beauvoir tells you off then.' She sounds hurt.

'It was you who wanted to know why,' I remind her.

'I'm just looking out for you, Eva. You need to grow up – school's important.'

'So says *Miss*,' I say. I'm the one being mean now. She turns and goes upstairs. I hear her bedroom door close. It's not often that I'm alone down here with Mummy. Usually, I'm the one who's shut out.

Mummy gives me a long look. 'If you just pinned your hair back a little more loosely, the parting would look nice, dear – that's all it would take. We could try it out tomorrow – for church. Then you could wear it like that at school.'

I am interested in hair dos and clothes – like she is, but I don't know how to explain to her that looking nice at school is pointless – you have to be fierce, or a saint, like Helen was, to survive.

'I'll look nice for church, I promise.' I don't mention school.

'Good. That's fixed then. Helen is giving you good advice, you know. She doesn't like you being in trouble, especially now she's going to be a teacher herself. And fitting in with other girls *is* important.'

She's right about Helen. But she doesn't understand school at all.

*

On Sunday, Mummy comes in to fix my hair, and we talk about the ladies in the front pews – *her* ladies, she calls them. We talk about everything – their dresses, their hair, their hats, their hems, their waistlines. It's a Sunday ritual. When she told us that the vicar's wife had an extra panel inserted in her dress – Helen and I laughed. Mummy likes it that I take an interest in the hats, but Helen is more interested in alterations – she's thinking about money.

The vicar's wife is wearing a beret decorated with leaves and berries. A plain beret would have been more stylish, I think. Helen is too busy praying to notice it. The King's plight dominates the opening prayers, and the vicar goes on about the national crisis. The service drags. We finally get out and I see Mummy talking to two ladies with colourful scarves, a bit like Miss Dessin's. Helen and I make our way over and listen in.

'My daughters go to Wellesley High School,' she's saying. The ladies are attentive. I've seen them before, but we've never spoken – Aunt Kate would call them *fancy*. Their tweed suits and silk blouses look expensive, and the scarves are pinned to their shoulders with huge brooches. The berets are plain, which is far better than leaves and berries. I can't wait to talk to Mummy about it.

'We're getting a few young people together for a perfor-mance.' The taller of the two rolls her *r*s and stresses every syllable. 'After all this terrible business, the country needs to come together, and my sister writes marvellous Christmas plays. Your daughters would be welcome – we need older girls to take leading parts.'

Mummy stands up straight. I start to feel excited and want them to notice me, but Mummy is in full flow. 'Well, if you're sure that she would be a help, though her studies are *very* important, especially now she's training to teach – but I'm sure she would love to...' She always thinks it's Helen who can do things because she's older. But this is a *play* – she must realise it's meant for me.

I have to say something. 'Hello, I'm Eva. I'm really interested in plays, and I'd love to be in one.' Helen jumps and Mummy flinches, but *she's* the one who said I could be a film star.

The shorter of the sisters speaks. 'If you're keen and your mother agrees, I think I have just the roles for Helen *and* you. Can you and your sister come around next Saturday when we have the auditions?' Mummy nods. They shake her hand and stride off in the direction of the vicar.

I sing and dance all my way home, even though tomorrow ... well, I've remembered what tomorrow is, even if no one else has. Despite everything, I think Mummy's proud of me for being bold. I'm over the moon all evening and the mutton dinner tastes like tender lamb and the rhubarb crumble like peach meringue. 'That was lov-e-ly.' I stress every syllable.

'She's already acting up.' Helen sounds happy, too.

At bedtime, I count down. It's five whole years – nearly a third of my entire life since he went. *You live with it*, I heard a woman saying to her friend on the train last week, about her dead husband. She thought no one could hear, but I did. Dead: not missing, but it made me think that it might be the same and that, maybe, I'm living *with* Daddy, even though he's not actually here. I can't help wondering what he would have made of the performance which got me an invitation to the big house. He would be proud, surely. *You've done it, Bunny*, he would probably say. *You nailed it.*

*

'What are you doing, talking to yourself?' Helen pushes her way into my bedroom on Wednesday evening.

'Just practising.'

She looks worried, 'You might not get chosen, you do know that, don't you? There'll be other jobs – like the prompt who helps actors with their lines. I wouldn't mind helping out with the costumes, either.'

She's as practical as ever but wasting her breath. Yesterday, I altered my walk home and counted the houses out, one by one, until I was at the end of the sisters' driveway. I could just see the rounded sides of a small black car, even though the house was obscured. I reached out to touch the rough surface of a giant stone pineapple on the top of the gatepost. Exotic for Haydon Cross. A sign said 'Kildara' which made me think of the sea.

I won't tell Helen. She's told me that the sisters are called the Misses 'Johnson' and belong to an organisation called 'The League of Nations' which makes them important but respectable, rather than Bohemian. Miss Dessin would be disappointed.

'Well, I won't get chosen if I don't practice, will I? We're doing *A Winter's Tale* in English, so I thought I'd read all the parts out loud. Practice makes perfect, aren't you always saying?'

'I always thought you liked art best,' Helen shoots back.

'I like the art *teacher* best, yes – but I've always liked English. You used to like lots of subjects, didn't you?'

'Yes, of course, but you shouldn't set your heart so on things, Eva. It makes life – well – it makes it more *difficult*. You're likely to be disappointed. I don't like to see you disappointed.'

This is a new angle on something but I'm not quite sure what. Perhaps she's worried *by* me, rather than *for* me. 'You don't have to look after me all the time, you know. I can look after myself... And eventually, I'll find a rich man to look after me,' I reply.

Helen laughs. 'Good luck with that. That'll make Mummy happy. But some of us have to work hard, not rely on our looks.'

Perhaps that's it – the fact that people look at me. 'Helen...'

'Hmm.'

'Why don't you take the part of Florizel and we can practice this bit together? You can help me, and I won't be disappointed if I'm not chosen, I promise.'

She looks relieved and takes the book from me. 'Well, all right. It'll help you with your English, I suppose. But rich people, even good people like the Misses Johnson, don't realise what our lives are like. They might promise something one minute and then forget about it the next. Just so long as you realise that. In the end, it's down to *you*, Eva. No one will help you to get what you want, except yourself.'

'Message received and understood.' Though it isn't, not really. She's the one who will be disappointed – I see the audience clap, as I take a bow. *I'm* not going to be poor forever.

*

I try and decide what to wear. I think black is right and put on thick tights under my school pinafore dress.

Mummy's annoyed. 'Make sure you keep that clean for Monday.' She doesn't like me to wear school clothes at the weekend. Helen is dressed in a skirt, blouse and plain wool cardigan.

'What on earth are you wearing that for?' Helen says. She doesn't see how dramatic my red wool scarf will look against the black. 'It's cold, you know.' She puts on her coat and then holds out mine.

'I won't bother with my coat – it's not far to go.' A coat will ruin the effect, so I wind the scarf round my neck and slip through the door, ahead of her. I run down the road and the large pineapple gatepost of Kildara beckons like an old friend. I stop when I reach it, so that Helen can catch me up.

The taller sister answers the door. There's a huge Christmas tree in the corner of the hallway, with a golden candle holder and candle on each branch.

'When will you light the candles, Miss Johnson?' Helen nudges me as I speak, which means that I shouldn't ask a question.

'We don't light them till Christmas Eve, dear – and by the way, I'm Ethel and my sister is Lillian. Let me take your coat.' I hear more voices. Ethel leads us into a vast drawing room, and I recognise a few of the children from my elementary school.

'We're having a run through of some of the parts, dear. Take a seat,' says the shorter sister. I hope I won't have to call her Lillian to her face. We sit by the fire and wait for our turns to come. Helen takes off her cardigan and puts it on the back of her chair. I unwind my scarf and feel drab. The tights are making my legs prickle.

When it's my turn, I read as if my life depended on it. The play is like the Christmas story – yet different from it, at the same time.

Lillian gathers us together. 'Eva, I want you to take the part of Martha – and Helen, perhaps you could be Mary?' I fight the disappointment that I promised Helen I wouldn't have.

'We'll run through again. I hope you see, dear, that the part of Martha is a *very* significant one. She's one of the children in Bethlehem who have heard about the birth of baby Jesus.' Lillian looks at me and I try to look grave. Then she looks at Helen. 'Mary's role is, of course, senior, but mainly symbolic, so you won't have many lines to learn, dear.'

My part is the bigger after all! Despite a throbbing head, I read the part again, with even more gusto.

'Yes, dear, you'll do. But don't forget to convey reverence for our saviour in your voice,' Lillian says. I'm not sure if this is good or not and my triumph ebbs a little.

On the way out, I take one last look at the tree and try to imagine what it will look like on Christmas Eve when the candles are lit, and we're dressed up to perform. Once outside, I start to shiver. The clouds have knitted together and look threatening.

'Borrow my coat, Pixie.' Helen uses the new nickname she has for me. 'You stopped them in their tracks with your reading. They were star struck!' I take her coat and curtsey, laughing.

'Christmas is going to be fun this year,' I look up at the thunder-black sky. 'Not everything is difficult, Helen. I just know there's whiteness under the clouds, ready to fall.'

Chapter Twelve

ARTHUR

Customers asked after little Eva all the time. Was she walking, talking? He answered as best as he could and tried to be interested when they told him their aches and pains, but he was bored by the tittle-tattle of shop life. He used to like it, but the war had shown him something different. Harsh but different.

It was early June and during the long light evenings, he sat in the corner of the sitting room and pretended to read the newspaper. The grainy images of men in flat caps holding placards bothered him. They looked like the men he'd fed and watered back at the camp in Salonika. Now, these men were seen as the enemy. He glanced across at Agnes's bent head; her hair smooth and clipped back from her brow; her face a study in concentration on her sewing. She had a sense of purpose, looking after their children. But what did he have? Just tittle-tattle.

Charlie dropped into the shop every so often. When he strolled in, a couple of weeks ago, he caught Arthur at a particularly low moment. He had a way of making the grass seem greener elsewhere. *You can't just stick around in one place and then scoot upstairs to your missus and girls every night. It's not what us men do, now is it? You need male company, Art. Why don't you have an afternoon off, eh?* It was as if he was reading his mind, and Arthur had to resist the temptation to shut the shop up there and then and go off with him.

He decided he would pay Charlie a visit when it

suited him and so Agnes wouldn't know – it would be his adventure and show that he was his own man.

A week later, the late afternoon still bright and sunny, he told Agnes he had a delivery to make. She was sitting with the girls reading a book and Helen was making Eva repeat words and point to pictures. It was a touching scene and he nearly decided not to go.

'Don't rush, I'll save your dinner for you, dear,' Agnes said, smiling up at him.

He tried to smile back, then grabbed his delivery jacket, ran down the steps and wheeled his bike round to the front. He knew where to find Charlie – he'd memorised the details – and it was, beyond doubt, a relief to be away from the shop and his family. The air was warm and slightly sticky after the long summer's day. He thrust his jacket into the large basket at the front of the bike.

The King's Arms was tucked away in plain sight behind Ealing Broadway. He parked his bike against the side wall and put his jacket back on. Finding a side door, he tapped on the chipped wooden panel.

'What do you want?' A woman half opened the door. She looked him up and down. He could see some worn flagstones leading to another door where he could hear voices. 'We're not open till half six.' She moved to close the door.

'I'm after Charlie. He's a friend – he said this was where I'd find him,' Arthur managed to say before the door closed in his face. It opened a bit more and the woman, probably in her forties and smartly dressed in black silk, looked at him again.

'You're not really Charlie's type, I'd say.' He wasn't sure how to respond but she opened the door and stood back so he could enter. He took off his cap and stepped inside.

'He's in there, but he won't want interrupting. Wait, and I'll let him know someone's here for him. He'll come out when he's ready.' The woman turned to go through an inner door. This was entirely another side of Ealing than he was used to. In a few minutes, she pushed, the inner door open again and beckoned him inside. The crumpled figure of Charlie was leaning against a wall and rolling a cigarette.

Charlie took a few seconds to recognise him. 'Art, my old man – it's you! What are you doing here? I thought you were a *family* man.' There was mockery in his voice.

'I am, and that's fine, but it's about what we all went through – you, me and the other chaps. We shouldn't forget it, should we?'

Charlie stood perfectly still for a minute, looking down at his buffed leather brogues on the worn flagstones.

'Indeed, no, indeed, no, Art,' his tone less mocking now. 'Come on in and I'll introduce you to some of the fellows who remember those things like we do. You've already met Annie here, our lovely landlady who looks after us.' The woman who'd opened the door pulled a face and eased past him.

He followed them into the bar. Three men were sitting round a green baize tabletop with cards piled up in the middle. The cards had a yellow sheen which glistened against the green of the table and the chairs round the table were shiny with use. A few notes and coins were pushed to one side as he entered the room. The men didn't look up, even when Charlie coughed.

'Relax, chaps – we've got a new member.' At last, they looked up and nodded towards him. Charlie pointed to a burly man whose legs barely fitted under the table. 'This is Harry, Annie's other half. He was in Greece like us, but a different unit. Tough, Harry, eh? Arthur here did the stores for us – he had an easy ride.'

Arthur raised his arms apologetically. Charlie then nodded to the other two. 'That's Will and that's Jack – you'll get to know them by the way they play.' This made them grin, so Arthur grinned back.

Charlie disappeared into the bar and came back with another wooden chair for him. He sat down and pulled himself up to the table.

'Now, Art, I know you won't have much to bet with, but these gentlemen could learn a thing or two from you if my memory serves me right.' Charlie addressed the three other men gathered round the table. 'Watch and learn, my friends, watch and learn – Art used to get his hands on all the ciggies. He's wasted on civvy street – should be a banker not a shopkeeper, eh, Art? What do you say?' The other men looked at him with interest.

'I say: what's the game, gentlemen?' Arthur was beginning to enjoy himself.

'Blackjack. What else, old man? And as I remember, you're a dab hand at this particular sport.' Charlie was his usual flattering and cajoling self. But it was true – Blackjack was Arthur's favourite and once upon a time, he'd been quick to calculate which cards were likely to be dealt.

'Just a flutter then, for old times' sake and all. I'll try and pick up where I left off when we were in the thick of it.' He looked up at them, wanting the other men to share in his nostalgia, but they looked back blankly. Perhaps they didn't want to remember. Never mind, the game was the thing – that's what had kept them going. He stroked his chin trying to look calmer than he felt. Before shutting the shop, he'd grabbed two ten bob notes from the till and stuffed them in his pocket. They wouldn't go far so he'd need luck as well as judgement.

The other men leant forward as Charlie started to shuffle. His fingers flicked backwards and forwards over the cards. He reckoned they were playing with four decks which made it easy for him to do the calculations needed. Charlie carried on shuffling with a showman's panache and each man pushed forward a wager. Arthur felt for one of his ten bob notes and placed it down on the table. It rustled pleasingly. Charlie dealt the cards and the Ace of Spades landed in front of him. A rush of pleasure soaked right down into his boots. The others whistled through their teeth.

'Told you he was a lucky bugger.' Charlie shook his head.

The next cards put no one ahead. He had the seven of hearts. Charlie had a three, so was unlikely to beat him. He watched as the other players calculated their moves. Harry was tapping his foot nervously and beckoned twice to the dealer for another card before he threw his hand down. The other two chaps were more thoughtful. He sensed that one of them was trying to calculate the odds. But if he was, his calculations were wrong, and he threw his hand on the table with disgust. Soon, it was between him and Charlie. Arthur calculated that the odds were in his favour. They were, and in a few minutes he had gathered up all the notes scattered over the tabletop. It felt very good indeed.

He won three of the next six rounds, finishing with a Blackjack, and wanted to play one last round to make his mark, but knew that Agnes would wonder where he'd got to. It was better to keep her sweet.

'Got to be off, chaps.' The other players dragged themselves in the direction of the bar.

'We'll need to see some of those notes back here again tomorrow, Art. Don't go depriving us of your winnings.' Charlie slotted the cards back in their wooden box. Annie was drawing back the curtains and he blinked as the daylight streamed back into the room. Suddenly, the room which had seemed full of rich colours, looked seedy and drained.

'Just seeing what you've been up to Charlie – seeing if I've still got the touch.' Arthur said, folding the notes inside his pocket as he stood up to go.

'The little lady stopping you, Art? Can't a man do what he wants in his own town?' Charlie was in full swing now.

Arthur was annoyed yet pleased at the same time. 'Perhaps next week then. Same time, same day, if it suits you.'

'That'll have to do, and keep it to yourself, pal – we're a club here, know what I mean? Private-like.'

Arthur let himself out and transferred some of the notes to his other pocket as he mounted his bicycle. The streets of Ealing had become the Salonikan mess for the afternoon – Agnes and the children were in the distance. This was men's business – women had other concerns.

When he got back home, Arthur found Agnes in the kitchen, and before she could say anything, he told her that deliveries were going to be a regular feature for customers that lived further away.

'But why don't they go to their own shop?' She looked confused.

'We have good stock,' Arthur said, turning away and making it clear that he didn't want any more questions.' It was easy to lie about the card game and it was satisfying to be in control for a change. 'Deliveries are lucrative. We should have started doing them ages ago,' he added, lifting a sack of flour onto his back in a show of strength that would impress her.

She still looked doubtful.

'There's five bob extra this month, if you need something new for the girls.' That stopped her doubts. He disappeared into the stock room.

*

'Why don't you put Eva to bed this evening?' It was an evening in early July and the uplift in Arthur's mood had cheered the whole family. 'She looks at you all the time – have you noticed that, Arthur?'

He had noticed her interest and sometimes even wondered if she knew where he went on Wednesdays. She couldn't, of course, but something about the way she looked at him willed him on.

'What do you think, Evie – shall Daddy put you to bed tonight?' He swung her into the air.

'Be careful now, Arthur. She's not a toy.'

'She's my special girl, though, isn't she?' He tucked Eva under his arm, and she shrieked with excitement. He saw Helen glance up from her book.

'Don't forget to shield her eyes when you wash the soap out of her hair, will you? And comb her hair slowly – you know how she hates tangles.'

'Aye, aye, captain.' Helen smiled at that.

Helen and he were mostly on good terms, but he especially enjoyed spending time with his younger daughter. Now she could toddle about and point and laugh, she was a proper member of the family – and one that seemed to like him without any complications. He couldn't understand why Agnes always went on about him wanting a son – didn't she understand anything about the war and how it had made him feel? It was because of war, that he still felt more distant from Helen, and he doubted this would ever change. Eva, on the other hand, put her arms out when he came in and wanted him to lift her up. She trusted him completely.

He ran the water into the enamelled bathtub – the hot water direct from a faucet still amazed him. Eva put up her arms for him to slip her dress off, and then her vest. He undid her nappy pin and carefully peeled her nappy away. Seeing her grasp the side of the bath made him choke up. She was so glad to be with him, he could barely stand it. How could such a perfect child have come from him? After the bath, he fixed her new nappy and put her in a night gown, then combed out her hair.

'Are you managing in there?' Agnes's voice rang out.

He winked at Eva. 'Eva says I'm managing fine, thank you.' He whispered in Eva's ear, 'Your Daddy will show your Mummy what he's made of!'

Next, he settled Eva in her cot. When he was growing up, his mother would weave characters into a tale that had him and Harold hanging on her every word. It was as if she'd absorbed all the tics and habits of their neighbours, for her sons' amusement. He looked over to the little stack of books on the shelf and picked up the top one.

'Shall we look at this one, Bunny?'

It was the book that his mother had sent her for Christmas. 'This is Grandma's story for you. It's about a little chick that wouldn't go to bed.' He turned it so that she could see the pictures. After a few pages, he tried using a different voice for the mother hen. It was easier than he expected, and Eva smiled, just as he had smiled when his mother had entertained him. She smiled even more when he put on a high-pitched voice for the chick.

'Would you like to visit Grandma?' He closed the book cover gently. She nodded, nearly asleep. 'Well, one day, Bunny, Daddy will get enough money for a visit.' He put the book back on the pile and crept out.

*

'Hope you're ready for a cracker of a game.' It was almost as if Charlie had been hiding behind the door ready to swing it open as he approached.

'I'll have to get back my winning ways lickety-split.' A couple of weeks ago, Charlie had completely outwitted him. He wasn't sure how it had happened and reckoned it must have been a fluke. Probability was like that – sometimes there were freak chances.

Back in the bar, the usual green baize table was set out. Two men he hadn't seen before hovered, ready to start playing. Charlie took his seat and they all followed. One of the new men looked as if he hadn't used a razor recently. There was a stain on his collar and when he greeted him, his voice had a strange accent, probably Scottish. The other man was thin and sharp looking. When he smiled, you could see black marks on a couple of his teeth. He wondered where Charlie found his new players – he doubted that these were ex-servicemen. Both men had come with a wad of cash in their pockets.

'We've got a couple of new players today, Art.' Charlie changed his tone to sound business-like. 'A couple of new chaps hungry for a good game.'

Arthur felt weary. It had been fine when he was the new player, but he was uncomfortable being a regular.

'Think you've got a chance against the mighty Art, do you?' Charlie looked from one to the other. 'It could just be your lucky day.'

Arthur sensed the men at the table searching his face for clues about his play. He sized up the bank notes they put on the table and decided to call their bluff and put down the maximum bet. Charlie raised his eyebrows, then started to shuffle and deal out the cards. He knew he was taking a big risk. He hadn't been able to borrow cash from the till because Mr Wood had started checking the books, but he still had a couple of pound notes put aside from the last time he'd won. Should be enough to get started, he thought.

He saw that he had a good hand – the chance of being beaten by the dealer was an outside one. 'It's a good one, gentlemen. Jack and a Queen.'

'Confident, Art – very confident.' Charlie flipped over his hidden card. 'Well, what do you know – it's a blackjack two week's running!'

He looked at the cards in disbelief. Freak chances could happen once but twice in a row? Surely not.

'It's unlucky Art, but there's always the next round, eh?'

Arthur sensed that the other men were smirking at him and felt sick with humiliation, but he kept his voice as level as he could manage. 'Why not? You'll have to sub me to keep me in this one, though.'

Charlie shook his head in mock surprise. 'You're going to need another couple of quid at this rate, old man, and that'll be another couple to pay it back, unless you can get it to me later today.'

'Easy.' Arthur reckoned that he could get back to the shop till before Mr Wood paid another visit.

'I'll call it a short-term loan to an old friend, then.' Charlie rifled through his wallet and tossed two grubby ten bob notes across the table to him. Arthur added them to a pound note he'd fished out of his pocket. The other men looked away as if embarrassed.

'Another round, then.' He looked directly at them. He wasn't going to be intimidated by these vagabonds. What were they doing with money in their wallets anyway?

The next couple of rounds didn't go his way and the new players got lucky. He drilled himself into his seat, determined not to leave until he was back on top. By the fourth round, he decided it was all or nothing and he wagered the remaining pound on one hand. His first two cards were a two of clubs and a three of diamonds, so he kept going after the others stopped. Then, risking all, he scratched the table as the sign that he wanted another card. Charlie paused dramatically before turning over the top card.

A Queen! Arthur was bust. The room felt clammy, but he kept his eyes riveted on the cards. He daren't look up at the others.

'Not your lucky day, once again, Art. Perhaps you need a change of tactics.' Charlie's voice cut through the air. It had an edge he hadn't noticed before. The sea of green and red notes that were swilling around on the table turned Arthur's stomach – he had to get out before he was sick. He pushed his chair back and grabbed his coat off the back.

'I'll get you the cash by this evening.' He willed his voice to sound even. The two new men had got up to go to the bar and he was sure that he heard the Scottish one laugh.

*

Arthur cycled back like a lunatic to find Mr Wood – Stanley – poring over the books. 'There seem to be some irregularities.' Mr Wood had the ledger in his hand and his voice was lower than usual. 'Agnes says something about deliveries... The takings don't seem to match the outgoings. Not by too much, and we can all make mistakes, but – well, what do you think is happening here, Art?'

Arthur considered his options for a couple of seconds and decided he had to give him a version of the truth. 'It's not to do with deliveries like Agnes thinks. It's a short-term loan.'

Mr Wood just stood there.

'It's not what you think. Some of the lads from the

front meet up for old times' sake and a bit of a flutter, so I need cash – at short notice, so to speak...' He left out where they met.

Mr Wood stared at him. 'You're gambling?'

'Agnes doesn't know and doesn't need to. Our lives have been a lot more comfortable, and I always pay it back – *always*.' Arthur tried not to sound desperate. He wanted to appeal to him, man to man.

'I'm sure you do, Art, but I have to say I'm surprised – I didn't think you were the gambling type – with the girls and all. My brother always speaks so highly of you...'

He felt wretched at this. This family had been so good to him and for such a long time. He pressed his thumbs into his temple, wondering what else he could possibly say to salvage his reputation.

'It's for Agnes and the girls, Stanley. I wouldn't do it for myself.' He knew Mr Wood was fond of Agnes and had looked out for her while he was away. He probably thought she didn't deserve him. He looked at the floor and awaited his fate.

'I see. Well, if you've paid it back, maybe I could let it go – maybe – but not if it happens again.'

Arthur took a deep breath and crossed his fingers behind his back. 'If I could just have a couple of pounds more, I can guarantee that'll be the end of it. You have my word.' He felt like a condemned man on a scaffold awaiting pardon from the King.

Mr Wood opened the till, handed him two pound notes and shook his head. 'I'll give you until the end of the month to pay me back, Art. But it's *got* to stop. If not – well, you'll need to consider a position elsewhere.'

Arthur felt his whole body relax. It showed that when the chips were down, he could still turn things around. 'You have my word. I'll work extra hours, too. One more thing – can we keep this between ourselves?'

Mr Wood shook his head again. 'That young lady has had enough to deal with, so I won't be adding to it.'

He sounded disappointed, but Arthur could only nod and pocket the notes. What else could he do? It was about time something went his way. Maybe his luck was returning at last.

Chapter Thirteen

AGNES

Her brother-in-law was the first to mention the bank notes in Arthur's wallet. 'I'll go into grocery if it pays this well.' It had been a Sunday lunchtime in June and he and Lou were crammed around the oval dining table in the flat.

'It's the deliveries and tips that pay, Freddy,' Arthur had replied. Agnes wondered if he was hiding something, but whatever it was, had decided it couldn't be that bad – he seemed so much happier. It was such a relief when he was happy, and she caught glimpses of the boy who had carried boxes into the milliners and made her smile with his awkward friendliness. If there was a bit of mischief mixed in with his shop business now, so what? It made her feel younger, too – almost as if the world hadn't turned on its axis and killed so many men of a similar age.

Now, it was the end of July, and Arthur's good mood had receded. His mouth was nearly always set straight and his expression grave, even though it was only six weeks since he'd been boasting to Freddy. It seemed as if his mood had darkened as the summer weather stagnated, and although Agnes tried to resist, she, too, was dragged back to the dark times between them. She would have to say something – she couldn't go through another period of unspoken tensions – she simply couldn't.

The next evening, when Helen was playing with Eva in her room, she caught his eye as he looked up from his newspaper.

'Tell me about the deliveries.' It came out blunt and to the point – she wanted him to know she'd had enough. He sat completely still. Plumes of his cigarette smoke drifted to the ceiling. 'Is that where the extra money comes from? You need to tell me – something's not right.' Her voice echoed round the room.

Arthur twisted in his chair, crossed and re-crossed his legs. 'There's nothing wrong with extra cash, is there? Money has to come from somewhere, you know. There wasn't enough money in deliveries, so I found something else – *and* it's better if you don't ask any more questions.'

'What on earth do you mean? What's *something else* when it's at home, and where have you been going every Wednesday for the past year?' Agnes had a terrible feeling she'd stumbled into a much deeper hole than expected. And her questions had only just started.

'It's just a bit of fun with some of the chaps – nothing to worry about... I'm good at working out odds – always have been.' He folded the paper and gripped it tightly.

'What do you mean? Which chaps, where...?' Her mouth felt paper dry. Odds meant only one thing and the light dawned on her.

'I'm good at it – *very* good. You don't realise,' Arthur's voice rose.

'That's not the point. You'll be mixing with the wrong sort and no good can come of *gam-bl-ing*.' That was it, she'd said the dreaded word.

'That might be what *you* call it, but it pays an income. How do you think I managed to pay for the dress you bought a couple of month ago?'

Her cheeks burned. 'I'll take it back, then.' Desperation was scrawled across his face, and it struck Agnes that it wasn't just the dress she needed to worry about.

Then he mentioned Charlie, and she knew he was in trouble. 'Why don't you just say *no* to him, Arthur? Like you said *yes* when you started with all this. You don't have to go there just because they're expecting you. Charlie's probably taking advantage of you!'

Arthur's face drained – she'd never seen him so pale. If he'd won some, she guessed now that he'd lost some, too – and he must have lost a lot because this was the lowest she'd seen him in ages. He looked down, then up at the ceiling. Eventually, he turned and looked her square on.

'If I'm totally honest, I wish I *hadn't* gone back, but I only did it for you and the girls – you believe me, don't you? He looked so sad; her heart was squeezed.

'I do believe you Arthur but it's not the way and you know it. You're too good to be mixing with that sort.' She reached out for his hand – she was certain she could make him see sense.

If you're sure you don't want me to, I won't go back again – we'll manage somehow.' He let her hand hold his calloused fingers.

He sounded repentant – maybe even glad that it was out in the open, but what did he mean about going back *again*? How long had it been going on and how had she missed all this? Worst of all, how could she be sure that he would stop? She daren't ask him any more questions until his mood changed.

The heat and the arguing had given her a headache. She was worn out when Helen peeked round the door and asked if everything was all right.

*

The next week the weather turned humid, and the skies were heavy. The flat was claustrophobic with tension.

Even Eva seemed low. Agnes decided that something must be done.

'We need a holiday. It'll make us all feel a lot better and when we get back, we can make a new start.' She chose her words carefully and saw Helen look at her father with anticipation.

'Maybe. It depends.' He'd said less and less, since the argument and she wondered when he'd forgive her for interfering with his Wednesday afternoons. She'd let him go for a long walk last Wednesday when he said he needed to clear his head.

'Depends on what?' Agnes said warily. What on earth did he mean?'

'Nothing really. Would Bournemouth suit you?'

Her heart quickened. '*Bournemouth*? Of course. Yes, it'd be just the thing – it'd suit very well.' Helen let out a whoop of joy.

By the end of the week, a holiday was fixed up. Mr Wood had a friend who ran a boarding house and had arranged for them to stay for a week.

'Are you sure we can afford a whole week, Arthur?' Agnes was tidying away the breakfast things and wondering if she should ask her father for a loan.

Arthur was on his way down to the shop. He paused – then turned around and sat down.

'You might not believe it, but there is a way we can have this holiday without paying *anything*. I don't quite believe it myself.' It was the longest sentence he'd said all week.

'What or who would possibly pay for us to have a week by the sea in the middle of summer?' She stood with a fork in her hand, completely confused.

'Well, it could be a practice run – a sort of a trial. The boarding house where we're staying is next to a shop just like this, with a flat above, and they need a manager!'

He was staring at her as if she was stupid.

'But how can we have a holiday, if you're managing the shop for the week?'

'It's a new position. They want a permanent manager, and having a holiday means we'll be able to take a look at it.'

'But why on earth would we want to go and live in Bournemouth, miles from anywhere?' Agnes put down the fork and grabbed the sides of a chair.

'It'd be a new start, like you said. Think about the children!' He turned round to go. She felt a sharp pain in the pit of her stomach – she wanted a new start in *Ealing*, not in Bournemouth. Why was he always making such a mess of things?

'What about Stanley? He won't let you go, just like that, surely?' She sounded desperate. They'd never even been to Bournemouth before, for goodness sake! The midday light illuminated the kitchen table, as her brain whirred at this latest turn of events. Arthur turned back to face her and started to pace the room.

'Stanley – Mr Wood – says it might suit us. He thinks we should consider it.'

She fought to stay calm. Going to the seaside would be a treat for them all, so maybe this shop idea was just a red herring. She shouldn't let it upset things.

'Well, if Stanley thinks it's worth considering and he's agreed to a holiday, I suppose we could take a look. But we mustn't be bound…'

Arthur stopped pacing. 'Of course not. The sea will be wonderful.' His cheeriness verged on peculiar, and he bounded down the stairs to open the shop as if they'd won a fortune.

Agnes started to clear the table and a framed photo of their wedding caught her eye. The Arthur she had just been talking to was utterly unlike the Arthur in the photo – *he* would have died rather than gamble or change jobs without a by your leave – let alone *move across the country*! Could it still be the war taking a toll on him? And what about her? Was she the same girl in the photo? She never used to be so suspicious of everything. Once upon a time, she thought life was on her side and she ran towards every opportunity with open arms. Perhaps the war had changed her too – made her harder? She had lost trust in Arthur, that was the long and short of it. She grabbed a knife off the table. Well, just maybe the holiday would make him see sense and he would come back to Ealing more settled. She certainly hoped so.

*

'It's cosy,' Helen announced. They had just sat down to eat supper on their first evening as Bournemouth shopkeepers. Agnes was too tired to reply and was wondering instead where they were all going to sleep.

The holiday, a few weeks ago, had gone well. They'd made friends with their landlady and her husband who owned the shop, and the weather had been beautiful. They'd spent every day on the beach, and Agnes had relaxed so much that when Arthur insisted they look at the flat above the shop, she'd ignored her previous doubts and thought she might have been hasty in dismissing the idea out of hand.

Back then, the sun had streamed through the small east-facing window, and she'd been taken with the light and shadows. She couldn't believe that it was the same gloomy room crowded with furniture that she now sat in. The enchantment had ebbed away the minute they dropped the trunks and bags stuffed full of their things for the winter. What had they done?

After supper, Arthur unpacked boxes while she slumped on one of the armchairs. 'I wonder how many other people have sat on this?' Agnes ran her fingers over the arms. The brocade material was thinning. The flat was a world away from the grand front they'd admired. 'Why did I think it'd be all right to come here? I feel completely at sea.' She winced at the irony.

'It's the change of weather. You'll get used to it. And you'll be helping out more here, so you'll meet more people.' Arthur sounded firm. At least he was happy again, she thought.

'I'm not sure I want to meet people – I was fine as I was.' She looked round at the abandoned boxes and felt desolate. She was surprised that Mr Woods, whom she trusted, had encouraged them to go, but she had gone along with it and told her sisters that the sea air would be good for the girls. Now doubts crowded in, she wasn't going to let her sisters know about her worries. She was far too proud for that.

The next day, Agnes set about finishing the unpacking while Helen kept an eye on Eva.

'When I've finished, you can go down and help Daddy in the shop. Tell him you need to do some adding up.' It wasn't ideal as a maths lesson, but it'd have to do until she started school again. They might go back home after a week or two – it'd be just like Arthur to change his mind – so school could wait a bit longer.

Later that afternoon, while Arthur was out getting stock, she sat at the till with Eva on her lap and Helen beside her. 'Add up the bills on your own. I'll write all the numbers down on this bag and let's see if you can beat me to the total.' She was pleased with herself for coming up with this idea and scanned behind the counter for something to encourage Helen to work hard. 'Every time you beat me, I'll put a sweet in the jar, Then, at the end of the week, you can share your winnings with Eva.' Helen smiled and adjusted her pinafore dress.

Their arithmetic entertained the customers all afternoon, and they were more cheerful when Arthur returned than when he had left.

'Helen, dear, why don't you take Eva now and show her some of the letters and numbers on the labels? Make sure you don't let her touch anything and make her repeat the letters after you.' Agnes was enjoying her success – she hadn't let things get her down which showed that she was the sort of wife she wanted to be – a resourceful one. As Arthur lugged in sacks from the lorry outside, she called after him, 'Perhaps I could have been a teacher, as well as a milliner!'

Arthur put down the sack and took a deep breath. 'But it'd be better if Helen started school, rather than you trying to teach her.'

It wasn't the response Agnes wanted. She steadied herself, disappointed that he couldn't see the effort she was putting in to make the best of things. 'I'm sure we can wait till after Christmas. Then she'll have more time to settle in,' she said, determined to keep her voice bright, even if he couldn't see when she was doing something well. She twisted her fingers together and felt her wedding ring rub.

She knew deep down that it might not be Helen that needed to settle in, but herself. The shop was tucked away down a side street which never got the winter sun. When she'd walked a few yards and looked down the street opposite, she could just about see the sea, but both the open sea and the cramped street were daunting. And she could swear that the rain was as salty as the ocean itself. The whole place felt watery with no escape. She struggled to understand quite how they had ended up here.

Over the next few weeks, her mood darkened further as Arthur got more into his stride. She was cooking breakfast one morning in early November when he came up behind her.

'The school's barely a few streets away. If we leave Helen at home till after Christmas, she might fall behind.'

She looked up from frying the eggs. 'She was way ahead of the others back home – you know that – and I'm helping her. Surely a few weeks more won't hold her back?' She sounded weak, even to herself, and was glad he walked away and didn't pursue the subject further.

It was the idea of Helen being left behind other children that made her waver most, so by the end of the week, she'd given into Arthur. The next Monday, she dressed Helen in her old school uniform and walked along the narrow streets to the school gates, holding her hand firmly. The gates were rusted – another casualty of the salty air, she thought with distaste. The children looked at them with curiosity and she held Helen's hand more tightly.

'I'll be fine, Mummy – Eva needs you – you'd better get back.' Helen pulled her hand free.

Agnes forced a smile and a wave as Helen disappeared. It was only a short walk back to the shop, but she took a wrong turning, and everything looked muddled. How was this possible when the sea was so solid and unbending? She retraced her steps, before a burst of salty rain battered down on her. When she finally found her way back, she told Arthur he could collect Helen after school.

For the rest of the day, she was beset by worry, and wasn't sure how much longer she could last in this strange and difficult place – the waves rolled into the shore regularly enough but each day their height was more unpredictable and often the spray washed over the seafront, only two streets away. The flat was the wrong shape, too.

'The table doesn't fit into the corner, and the chair sticks out,' she wailed, as Arthur appeared for his dinner that evening. 'The angles are different here.' She felt queasy and disorientated.

Arthur threw up his hands. 'Well, let's get a smaller table then.'

'What's the point? I just want to go home.' That was it – she'd said it now, but he just sat down with a thud and started to eat.

*

Life settled into a predictable routine. Helen was at school during the day, while Agnes was upstairs with Eva, and Arthur was in the shop. On the surface, it was the same routine as life in Ealing, but underneath the surface, things were very different. She found her moods nearly impossible to control and Arthur suggested that she see a doctor. The idea infuriated her. A doctor couldn't put things right. One Friday evening, six weeks after they had first arrived, instead of sitting down in his usual spot, Arthur put on his overcoat.

'Won't be long, I just need to check something with the supplier.' He headed out before she could reply. She heard the door close and knew with a wife's intuition that he was heading to the pub. That evening, he would drink – and God knows what else – but she didn't care anymore. It was more comfortable without him sitting in the corner rustling the newspaper every few minutes and trying to start conversations that she didn't want to have. She settled in her usual threadbare armchair. Christmas on the horizon felt like a trap. Her sisters had suggested that they come for Christmas, to see how she was getting on. But the last thing she wanted was them visiting when she was so miserable, so she'd written back to say that they were too busy in the shop to have visitors. When Kate offered to come and help, she said that they were going out on Christmas Day to have dinner with new friends.

Nothing could be further from the truth. Agnes's life was narrower than it had ever been, even compared with the years when Helen was a baby and Arthur was away. She avoided the customers and used Eva as an excuse for staying in all the time. On the few occasions when the sun came out and Arthur suggested she take Eva for a walk, she always said that it was too cold, and she was worried about Eva's chest.

So now he was going out without her. Well, so be it, she thought – she simply didn't care about anything anymore. When he appeared back, two hours later, she was still sitting in the threadbare armchair with her hands folded.

'I suppose you'll have to go out again, tomorrow. Too much to expect you to stay in with your wife and children!' she spat out.

'I'd stay in if you were better company. More like you used to be.' He had definitely been drinking, Agnes thought.

'I would be if I knew what we were doing here. What was wrong with the shop in Ealing? What happened to us?' She dredged up every ounce of the old determination she used to have. It was the most she had said to him for weeks.

Arthur stood stock still for a minute then sat down with a thump. 'It was a good opportunity for me,' he said. He sounded weak and unconvincing.

'It wasn't a good opportunity. *It wasn't*. Something

happened that you're not telling me about.' Agnes was emboldened now.

Arthur heaved himself up and started to leave the room. His bulky shape was silhouetted in the doorway, and he stopped with his back to her. Suddenly his shoulders sagged, and he dug his hands into his pockets. 'Mr Wood said it'd be for the best.' He turned to look at her.

'Stanley? But why? The best for whom? There *must be* something you're not telling me.' Her spirit was returning. Suddenly she saw that there was a reason for her weeks of decline – it wasn't her being awkward.

'The till was short again, that's all... Charlie wouldn't wait for payment and Mr Wood wouldn't lend me it.' Arthur was looking away from her now.

It only took a few seconds for Agnes to piece together the facts that had hung over her head like a sharpened axe. She started to shake. 'So, you stole, Arthur – you mean you *stole* from Stanley?' Her voice was staccato. He stepped back into the room.

'I borrowed, that's all and I was going to pay it back. Cards have their ups and downs – like life – but it was nothing I couldn't have handled if he'd given me a bit of leeway.' His voice was eerily soft.

She sniffed the cold, salt-encrusted air. It all made sense, now. Mr Wood, kind, *respectable* Stanley Wood, had had enough of his unreliable shopkeeper and had found a way to get him away from Ealing. Of course, Arthur hadn't given up the cards. Of course, he owed money. His luck had been more down than up, and he couldn't get himself out of trouble.

'If he'd lent me the money, I'd have started winning again. It was under control, but then you interfered and made it harder for me to play and pay him back.' His tone was sharp now. At last, a pure white-hot fury engulfed her.

'Because of you, ALL because of you, we're here in this God-forsaken hole and *you* blame *me*?' Her voice was a controlled scream. Arthur turned away and thundered down the stairs. The shop door crashed as he left.

Life streamed back into her – blood pumped round her body as she paced round the cramped room. She went into her bedroom and pulled out the battered trunk from under the bed. Then she opened the wardrobe door and started removing her dresses from hangers and folding them on top of each other on the bed. She worked her way through her side of the wardrobe, then pulled out each drawer, scooped out their contents and squashed everything together into the trunk.

She didn't want to leave any of her personal items here. She would pack up the girl's things first thing in the morning. Let them sleep first. She felt absolutely fine – wonderful, in fact. He could stay in Bournemouth, but *she* was going home for Christmas.

PART TWO

*Perhaps that's what it means to be a father –
to teach your child to live without you.*

Nicole Krauss, *The History of Love*

Chapter Fourteen

EVA

'Eva!' Miss Alexander eyes me like a hooded crow. 'Please see me after school. I want to ask you about your plans.' The final history lesson – what is there left to ask?

I take a last look out of the window. The cedar trees roll up the lower slopes to the hockey fields, currently an athletics track. On Sports Day, the headmistress had to step out of the way when my javelin went further than anyone thought possible. It might be the only mark I leave here. I'm wistful about leaving school. I like that word, *wistful* – it's sad, but wise too. *Everything changes*, Helen says, *the trick is to keep up. Secretarial work will be fun.* Will it? The thought of having my first pay cheque is the main thing that excites me.

Miss Alexander's room is at the top of the sixth form block. I mount the steps thinking of all the school leavers who have stood on these worn stair treads. I knock and hear *enter*. She's at a wide desk, writing on an exercise book – a pile of them stranded to one side. She doesn't look up.

'Thank you for coming in, Eva – please take a seat.' I do as she says and wait for her to continue. Eventually, she looks up.

'As your form teacher, I want to see what your plans are. What your *educational* aims are. Helen did very well in the sixth form...' That familiar sinking feeling pitches into me. I place my hands firmly in my lap. 'You, on the other hand, haven't always studied as hard as we expect at Wellesley, but are a girl not without some talents.' I try and work out if this is good, or if I'm in trouble. She carries on. 'In fact, Miss Isaacs and I have been wondering if your mother might let you stay on at school – at least for another term.' Her eyes are hidden behind thick reading glass lenses. 'Hmm?' My hands are sweaty.

'I'm not like my sister, Miss.' She tries to interrupt but I don't let her. 'I'm not Helen, or anything like her.' I'm wringing my hands together now and would like to get out of this room as soon as possible, but she isn't going to let me go.

'I know being Helen's sister isn't easy for you, Eva, but if you worked a bit harder, you could be one of our brightest sixth formers.'

I can't believe it. Don't the teachers know? When we pretended school trips weren't convenient, I thought they realised that we couldn't afford them. Are they stupid? Can't they see that Helen only stayed in the sixth form so she could be a teacher and earn enough money to keep us? Most weeks, the vicar's wife gives us their 'excess' meat after church – we live on scraps and the shame nearly kills Mummy, but if I tell Miss Alexander this, Mummy really *will* die from shame. I reach for something else to say.

'It's not the right time for studying. The world is muddled up and dangerous. Look at the girls that came to us from Bilbao. They had to flee, so who knows when the war will reach us?'

Miss Alexander's tilts her head sideways. She's weighing me up – the scales tipping this way and that. 'You shouldn't be worrying about that at your age, Eva – you should be thinking about *your* future.'

'That's the point, Miss. I'm not sure that I have a future. But at least with a job, I can do my bit to help.'

She stares at me, and something closes in her – she's lost interest. Perhaps she realises that she doesn't have any idea about my life, nor ever has had. But she's a teacher, so has to finish the conversation. 'Your education is important, dear. Don't dismiss the idea of sixth form without a bit more thought.' She's detached from the outside world, too. How ridiculous school is!

'Thank you, Miss. I'll think about it,' I say. It's a good thing I'm leaving school if teachers are like this.

*

'Good – you're back,' Mummy all but screams at me as I walk in. 'I've got some news. Mrs James – you know, at the chemists – says that Mr Pettigrew, her brother, works at the bank. *The Bank*, that is, in London. You can do the secretarial training, Mrs James says, and it won't cost you a thing!'

She's not worried that I'm late back, or why. I run upstairs to my room. Everyone knows what's best for me, except for me! I try to breathe evenly, but the stale air in my bedroom tickles the back of my throat. The window is stiff, so I give it a shove. My future is a seesaw with Mummy at the centre. Perhaps Daddy was tossed about too, and that's why he went. I see his hair glistening with brilliantine, smoothed back from his forehead and the shadow of stubble under his chin. Then the image blurs and disappears.

The day after he left, his cigarette case was in plain view on the sideboard. He must have left without it, so I kept it and hid it behind my *Pilgrim's Progress*. He would see the joke – he used to read me bits when I couldn't sleep. I yank its dull green spine forward on the shelf and feel behind for the secret silvery curves of the case. I can hear Daddy's voice and see his lips moving, as he reads to me – like magic.

In the corner of the case, there's a small '*B*'. I tighten my fingers over it. Despite what I said to Miss Alexander, I did once think that I'd be a sixth form girl school – carry round books and walk the stately corridors. Until I realised about the situation at home, that is – Helen has another year to train, so I need to pull my weight. If Miss Alexander hadn't trapped me, school wouldn't feel like a wave pulling me back out to sea.

I imagine handing Mummy my first wage. What would Daddy say? I remember him once snapping open his wallet and saying, in a stage whisper, *Take a peek at that wad, Bunny*. The notes bulged out of his wallet, as he pulled it from his pocket. *Shall we make Mummy happy?* he said, and I smiled. His co-conspirator.

It's worked – back to the shore and feet on the ground. I squeeze the case one last time and slot it back on the shelf. I will read – perhaps on the train like I've seen others do – I don't have to be at school to do that. The sixth form girls carry books just to show off. *Rude*, Helen once muttered, a little too loudly, when a sixth former spilt books over us, coming out of school. You never actually saw them reading them, like Helen and I do.

I straighten the bedcover and give my hair a cursory brush. A few weeks ago, I thought an angular cut was interesting, but a softer style might be better for work. I'll be a smart secretary and I'll be good at it. I grip my brush handle tightly. Everything is about money when it comes down to it – teachers must be blind if they don't see that. School, home, Haydon Cross itself, they're all about money – or the lack of it – so the sooner I start to earn it, the better for everyone.

Chapter Fifteen

ARTHUR

He couldn't feel it – but knew it would creep up on him, just like the first time, and then he would be floored – lost. Seeing Agnes pack up and leave was like that day on the Liverpool docks when his mother receded into the distance. There was nothing he could do about it – that was the terrible thing. He told the customers that Agnes and the children were away on family business and made sure that he kept on top of the stock keeping. The stock took his mind off things.

In the evenings, it was different. He sat on a wooden kitchen chair rather than sink into an armchair, and he dreaded the silence – no Helen playing with Eva in a corner and no Agnes bending over some needlework. After eating several slices of bread and dripping, he went to the local pub one street away. The men in the smoky atmosphere looked as lonely as he probably looked to them. There was a blur in his mind where clear facts should be, and the blur was edged with a sense of shame which wouldn't go away.

It was a late March evening and unseasonably cold with flurries of sleet blown in by the sea. He pushed open the heavy pub door and lifted himself onto one of the empty stools by the bar. Joe, the landlord, appeared out of the back.

'The usual, then? Good thing you're in – quiet tonight – wives stopping them from coming out.' Joe knew Arthur had a wife, so it was as much a question as a statement, and it was getting harder to pretend to people that Agnes was visiting family.

Arthur pulled at the collar of his jacket and Joe bent forward to fill the tankard for him. 'My missus can't do winter by the sea – she's not cut out for it.' He thought this might stop further questions.

'It takes some people like that when they've not been brought up to it. Too open, and they're expecting candyfloss and rock all year round. Take my wife. She came down from London – thought she'd be able to sun herself on the beach in the summer and work behind the bar in the winter. But it doesn't work that way. The work here is in the summer. When the cold days come, there's not so much to do – everyone's gone home.'

'Where's your wife now?' he asked. Arthur was relieved to hear that other men's wives also found the seaside hard to take.

'She left me two years back – went back to her mother. I haven't seen my son for over a year. She said the pub was no place for a young boy, but she doesn't mind the money I send her, does she?' Joe thumped the tankard onto the bar.

Arthur shifted sideways on his stool and looked around as if he was seeing the empty bar for the first time. He grabbed the tankard. 'And how many of the men that come in here lay in trenches getting shot at while their wives had no idea what was happening to them?'

The barman started wiping the glass he'd just picked up. 'Not many good men left and those that are, still struggling to get by.'

'Struggling to get by just about describes it. What does a man have to do to earn respect?' Arthur gripped his tankard more firmly.

Joe looked at him more closely. 'Money's one thing and a wife's another. If I could get my wife to come back to me, I'd give this job up in a flash but it's too late – she's stuck with her mother for good now. Two brothers dead and a third crippled, so she has to look after them – never mind me. She says she can't leave her mother on her own.'

This was the first conversation of more than a couple of words that Arthur had had since Agnes had gone – and it felt as if Joe knew his situation intimately. Yet how could he? He scanned his face – he wasn't much older than him but was scarred on one cheek – he'd seen combat, Arthur reckoned, but he wasn't going to ask him when or where. What was there to say, after all, about seeing hell and tasting damnation?

He raised his glass to show solidarity, not just about war, but about wives, too, then moved over to sit at a corner table where he could think things over. The war had been a mess for others. But just because he'd got back in one piece, it didn't make it any easier to be a husband and father afterwards, and he'd been tempted by Charlie's promise of easy winnings. Could he have talked Mr Wood round to giving him longer to pay the money back instead of agreeing to leave Ealing? Maybe, just maybe. If he was honest with himself, he'd been worried about Charlie getting the better of him again, so had grabbed the chance to run away. He downed the last of his beer and felt a hollow in the pit of his stomach – she might not have him back. He must prove himself to her, show he was respected – but how? He wasn't sure. He just knew he had to try, that was all.

The next day, he was in the shop sorting through orders. Packing the cans and packets neatly into cardboard boxes made him think of the mess stores in Salonika. He'd run a tight ship – even Charlie would admit that. Surely he had the moral fibre to make a go of things now? At nine o'clock, when the last of the orders had been collected, he slumped onto the chair by the till and waited for the regular customers to arrive. He dreaded days when regret loomed large. The post boy was the first to call. He took the letters he held out, wanting a distraction – even a bill would give him something else to think about. He needed to get Agnes out of his mind. But the top envelope wasn't brown, it was pale blue, with his mother's familiar handwriting staring back at him.

He unfolded the pages and knew straight away that something was different. The paper felt crisp, and her handwriting was more curvaceous than usual. He skimmed over the words. There were a scattering of exclamation marks and news, in turn, about each of his siblings. He quickly homed in on the heart of the letter which was that Maude had got engaged to a chap called Ed Walters. But that wasn't all. This Ed's father had a couple of grocery shops in Edgbaston, near Birmingham. *They would love to meet you!* she'd written. *Just think what they could do to help you! I've told them how long you've been in the grocery business* – no exclamation for this. What amazed him was that his mother had guessed he was looking for an opportunity to prove himself – even across the ocean. He bit his lip in anticipation. But then again, would he have anything in common with this family and why should he care about Ed? He might never meet him, and it would be just another missed family wedding.

After a glut of contradictory emotions washed over him, he shifted on his chair. He'd heard of Edgbaston because of the cricket ground but had never been to Birmingham or even wanted to go there. On the other hand, meeting these people might lead to something and perhaps a trip would do him good. He imagined telling Agnes that he was leaving Bournemouth and making a new start. She'd be impressed, he was sure.

A couple of regular customers came into the shop,

so he put the letter away, but with something new to think over, he started to feel a lot brighter – he could almost feel a path leading him out of his current mess. By the end of the day, he'd decided that it couldn't do any harm to write to Mr Walters and introduce himself. He would suggest a visit over the Easter weekend, and if all that worked out, he'd travel back via Haydon Cross and see Agnes and the girls. For the first time in several weeks, he could see the contours of a plan.

*

Rain battered the train windows all the way up to Birmingham. As he gazed at water snaking down the windows, his life seemed like one of the dark tunnels where daylight took an age to resurface. It cut him to the bone that Agnes had taken a job as a housekeeper, in a place neither of them knew. It wasn't what he wanted for her or his girls. She was still his wife, after all – the situation was shameful for them all.

The eldest son of the Walters family met him at New Street station. He was about Harold's age and dressed smartly – his light sandy coloured hair slicked back to display a handlebar moustache – he didn't look at all like a grocer. The mother was there, as well – a small, lively-looking woman who took charge.

'Maude's a pretty girl. She and Ed look well together. We're pleased he's found an English girl to marry. Do you think they might come back and settle?' She didn't wait for him to reply but carried on. 'Mr Walters has given Bert the afternoon off to show you round the place. Have you been to Birmingham before? It's a grand place – you'll be used to London and Bournemouth, of course, but Birmingham is a grand place. Bert will show you the sights.'

He stopped in surprise as Bert loaded his suitcase onto the rack of an enormous car.

'It's a new 14 Crossley – fit for royalty. You can have a go at driving it, if you like.' Bert opened the passenger door. 'See what she's like, then you can decide.' Arthur wondered how to say that he'd never driven a car.

They sped between magnificent buildings whilst Mrs Walters carried on talking. 'Mr Walters and I are busy tonight but Bert's going to take you to The Scala Theatre, aren't you, dear? They're opening one in Edgbaston next year, so we won't have to go far to see a show. Have you got a theatre near you in Bournemouth? Shall we head home now, Bert?' Bert kept his eyes on the road and didn't respond to anything his mother said. Arthur wondered if he'd seen combat and if so, how he coped with his garrulous mother.

The car was impressive, but their front door was elaborate on a scale he had only ever seen in London. To think that little Maude was marrying into such a family! He was shown to his room where he sat on the bed and stroked the towels that were laid out – not one, but two. An hour later, he wandered back downstairs to the kitchen where a light dinner of ham and salad was laid out – it was like being on a very grand holiday.

A few minutes later, Bert appeared. 'Come on, old man. Look lively – mustn't miss the start of the film. It's something to do with London fog. Come all the way to Birmingham to see a film about London!' Bert bared his teeth and forced a high-pitched laugh. Arthur got up with a lingering look at the ham still on his plate.

They set off in the car with Bert shouting above the rattle of the engine. 'In case you're wondering, I'm the one left to carry the can round here and run the business. Ed cleared off to Canada before the war, like your brothers.'

'Avoided being called up, then.' Arthur still couldn't work out if Bert had served. The long manicured fingers on the steering wheel seemed to say otherwise. Bert swerved into a space outside the cinema, then pulled up the handbrake and turned the engine off. He leaned back and turned to look directly at him.

'Let's just say I was "too busy" to be called up.' He tapped his nose and grinned. Arthur shifted uncomfortably on the red leather car upholstery. He hated men who'd avoided conscription, and if he hadn't crouched in Somme ditches, how had Bert spent his time? Shifting flour sacks? It didn't seem so. He decided not to ask him any more questions.

The Scala was a grand building lined with terracotta tiles on the outside and large illuminated signs across the front and down the sides. There were two strange mythical beasts over the stage that he thought might be called griffins. There wasn't anything to compare with this in Bournemouth – it was magnificent. He crossed his legs and leaned back to enjoy the film thinking about how Agnes would love it. Birmingham was definitely a place on the up.

The minute the final music started to play, Bert jumped out of his seat and set off back up the aisle. Arthur ran to catch him up.

'My wife would love it here. Do you take a lady with you, sometimes?' He wanted to make conversation and get to know him better.

Bert shrugged as he headed outside. 'Maybe I do and maybe I don't. I'm not like Ed. Us men need to stick together, if you follow me.' Arthur wasn't sure what he meant, so he buttoned up his jacket and got into the car. When they were back at the Walters' home, Bert waved him into the drawing room, grabbed a bottle of Scotch and poured a couple of slugs into two heavy tumblers.

'Right, old man, we've done the film – so when can you start?' He thrust a tumbler in his direction and some whisky splashed onto the leather settee. Arthur took the tumbler and grabbed a hanky from his pocket, but Bert held up his hand. 'Don't bother with that – the maid will clean it up. Now, how about next week?'

Arthur shoved his hanky back in his pocket and sat on the edge of the huge settee. Was Bert joking? He looked at him and decided not. 'Well, of course, there'd be lots to sort out. I'm hoping my wife...' He couldn't get his breath to say much more before Bert interrupted him again.

'Yes, yes – details. You're up for it, that's the main thing.' It wasn't a question. Bert looked at his watch and slammed his empty tumbler on the table. 'How about we show you the ropes in the morning after you meet Father? Then you can see what you make of the Walters's Emporium! Bit of a rush right now – you know where everything is, so make yourself at home.' He whipped round and strode out. In a few minutes, the car jumped into life again.

Arthur slid back on the settee and sipped the malt – he was exhausted and not sure what to think about this impatient man. He looked around at the lavish furnishings – the Walters had money, plenty of it, and thanks to his sister, they were offering him a job with no questions asked. He'd see what the morning brought – there was no point putting things off any longer if they had a position for him. Sometimes you had to take the plunge, he thought, finishing the whisky in one final gulp.

*

'Bert does what he can, but he's got his own life to lead.' Bert's father, also a Bert, but referred to as 'Albert', was apologising for him, or was he imagining it? Bert wasn't at breakfast, and no one seemed to know where he was. 'He's told you our situation, then?' Arthur wasn't sure he had but nodded anyway. 'Well, the job's yours as soon as you're ready to start. Sooner the better, so Bert can do other things.' Albert Walters was as tall as his wife was small and as serious as she was frivolous. He was keen to talk about the stock which was a huge relief to Arthur who couldn't stand Bert talking to him in riddles. Albert seemed to understand grocery.

'And as well as managing grocery, Ed tells us that you're a strong family man, even when times are hard.' Albert's gaze made him wince. He couldn't say that his wife had left him, so before they sat down, he clutched his hand in an awkward handshake – after all, this man was going to help him win her back.

'You can rely on me.' It was ridiculous but after only a few minutes, Albert had begun to feel like a father figure. They settled down to plates of bacon and eggs and Arthur's mind raced ahead – how would he find somewhere for them all to live? The shop didn't have accommodation over it, as they'd been used to.

Albert held his napkin to his mouth, coughed, then turned to face him. 'Perhaps I can help you get set up so you can bring the family up here?' Arthur's heart thumped with relief. This man understood without him having to explain.

'That'd be marvellous. I'd like my wife and girls to join me here as soon as possible,' Arthur gushed.

'We'll have a look round the shop, and I'll sort out a house today.' Albert sliced into his fried egg and the yolk spilt onto his toast. *A house*! Arthur's hand trembled with excitement as he lifted the last rasher of bacon to his mouth.

The shop was a solid building, almost as impressive

as the Walters' house. The shelves were crammed with so many tins, packets and produce, Arthur ached to tell Agnes about the range of stock – it was a much bigger concern than the Ealing or Bournemouth shops and surely a gold mine. It was well within his capability, though, and he could already see where some improvements might be made. He felt just like he did when he got his first job in Caversham – it was almost as if the last ten years were erased. Albert wanted him to manage things when Bert wasn't around which Arthur guessed was most of the time – and he'd be in charge of several part-time staff, too. How quickly his fortunes had changed! His mother had got him out of a hole which she'd never known he was in, and found him a new family – well, sort of.

After examining the stockroom, he just had enough time to get a cab and make the last train with a connection for Haydon Cross. Sun lit up the fields along the way and the engine beat a jolly rhythm. Arthur glanced at his reflection in the train window and adjusted his tie – Bert wasn't the only shopkeeper who could dress smartly. He'd make the trip sound like a funny story and describe Bert in detail to make the girls smile. They'd laugh out loud when he told them about the offer to drive his expensive car. Thank goodness he hadn't done it and made a fool of himself!

Chapter Sixteen

AGNES

The first of February was a bitterly cold day, but Agnes felt only relief as she walked up the driveway of 'The Laurels'. Her thin stockings gave her legs little protection from the wind, but oh, the relief! Relief to be away from the vast rhythmic emptiness of the sea and relief to be smoothing down freshly laundered sheets and folding back a beautiful patchwork eiderdown.

From Bournemouth, she had gone straight to Lou and Fred's, but it'd been too crowded there, so her sister suggested she look for live-in work. It had meant another move, but Lou helped her to find a position with an elderly widow who liked children. She warmed to the old lady the minute she let Helen look at one of the books on her shelves, and Haydon Cross, where she lived, was a pleasant town. *We'll be near enough to visit, but we won't get in your way any longer*, she told her sister. Best of all was the address, 'The Laurels'. It rolled off her tongue pleasingly.

She'd ignored the first couple of letters from Arthur. Then she'd written back and told him about her job. He wasn't a bad man, she knew that, but she was exhausted by following all the twists and turns he'd made of their fortunes. She needed time apart from him, unless he could offer her something she could make sense of. Marriage was a conundrum – she'd tried, *really* tried to do the right thing but every time she thought about Arthur, he seemed curiously empty – she simply couldn't see anything inside him, and it scared her. So it was a relief to manage things on her own again.

By early April, Eva's questions about when Daddy was going to come had nearly stopped. 'The Laurels' was set back off a wide avenue and Agnes marvelled at how each house remained partially out of sight, yet also made its presence felt. The shrubs and trees at the front were tended by a gardener who came once a week. The thick trunks beneath the waxy leaves of the laurel bushes that lined the drive made the whole plot feel substantial, and most importantly, it felt private.

Mrs Atkinson, her employer, had vacated the attic rooms and provided basic furnishings which Agnes found less oppressive than the threadbare clutter of the Bournemouth flat. Once again, she and the children mounted steps to their quarters, but how different from living over a shop! The house lay under a quilt of calm. She and Helen liked the seclusion, but Eva kept asking where everyone was. *You were born above the jangle of the shop doorbell*, Agnes told her, hoping she would realise that living above a shop wasn't how most people lived. She decided that this was the tonic they needed to recover from Bournemouth, and she was sure Eva would settle down soon.

Haydon Cross was further out of London than Ealing. It had a fine open common with large beech trees and a grand pond which had gradually been surrounded by genteel houses. For white-collar working men, there was a railway line to Marylebone Station, and for the upright, an impressive parish church graced the edge of the common, its Italianate dome lending the town a stylish edge. Agnes soon worked out how the streets interlinked and laced around the wide space of the common. When she came across the curved window display of an opulent dress shop, she wondered if maybe one day, when the children were older and she had a home of her own, she would work there. But, the best aspect of the town was that the children who streamed through the primary school gates looked far better clothed and fed than the rag-tag urchins in Bournemouth, and Helen settled in easily.

*

Good Friday in 1927 fell on the fifteenth of April, and Mrs Atkinson had said that she could have the whole weekend off. Late in the morning, the sun emerged from a bank of clouds and Agnes felt her spirits lift. For the first time in months, she could see the outline of a future emerging from the chaos of the past few years. She had a roof over their heads and money in her purse, and a morning doing her own housework felt like a luxury.

In the afternoon, she and the girls set off for the three o'clock church service. The Common was between the house and the church and she'd promised Helen that they would walk back the long way round to look for spring flowers. Helen took Eva's hand and pointed up into the tall branches of the beech trees that were starting to bud. 'We'll pick some on our way home and put them on our table to watch them open,' she said. As Eva started to skip in excitement, Agnes reflected on how close the girls were and how lucky they were to have each other.

Agnes loved hearing her feet crunch on the gravel of the entranceway which led to the large oak church door. She and the girls filed into a pew near the rear of the church and waited for the service to start. The vicar's voice was low and monotonous, and the smell of beeswax polish made her slightly queasy. She ran an eye over the hats in the front row, remembering what she had learnt at the milliner's shop in West Ealing. Further back were seated the less wealthy members of the congregation. These women did the church flowers on the altar, and she wondered if there might be an opening for her there. Eva was swivelling on one leg and pulling at her hand, so she leaned down to shush her.

When they emerged into the late afternoon, the sun was still high in the sky. Eva sped out ahead and Helen hurried after. Agnes made her way to join the small group of ladies who had welcomed her when she'd first arrived.

'That must be your girls.' One of them pointed at Helen who was dragging Eva laughing and skipping in their direction. The whole group turned to watch. 'There's quite an age gap, isn't there? Was your husband in the services?' the high-pitched voice continued.

Agnes adjusted her dress. The girls' charm usually drowned out questions – Helen, clever and kind, and Eva, lively and pretty, meant that she didn't need to explain anything, and that was for the best, she'd decided. People could think what they liked – after all, there were so many men missing these days, it was nothing out of the ordinary.

Just as she opened her mouth to say something oblique about Arthur, Eva piped up.

'Mummy, can we count the primroses on the way home?' Agnes looked down at Eva's excited face. If such joy seemed a bit out of place on Good Friday, well, so be it, she thought. Indeed, her companions had already forgotten what it was they wanted to know because Eva had captivated them. So after some pleasantries, she made their excuses to go.

There were celandine and stitchwort, as well as primroses, on the path home. They encircled the common, then found a path through the trees and ventured into the heart of it. Helen's step quickened and Eva ran by her side. The air had cooled, and the chill of early spring blotted out the smell of fresh leafiness the sun had brought. 'It's like a tunnel, Eva. Look for the light – that's where we're going – that's our way home,' Helen said, pointing ahead.

Agnes looked too and felt happier than she'd been in a very long time. She had her girls and a place in the world again. The memory in the pit of her stomach of the bad times with Arthur was fading, and she could even picture his boyish enthusiasm and affection for the girls. It was sad that he would be missing them while she held onto them. Well, let him prove himself then, she thought – she'd done what she had to do. It was his turn now.

*

The next day, early morning cloudiness threatened rain. Helen copied flower pictures from one of Mrs Atkinson's books and Eva sat close and covered sheets of paper with every colour in her set of wax crayons. The rain came and went.

Agnes looked at Helen. 'Put Eva's shoes on and let her into the garden while I get ready. She might be able to find some green shoots in Mrs Atkinson's flowerbeds.'

Helen finished her drawing, then fetched Eva's shoes from the mat. She fastened the straps, then buttoned up her cardigan over her pale blue dress. 'Out we go!' she commanded as Eva followed her down the stairs.

'Keep an eye on her and I'll bring your outdoor things down with me,' Agnes shouted after them. After a few minutes, she put on her coat and followed them down into the garden, carrying some stout lace-up shoes and a spare coat. Eva had disappeared, but Helen was waiting for her. 'You didn't let her go on the lawn, did you? She'll have wet feet before we've even set off.' Agnes said sternly.

Helen bent down and laced up her shoes, then dragged on the coat. 'She ran off, but I'll go and get her.' Agnes heard her calling Eva's name, but she appeared again, red-faced and breathless, and without Eva. 'I've been round the whole house and can't find her – she must be hiding. What shall I do?'

Agnes fastened her own coat and shoes and set off to the central flowerbed where clumps of daffodils were beginning to come into flower. 'Eva, we're off to the common now and we'd like you to come with us. Come on dear, let's go while the sun's shining and look for more flowers... Helen needs you.' Helen followed her. They looked in the sheds and the greenhouse and even went back into the house, but after an hour of looking, including scanning the branches of the tallest trees, the only answer was that Eva had gone out of the side gate, and onto the driveway and avenue.

Helen's face crumpled, as Agnes took her shoulders and dug deep to appear calm. 'You stay here. I'm going up the avenue to look for her. Don't move, in case she comes back.' Agnes ran up the driveway and stood looking up and down the leafy avenue. Other driveways led off the road. Would Eva have wandered down one of these? Her panic was a suffocating weight. She turned her head wildly from left to right, heart thumping and breath coming quickly. Perhaps one of Mrs Atkinson's neighbours could send out a search party? Surely a child can't just disappear? She can't have got far. As these frantic thoughts shot through her mind, she turned round one last time and peered up the avenue. She could just about make out a couple of figures in the distance coming from the direction of the town. She screwed up her eyes a bit more till the images came into focus. One was an adult, male, tallish, and the other – the other was a child with a pale blue dress on. She clutched her stomach as it somersaulted. Thank God! Someone had found Eva and was bringing her back.

Agnes's knees buckled as the pair came into clearer view – Eva was holding the man's hand. She started to run towards them but then stopped. Surely not! The man with Eva was Arthur – *Arthur* in a suit and hat, with a stupid grin on his face!

'What on earth are you doing with her?' Agnes snatched Eva's hand as they came alongside her.

Arthur tipped his hat, but his look of amusement drained away when he saw her expression. 'Hello, Agnes. Bunny was just showing me where to get some cigarettes, on this fine day near your fine house'.

'We've been looking *everywhere* for her. Helen and I were sick with worry. You should have told us you were coming. Why on earth are you here, anyway?' Tears muffled her voice.

'Well, if we could go inside this grand place of yours, I'll tell you my news.' He seemed undeterred and her heart quickened with anticipation. Just then, Helen appeared on the avenue, and with a yelp rushed to hug him. Agnes tightened her grip on Eva's hand, waited for Helen to break free, then stood back and pointed down the driveway. She was so relieved, nothing much else seemed to matter.

'You'd better come in, then. Helen, could you stay with Eva in the garden while I talk to your father? And keep an eye on her this time!' She led Arthur upstairs and motioned for him to sit on her small settee, then went to make him a cup of tea. Her hands shook on the tap as she filled the kettle. So many unexpected events had happened in the last few minutes, she desperately needed to take stock. What on earth was Arthur playing at giving her a fright like that and what was going on to make him turn up like this? She composed herself and made the tea, then carried it in carefully. As she glimpsed his profile through the doorway, she caught her breath. He looked good, there was no denying, and for the first time since who knows when, she was a little bit proud that he was her husband.

'Well?' She raised her eyebrows and looked at him as he took a sip from the cup. He looked happy, too, and his happiness made her want to smile – but she mustn't. She smoothed down her skirt and composed herself – whatever he had to say, he mustn't sway her – not when she was starting to feel settled again.

When he started up, she couldn't stop him talking, and it took a while for her to piece together what had happened. 'It's a lovely area – you'd like it. I know you would. There's a park nearby and big houses – and the cinema is really grand. You were right about the seaside. It doesn't suit us – not at all. We need city life. The seaside is for holiday, not every day.' Arthur was in full flow and gradually she realised what he was asking of her.

It was hard not to be impressed. Maybe he had found his feet at last, but she had to stop him before he said any more. His enthusiasm for Bournemouth flashed into her mind and look how that had ended! She twisted her hands together, willing herself to stay calm. 'I can't just up and leave again, Mrs Atkinson has been kind to me, and Helen is doing well at school. And *Birmingham* – well!'

'Once you see it, you'll feel differently. We'd have a house to ourselves!' He was persistent, but she simply couldn't trust him – she'd come too far on her own. She felt a wave of something and wondered if it was pity.

'I suppose I could bring the girls to see where you are – that's all I can say at the moment.' She forced herself to stand up – she had to make him leave before he said anything else. 'You'd better go before Mrs Atkinson sees you. I'm glad you've found something, I really am, but you can see how settled we are.'

He looked up at her, then slowly got to his feet, ducking to stop his head hitting the sloping roof. 'Right – I'll get out of your way then. I can always sleep on the platform at Paddington.' She dug her fingernails into her palms as he scanned the room again. 'The houses in Edgbaston are vast compared to this. It's a chance to put things right. You'll see.'

'I've worked for this, Arthur.' She gestured round the tiny room. 'It's *mine*. But I want you to be all right – I do, really – maybe Birmingham will suit you.' It took all her effort, but she had to make him go. If he stayed now, she'd lose everything she'd worked for. When she'd had time to think things over, perhaps she could make sense of it, but he was rushing her, and her head was aching.

'It's Edgbaston really, not Birmingham as such. I'll let you know when I've moved, and you can bring the girls to visit. It'll be easier when you see it,' he said, as what felt like a last ditch attempt to win her over.

She picked up her cardigan from the chair, then put it down again. 'Maybe – I don't know. But maybe you could come and see us, sometimes. Just let me know next time.'

He smiled and her heart softened again, just a little. They traipsed down the stairs and into the garden where he hugged Helen and gave Eva one last swing in his arms. 'Be good, Bunny,' he said as he put her down. 'And thanks for showing me round.'

Agnes shut the gate firmly after he'd gone. The heels of his shoes clicked an even rhythm on the drive, and she watched his hat bob up and down till he turned the corner onto the avenue. This was another shift in things, but she couldn't leave her new home for something so uncertain. He had to *earn* her trust again – and if she was honest, she wasn't sure that he could.

Chapter Seventeen

EVA

Working in the City is a big step up for me. I march along its streets with the 'bowlers' – the men who cover the pavements in the first light of morning – and we wait for bombs to fall, but so far there have been precisely none and I've made it home every night. If Mummy could taste the sense of anticipation in the London air, she'd never let me go to work. I've surprised everyone, including myself, and I like my job. Daddy would be amazed to see me – perhaps his love of money got under my skin. *Look where that got him*, Mummy once said, and I wanted to say, *and where's that?* but didn't dare to. I look for him on the train and in the streets. There are men who might be my father, but I'm not even sure if he still has a moustache, so would I recognise him?

When men look at *me* – and they do look – I forget about the freezing house and cold water that I come home to every night. Luckily, they can't see me scraping potatoes and stoking the fire. I prefer clean-shaven men – the Cary Grants, I call them. Girls like me live in Hollywood because the posters in the tube stations take us there. In the office, they even call me *Ingrid*, as in Bergman. Mr Wells, my manager, says there's a passing resemblance and I wonder what it's like to be a film star, rather than a girl who looks for her father in dreary trains.

The men in the office mostly have wives, and some of them have daughters, too. I smile at them, but that's all. Helen says I need to mix with boys my own age and stop thinking about film stars. *Hmmm*, was all she said when I told her about my nickname in the office. Mummy, on the other hand, looked pleased. Helen didn't see that, but I did.

Last Thursday I talked to a boy called David. He turned up at Helen's church youth group a few weeks ago because his school was evacuated to Haydon Cross. It's rich, considering that I go into London to work every day and he's come here, but there you are – some people are protected more than others. Peter Barnes, the butcher's son, was teasing him for being posh, saying how bombs are a real nuisance when you're trying to read. David didn't laugh, so now Peter and the other boys aren't sure how to treat him. They'd like to cut him out of their group, but he doesn't let them. He's staying at the vicarage which can't be easy – the vicar and his wife are kind but they've no sense of humour. Even Helen's eyes glaze over when they talk, so David could do with a friend.

Funnily enough, he reminds me of some of the older men at work, even though he's younger than me. It's his confidence. He's what I would call *slight* but he's quietly self-assured – not shy and not a pushover. When he smiles, it's crooked, as if he can see something that no one else can. The second time he came to the group, he kept asking Peter about the different ways to butcher a lamb. I could tell Peter was worried by it, but David persisted and by the end of the session, Peter was hanging on his every word.

I left home later than Helen, thinking I could catch him on his way to the group and get to know him better. The gravel at the end of the vicarage drive was making that crunching noise and then he appeared with a crooked smile, just as I'd hoped. We walked the last few yards to the church hall, and I asked him how it was staying at the vicarage. He said, *a bit stuffy*.

I can't believe I said it, but I did, *Would you like to go for a walk on the common on Saturday?* He didn't even look surprised.

Helen wasn't impressed when I told her. *Isn't that a bit forward?* she said. I suppose it is, but then we looked at each other, thinking of the vicar. *I suppose he could do with a friend*, she said then.

*

Mummy tries to button up my cardigan, as I shuffle past her to the kitchen door. It's midday, exactly.

'It might get chilly later.'

'And I'm nearly eighteen.'

'He's a grammar school boy, you say?'

'Yes – and I used to be a high school girl once.'

'So you know how to behave, then!'

I've told him to meet me at the bench by the pond. As I turn down the street, I can just make out a slim figure where he should be. My heart gives a little jump and I wave. It's nice – he's waving back. Then I'm nervous and don't know why. He's nearly a year younger than me and still at school, for goodness sake. If he wasn't clever, I wouldn't even consider meeting him.

'How are you, Eva?' he says. I like the way he uses my name.

'Fine, thanks. And we've got a lovely day for a walk.' I feel his eyes on me. We walk towards the common. 'You must miss your parents.' Risky place to start.

'They come up occasionally. Well, my mother does, anyway.' He doesn't seem perturbed by my question, but perhaps he has an absent father, too.

We walk right up to old 'Agee', and I rest my palm against the deep ridges of the trunk. 'This is my soulmate. I used to climb it when I was seven or eight – Daddy showed me how to.'

He gives the tree a long hard look. 'Ancient oak. It's seen a lot.' He looks up into the branches. He's like a dark green statue for a moment, then a beam of stray sunlight breaks through and strikes him on top of his fair head.

I laugh. 'You look saintly.'

He looks at me with his odd grin – it makes me shiver. Then he looks down. 'Do you like poetry?'

'Sort of. Drama more,' I reply. He beckons me to walk back onto the main path. It was meant to be *me* taking him for a walk but already he seems in charge.

'Am I taking over?' he says, and I wonder if he's reading my thoughts.

We wander along and he tells me about the poets he's reading – Eliot and Pound. I've heard of them but they're more difficult than the poems I've read at school, like Tennyson. I describe the bank and the vault where we go during air raids, and he laughs when I tell him that Mummy thinks it's a safe job.

'She has no idea,' I say. No one has listened to me this hard before.

'I'll go up to Cambridge soon.' He's looking ahead, as if the college is just there at the end of the common.

'How do you know you'll get in?'

'I will,' He replies.

That's all – just that: *I will*. I can almost believe that Cambridge is waiting for him, rather than the other way around. When a couple of girls from the High School went to Oxford, I tried to imagine what it would be like. *You're the clever one, Bunny*, Daddy used to say. So what? The war stops most people going now.

But not David. He tells me he speaks three different languages – French, German and Italian. He has *a gift*, he says. It makes me wonder what I might have done if I'd listened less to Mummy and stayed on at school. Perhaps I had a gift, too. Maybe even have one, still.

We walk off the main path and into the shade. I crouch down and point to a violet.

'Half hidden from the eye, like Wordsworth says. We don't get many flowers in Hammersmith,' he says. Why doesn't he talk about his parents, or brothers, or sisters, I wonder? I look at my watch and think that we should be getting back.

'You must miss your home. I'd love to know about it. I mean, I love it here *because* it's my home, but it's exciting going up to London every day, too… You're so close to what's really going on.' I'm gabbling and my pulse is thumping, but a mad idea has just come to me. 'What would the vicar think about you coming up to meet me in London one evening?'

He looks up and straight into my eyes. 'Why not? It's not my sort of place here. I mean I'm grateful and all that, but it's a bit predictable. Not where I want to be for very long. We could go to a show or something. Back in The Old Smoke.'

It's clear from his response that I'm not asking a local boy who doesn't know his way around London. I get my breath back and plant my feet slightly apart with my hand rakishly on my hip. 'Well, that'd be marvellous. Mar-vell-ous,' I sound like the Misses Johnson. We both laugh. Oh, I like this boy *very* much and I think he likes me. Daddy would approve and as for Mummy – well, she needn't know just yet – or Helen. It's between me and David. We have an understanding.

Chapter Eighteen

ARTHUR

Being constant was once his strong point – he'd put his younger siblings right about several situations. But not now. Dennis was more or less running the farm he worked on, and it was only a matter of time before he got a proper share in its profits. His father had retired from the railroad and Maude had a job in a store – and was planning to marry next year. Last, but not least, Harold had, of course, landed on his feet. Despite Arthur's predictions, they had survived – *and* survived without going to war, whilst here he was in another room in another town with no one to talk to in the evenings. *But* he wasn't in debt any longer and was able to set aside a monthly amount to give to Agnes. Maybe these counted as good times, so why didn't he feel any better?

It was a quiet Monday afternoon in early September. Nights were getting cooler, and the winter stretched out in front of him. Was stacking shelves all he had to look forward to? He locked the till and went to see what was left in the cellar storeroom. It was like being underwater down here – dank with green moss growing at the corners. The noises from the shop above were muffled and the sharpness in the air helped him to concentrate. Agnes had been a wall of silence this weekend and the journey back had simply added to his frustration. He must try to get her to visit him *here,* rather than him trailing down *there* all the time. It wasn't what he'd planned.

'Arthur. What are you up to down there?' It was Bert. He could do without him paying one of his visits.

'I'm on my way up.' He dragged a heavy box of cans onto his shoulders and started to mount the stone steps. Bert Walters's silhouette hovered over the entrance. He squeezed past him and eased the box down at his feet. There was a young girl by his side.

'Arthur, this is Jessie. I'd like you to show her the ropes.' He noticed that she was fiddling with a pencil. 'Start by showing her the stock system and where things go on the shelves. Then we'll work up to letting her loose on the customers.' Bert grinned at them both. 'I'll leave her in your capable hands. Take care of her – but not too well, if you know what I mean.' Bert turned away before Arthur could answer and did his usual disappearing act. Always flitting in and out and never helping out, Arthur thought for the millionth time.

'Well, Jessie, you'll have to learn quickly. We're on our own this afternoon,' he said, shaking his head.

Jessie Jones had jet black hair tied neatly into plaits. She spoke with a flat Birmingham accent but didn't talk much – she was more of a listener. Luckily, she was able to work out the stocking system and he saw that her hands, though small, were deft. She was a quick worker as well as a fast learner, and they passed the afternoon together in companionable silence. Very different from the silence of the weekend, he thought.

'Are you with us now for the rest of the week?' Arthur asked her.

Jessie was folding her apron ready to leave. She looked up and he noticed the pale blueness of her eyes. 'Mr Walters says there'll be a position for me if I work hard, so I hope I've been of some assistance to you today, Mr Borton. You've been very kind.'

He folded his arms, leaned back and smiled. 'Indeed you have, Miss Jessie. If you keep up your work, I reckon you'll get the job.' At least someone appreciates me, he thought.

By the following Friday, Jessie was a fixture in the shop. It was marvellous how quickly she'd fitted in. He closed the shop for lunchtime and started to think about his evening trip down to Haydon Cross. Jessie sat opposite him in the kitchen at the back of the shop. The morning assistant had left and the women who worked in the afternoons were due in. She delved into her large canvas bag and brought out a small box wrapped in silver paper and tied with a green ribbon.

'For you, Mr Borton. You've helped me so much.' He stared at the silver box and ribbon – goodness, it made him want to cry.

'Well, thank you, Jessie. You really didn't need to get me anything.' He put his sandwich down. 'I don't think anyone has bought me a present like this before.' He was unprepared for her – what was the word? Purity? Perhaps, sweetness? He turned away in case she saw his eyes water. The silver box lay on the table between them, unwrapped.

'I'll open it later.' He picked it up as if it might break and placed it well back on a corner shelf where it wouldn't attract attention. 'I'll let Mr Walters know that you're suited for this type of work.' His heart ached when he saw her smile up at him. How easy love would be with a girl like this. How difficult it often was with Agnes!

When he found a minute to open it, he found five beautifully hand-decorated chocolates inside. He put the lid back with care and decided to leave them on the corner shelf to eat at work. He couldn't take them to Haydon Cross – Agnes would want to know where he'd got them – and it wouldn't do for the other assistants to know that she'd given them to him. It would have to be a private secret, and why not?

He was in fine spirits on the train later that afternoon – and thinking of the silver box comforted him as he hunkered down on the settee in 'The Laurels' later. He'd arrived late and Agnes hadn't waited up. Living apart was a strain yet living together seemed impossible. Why was it that he seemed to be everywhere but also nowhere at the same time, with life a conundrum he couldn't ever seem to fix? He thought of his daughters – Helen was still often distant. He knew his relationship with her was complicated because she was so protective of her mother. It was Eva who kept him going. She alone seemed to have faith in him. Well, her and Jessie, so it seemed.

*

Bert said that Jessie was on trial for a couple of months, so Arthur made sure that he passed on lots of tips to her. The other staff made the odd comment about the attention he gave her, but he didn't care what other people thought – it made a nice change for someone to look up to him.

One day in late October, they were alone in the big kitchen at the back of the shop and Arthur took Jessie aside. 'It was busy this morning – I'm not sure how we would have managed without you,' he said, smiling at her.

She flicked a plait over her shoulder and raised her face to look at him squarely. 'I've learnt a lot from you, Mr Borton – I'd like to learn everything you can teach me.' She paused. 'If you were my husband, I would be by your side all the time.' Arthur was surprised but also flattered by her forthrightness. Her face had gone bright red. 'I'm sorry – I'm so sorry, Mr Borton. I didn't mean … but we get on so well, I…' Her shoulder heaved, as she leant forward and started to cry.

Without thinking Arthur reached for her hand. 'Please don't cry. I'm hopeless when people cry.' She looked up. The question in her eyes pierced him, and he instantly recoiled. Whatever he'd said or done, he hadn't intended this. She reminded him of his sister Maude. Goodness knows, she might even be young enough to be his daughter. Gently, he withdrew his hand and looked away. With half an idea of how to set things straight, he faced her again.

'I like you, Jessie, but I've got responsibilities. My wife and I live apart but that doesn't mean that I'm not a married man. I've got children, too.'

Her eyes, a minute ago like rays of light, switched off. 'I just thought... I thought you...' The shop door rattled, and footsteps could be heard coming towards the kitchen.

'That'll be Mr Walters. Can we have a word later?' Arthur said, barely hiding his relief. The door opened, and Bert shook a set of keys at him.

'I'm locking up tonight, Art. Perhaps this lovely girl will stay behind and help me, eh?' Bert said, as Jessie swept past him into the shop.

Arthur managed to work the rest of the afternoon without getting too close to her. As the last customer left, he turned to where she'd had been stocking shelves, but she wasn't there. His stomach tightened as Bert, who for once had stayed around, emerged from the kitchen.

'It seems that the young girl doesn't like us, Arthur old man. She doesn't want to stay, after all. Did you expect too much?' Bert looked at him as if he knew everything. Arthur felt his legs go weak. He'd spent the afternoon wondering how he was going to sort things out.

'Well, so what? Plenty more girls like that, eh?' Bert said with a grin.

Arthur tried to smile back but felt sick to his stomach. 'I'll do extra until you find someone new. Perhaps a more mature woman will stay. The young ones don't have it in them.' He was desperate to stop Bert from jumping to conclusions.

Bert's forehead creased as if he was working out a particularly difficult puzzle. 'You could be right Art, my man – you could be right.'

The business with Jessie unsettled Arthur for the next few weeks, and still Agnes and the girls didn't visit. Maybe it was just as well. Behind the impressive olive-green front door of his Victorian villa lodgings, he was confined to a first-floor room that overlooked the main street – it was hardly the 'house' he'd been promised. Then there were the Walters'. Albert was fine, but Bert wasn't his cup of tea at all. When he talked to Agnes about him, she said, *He sounds awful, but what did you expect from a family in Birmingham?* Could it be that the city of Birmingham was as unsuitable for his family as the seaside of Bournemouth?

As the year drew to a close, Arthur forced himself to face this possibility. And if he *did* give in and admit to Agnes that she'd been right all along, maybe she'd let him come and live with her for good. Maybe they could even rent a house together. He had to do something for things to right themselves. Casting his mind back was difficult – especially with the war in between – but he wondered if things had started to go awry when they'd moved from Caversham. Still, whatever the mistakes they'd made, living apart was not the way forward. In the New Year, he decided to try and find a job near Haydon Cross.

*

Arthur was at a pub near Paddington on a Friday evening in early February. Despite a few misgivings, he thought it was worth a shot to see if Charlie could help him to get a suitable job down south. If anyone had a knack for survival, it was Charlie, who was now *playing with the big boys in the city*, or so he said.

'You're good with the ladies – I've always seen that about you. I don't know how you do it, but they seem to like you. How about using that, Art?' Charlie said, as he put his tankard down with a thud. 'Now, as it happens, I know a man who needs someone to sell trinkets – that'd use your looks and charm. Hatton Garden. Knows all the boys down there – Abe Goodman – good by name, good by nature, I don't think!' He nudged Arthur who smiled weakly. 'You'd need to shift stuff that has a higher markup. *That's* the way to make proper money.' Charlie rubbed his fingers together. 'That and the cards, of course.' He grinned and Arthur felt his face go red.

'No more cards. I've finished with that. It's a mug's game, as well you know,' Arthur said, gripping his beer glass.

'Well, maybe, and maybe not. It's all right if you know how to take the rough with the smooth. There's always a rough with a smooth. But I can see it's not for a man with a wife who rules the roost.'

Arthur shifted in his seat. 'Look – the thing is, well, London's a bit of a stretch from Haydon Cross and it's not quite what I had in mind – jewellery, that is. What about your contacts in Ealing?' He wasn't going to talk about Agnes, or cards, for that matter. As for being *good with the ladies*, his experience with Jessie still smarted. But the idea of being his own man did appeal. He glanced at his watch. 'Train's due soon... If you think there's something for me in it and I'd be my own boss, I'll consider it, but I'd rather find something in grocery and be somewhere I know better...' Charlie looked blank, so Arthur finished off, 'I understand grocery.'

'All right, old man, I get the picture. I'll ask around a bit more and get back to you. Grocery isn't going to make you a fortune, though, is it? And what about your other talents, eh?' Charlie stroked one of his cufflinks and sighed. 'My man in Hatton Garden won't wait forever ... but let's see if I can pull a few more strings – a few *lucrative* strings. We go back after all, don't we?'

Arthur felt the air being sucked out of him. He would crumple if he stayed there any longer, so he grabbed his coat and got ready to dash. 'Same time next week then?' It wasn't what he wanted but he had nothing else to go on – Charlie's contacts were his best chance of getting away from Birmingham.

'Wouldn't miss it for the world. I'll start asking around.' Charlie tipped back the last dregs from his tankard. 'Leave it with me. People to see, places to go...'

Arthur didn't wait for him to say who or where – Agnes was expecting him to arrive soon and had no idea that he'd asked Charlie for help. He couldn't face questions from her, so he had to be on the next train. He dodged a few drunks and headed for the door without looking back.

Chapter Nineteen

AGNES

The Sunday church service was entirely Agnes's domain, and a way to make her mark on the social life of Haydon Cross. If Arthur visited for the weekend, he left early on Sunday, and she told the ladies of the congregation that her husband worked away. Despite what he said, she doubted he'd find a job nearer them, so overall, this was the best arrangement – in fact, it was an arrangement that seemed to work. The girls looked forward to his visits, and so did she, if she was honest. But his visits made the flat feel cramped, and she didn't want to live in with Mrs Atkinson forever. She needed to find ways to earn some extra money so she could afford a place of her own. Then, perhaps, they'd feel more like a family again.

One hot Sunday in July, she and the girls set off for a service to honour four sons of a wealthy family who had lost their lives in the Great War. She wore one of the last hats she'd made for herself. It was dark grey felt with a scattering of colourful feathers tucked together under a black band. It went well with the plain black dress and wide belt she'd designed. It was warming up for a hot morning, so they took the shady route under the wide beech trees lining the common.

'It's important to look our best today. That poor family have suffered for our country, and we must show them the respect they deserve.' Agnes stopped to adjust her hat pins. She had told Helen and Eva that they could forego coats, so long as they pulled their cardigan sleeves down to cover their arms. Eva's dress was perhaps a little *too* colourful for the occasion, but it was one of her best patterns. The ground had the heavy scent of summer, and the leaves were vivid lime green against the blue sky. Halfway across the common, Eva pushed her sleeves up. 'Eva...' Agnes warned. She felt once again for a loose hat pin, took it out, then jabbed it back in again at an expert angle. Eva dragged her sleeves down again.

The service was long and despite the high domed ceiling, the church felt stuffy. The family at the centre of it were well known in Haydon Cross – the father a local magistrate and the mother, now permanently disorientated, had set up a home for orphans. That she had lost her own children was a cruel irony, but many people said they had given their lives for the greater good.

Agnes pulled out her hanky from her jacket pocket and dabbed her eyes, thinking of Kate's Jack and quietly thanking God that she had girls. The weight of sadness in the church felt like a heavy coat dragging her down, but you didn't have to have a son or fiancé die to be infected by loss. Look at her brother. Sure enough, he was alive but not the *same* as before – it had all but killed her mother. And then there was Arthur. He hadn't been a gambler before he went out to Salonika, and would she ever be really sure that he'd given it up? He certainly wasn't the man she'd thought that she'd married. Was she different then as well? War certainly complicated marriage.

Finally, the service was over. She put her hanky away, grabbed Eva's hand and followed the sombre trail of people to the blazing arch of light framing the doorway. When she was a few yards outside, she stopped to take a breath and look around.

'Hello, dear – lovely to see you and your girls today. I was hoping to catch you. Mrs Atkinson tells me that you're a dab hand at dress alterations and there are ladies in the Guild who are trying to find a reliable seamstress,' a voice rang out.

Agnes shielded her eyes from the sun, so she could see the speaker better – it was one of Mrs Atkinson's friends. Her tailored suit made the best of her stout figure. 'Yes, of course. I'd be very happy to take on needlework in the evenings. I make patterns up, too.' She racked her brains to try and remember the woman's name. She could picture her sitting with Mrs Atkinson in her drawing room. She let go of Eva's hand and propelled her forward. 'I made this dress last week.' It was sky blue with orange and yellow embroidered flowers on the bodice and Eva twirled the skirts and cocked her head to one side.

'Grace, what do you think of this sweet little dress that Mrs Borton has made up?' Another taller woman then appeared.

'It's lovely, dear, and what a sweet child! Perhaps we could ask Mrs Borton to our Guild meeting on Monday, Mary?'

Mary – yes, that was it. But Mary who? If only she'd paid more attention when Mrs Atkinson's friends visited. 'Of course, I'd love to see what I can do to help you out, Mrs...' She touched the brim of her hat lightly and smiled.

'Fox. It's Mrs Fox. But do call me Mary, dear. Everyone in Haydon Cross does. And I must say that hat is wonderful. Surely you didn't make that, too?'

Agnes felt warmth spread right from her head to her toes, even as the remnants of the black dresses and jackets of the congregation filed past her and spread out across the common. The vicar's closing words: *Give thanks to the Lord for He is good ...* rang through her head.

*

It was ten-thirty, precisely, the next day when Agnes took off her apron and tidied her hair. 'It's time to go – we can't be late.' There was no sound from Eva's bedroom and she had a horrible flashback to the dreadful time she went missing. 'Come *on,* Eva. It's only a visit so the headmistress can meet you. Imagine that – meeting a headmistress! And she won't want to be kept waiting – you know how strict she is. Helen has told us about her rules.' Agnes still couldn't hear anything, so she peeked round the bedroom door and saw that Eva was sitting perfectly still on her bed, appearing to read. 'Did you hear me? We have to go. We can't be late,' she said firmly.

Eva was as rigid as a statue. 'I don't want to go to school. I want to stay here with you – forever.'

'No, dear. You have to go to school, you know that. Helen will be there – you'll be perfectly fine.' Agnes urged herself to stay calm.

'Helen goes to school, but I don't have to – I heard you telling Daddy once.'

Agnes froze. It was true that when they were in Bournemouth, she had told Arthur that she was going to keep Eva at home – she'd hated that rag-tag school – but she had no idea that Eva had heard her. Now, it was as if she sensed her reluctance to let her go. And she knew that when Eva dug her heels in, it took ages to change her mind. She let out a long sigh. 'Well, maybe just this once I could go on my own – but school isn't going to go away, you know. Every child has to go in the end.' She turned and went downstairs to ask Mrs Atkinson to keep an eye on Eva while she went off alone to the school.

Mrs Oliver, the headmistress, pursed her lips when

Agnes arrived hot and flustered and without her child whom she said was poorly. 'We'll expect her to start full-time next Monday morning, first thing.' She glanced down at her watch. 'And you do realise, Mrs Borton, don't you, that we don't tolerate children arriving late? Helen has set a good example. I hope Eva will be as prompt as she is.'

'Oh, I thought she'd be starting properly after the summer holidays.' Agnes's voice was higher than usual. She could already see Eva digging her heels in.

'No, that won't do, I'm afraid. She's already older than most of our new children. She needs to start as soon as possible and make up for lost ground.'

'But she reads on her own. She loves reading – I've taught her.' Agnes's confusion had an edge of anger. How dare this woman suggest that she had neglected her child!

'She'll start at the beginning – we have a method that works. Mothers don't know the best way. Now, I'm afraid I'm very busy this morning, so I have to go. I hope Eva feels better soon.' Mrs Oliver stood up.

Agnes's face burned. She looked at her blankly then remembered that she'd said that Eva was unwell. 'Oh, she will, and I think you'll find that my younger daughter is as clever and as ... *diligent* as my older one.' She clutched her bag and stood up. Her annoyance was as steely as flint. Who did this woman think she was? She wasn't even a Guild member!

Mrs Oliver held out her hand and Agnes shook it unwillingly. It was icy. She prayed that Eva would do as she was told, so she wouldn't have to have anything more to do with this rude woman. Thank goodness she had Helen to help! Between them, they would persuade Eva to go to school. As she closed the huge school gate behind her, she wondered if perhaps she *had* been too soft with Eva – what with her own struggles. Well, this would be a new chapter.

The next Monday, Helen held Eva's hand till she was through the school gates and into her classroom. Exactly an hour later, Eva appeared back on the garden path of 'The Laurels', just as Mrs Atkinson sat down to rest under a tree.

'I'll get your mother, dear.' Mrs Atkinson hauled herself out of the wicker chair, took Eva's hand and led her into the laundry room where Agnes was busy at work.

'We've an escapee here. You'd better go up to the school and tell them that she's run home. I'll keep an eye on her while you go.'

Agnes stopped folding clothes and dropped a blouse onto the pile at her feet. Her pulse started to race. This was just what she'd feared. 'What on earth do you think you're doing coming home like this, giving us all a nasty shock?' she said, her voice rising. She turned to Mrs Atkinson. 'I'm so sorry we're causing you such trouble.' She glared down at Eva. 'You know I have to work, not chase about after you. I can't look after you anymore.' Her voice was loud and wobbly.

Eva's eyes widened. Her head slumped as she clung to Mrs Atkinson's wrinkled hand. 'I'll help you with the washing, then go to school tomorrow.' Her voice was a whisper. Mrs Atkinson looked over at Agnes.

'Well, dear – what do you think? Maybe we could let her stay for the rest of today? It won't do any harm.' Mrs Atkinson then looked down at Eva. 'Tomorrow, Eva, I need your Mummy to do things for me that little girls can't help with, because little girls should be at school.'

Agnes steadied herself. 'If you're quite sure you don't mind keeping an eye on her again. Eva, be good for Mrs A. She's been very kind – letting you interrupt her morning, but this *can't* happen again.' She pushed the laundry basket to one side and ran upstairs to get her bag. She should be angry, but she couldn't help thinking that making her way home alone was clever for a child of Eva's age. Perhaps Eva had a bit of the grit and determination she had shown when she left Arthur?

Agnes walked briskly up the road, her mind whirring with what to say when she got to school. Eva might be brave, but she had to prove that with Arthur 'away', they were as good as any other family. Imagine the shame if Mrs Oliver thought she couldn't cope! Eva had spirit and she might turn that to good one day, but for now there was no way around it – Eva would have to stop these antics and go to school. Spirit was for later on in life, she thought wryly.

*

Over the next few months, the alteration work for the Guild ladies snowballed, and Agnes's purse was fuller than she could ever remember. She allowed herself to buy some silk to make a slip, and as she handed over the shillings, she had a clear sense that she'd always been destined, not just for fine things, but for the means to buy them herself. If only her father had realised that one day she'd be financially independent, he'd have been less jokey about her 'airs and graces'. How the mighty are fallen, she considered – he and her mother were looked after by Kate now and barely aware of what was happening to the rest of the family. At least *she'd* proved herself to Arthur, even if her mother had never broken free from her father's influence.

One Thursday in late October, she set off to collect the next bundle of sewing from a Guild member called Mrs Crowther who lived at the end of their avenue.

She checked the names on each grand driveway until she came to the right house. At the side of its lawned garden was the main road and on the other side were six semi-detached houses leading onto a row of grocery shops. It was less grand than the rest of the avenue but very convenient for the town.

'Do come in, Agnes.' Mrs Crowther's permed hair was streaked with iron grey. She looked smart in a fine wool jumper and tailored skirt. 'Excuse us for a moment, my husband is just on his way out to deal with our cottage over the road – it's vacant again and there's so much to sort out.' A short man tipped his hat to her as she entered the wide hallway. 'Wellesley Cottage is such a dear place. I don't suppose that you know anyone who needs accommodation at the moment? Obviously, we'd need references.'

Agnes felt a rush of blood in her veins. 'Well, Mrs Crowther, I...'

'Please do call me Angela, dear.'

'Angela...' She felt her face redden at the use of the Christian name. 'If you're looking for a tenant, I could be interested myself.' Agnes could hear her heart thumping.

Mrs Crowther opened her eyes in surprise. 'But I thought you were living in with Mrs Atkinson, Agnes. May I call you Agnes?'

Agnes nodded. 'That's just a temporary arrangement until I find my own place – because of the children.' She shifted her weight, so she was standing as tall as possible.

'I'm not sure.' Mrs Crowther folded her arms. 'Of course, I know you're trustworthy, but what does Mrs Atkinson think about your plans to set up house?

'She knows that the children need their own rooms. Helen has just started at the High School and has more homework to do. I see Wellesley Cottage every day when I go to the shops – it looks just right for us. I'd make sure I looked after it well for you.' Agnes hadn't actually talked to Mrs Atkinson about all this, but surely she would agree that they needed more room? There was no way round it, especially when Arthur turned up. And Wellesley Cottage would be close enough to pop over and see to Mrs Atkinson whenever she needed it, whilst the extra sewing would help pay the rent.

Mrs Crowther's face opened up. 'Well, how *marvellous* that your daughter has got into the High School! She must be such a bright girl. Well now – this wasn't at all what I expected, but if you think Mrs Atkinson would be favourable, then maybe we could come to an arrangement. You might even be able to do a few jobs for me in return for a lower rental.'

Agnes felt as if she was playing a game of snakes and ladders and would land back on bumpy ground any minute. She dug her nails into her palms to keep calm. 'That would be an agreeable arrangement. And my daughters could help out, too, if you have anything for them to do.'

Mrs Crowther smiled at her then looked down. Agnes wondered if she was going to reconsider. Finally, she spoke. 'And what about your husband, dear – will he be moving in too? I do see him occasionally – at weekends…'

Agnes was used to this sort of inference. 'He works away.' She narrowed her eyes – most people withered under her unflinching stare.

'Oh, of course. I see. How *difficult* for you. Do you want to look round today?' Mrs Crowther said quickly.

'When the girls get back from school would be best.' Agnes felt triumphant that her determination had been rewarded and she was already doing the sums in her head as Mrs Crowther went to get the pile of sewing for her. They would be proper residents of Haydon Cross at last! If Arthur wanted to stay in Birmingham, that was up to him, but if he came too, she would welcome him for the girls' sakes. But what really thrilled her, as she placed the sewing into her basket, was that it would be her name on the new rent book. By the new decade she would be a householder – it was a marker that she had been right to leave and was now right to stay. Finally, she had control of things.

Chapter Twenty

EVA

I look out for David, but he's not at church and doesn't call. It's the week after our walk on the common and I haven't told anyone, least of all Helen, about asking him to meet me in London. I wonder what possessed me to be so forward with a boy – and he is only a boy, after all – I'm a year older than him and know nothing about his family, or about him, really. All I know is, he's clever and knows he's clever and other people think he's clever. I'm almost beginning to dislike him, because of it. Yet I find myself wanting to live his life – his air of mystery is potent.

On Thursday afternoon, one of the delivery boys at the bank tells us that the trains are messed up by a blockage on the line. Everyone thinks it must be a bomb, so I clear my desk, hoping to get away early. Most of the secretaries have slipped out with practised ease. There's one letter on my desk to finish typing.

'Eva, can you take shorthand here.' Mr Wells smiles in my direction. He's spotted that I'm still typing. Brenda, who sits next to me, puts on her coat to go.

'I have to catch the train, sir. There's a delay on the line.'

Brenda winks at me, as she slides expertly towards the door.

'There's always a delay – it won't take long.' Mr Wells gets out from behind his desk and heads in my direction. His forehead glistens under neatly Brylcreemed hair. He only lives half an hour's walk from the office, so how does he know about train timetables, I think?

I grab my biro and pad. 'I'll come over to you, sir.' If he settles down beside me, I'll never get away – everybody knows he likes to chat.

He shrugs, turns around and sits back at his own desk. 'It's just a memorandum.' Mr Wells, or Bert, as some girls call him behind his back, takes ages over the shortest note. He's in charge of the air raid drill, and everyone laughs when he puts on his warden's helmet and chivvies us downstairs to the gold vaults. I adjust my top and smooth down my skirt before joining him. As I expected, he fusses over the wording. It's just a memo, for goodness sake. Finally, he gets to the end.

'Thank you, Eva. I'm sorry to keep you. It's Mrs Wells' birthday this evening, so we're off to see the new film at The Ritz.' He's making the effort to do something normal – and I'm impressed that he's doing it with his wife. Us girls should be kinder to him. He mentions the film, *A Window on London,* and I wonder if it's something that David would like. If he meets me one afternoon after work for the early showing, we could make the last train home.

'I hope she enjoys the film, sir.' Finally, I can go.

It feels as if everyone heading for Marylebone is expecting the big strike, even though, like Mr Wells, they're also trying to pretend things are normal. It'll be fun to show David what it's like – the hum of excitement with a large dose of fear thrown in. A train has been diverted to call at Haydon Cross. I could cheer. I squeeze into the corridor and look for something to hold onto. In one of the compartments, an elderly man stands up and points to his seat. Perhaps I should refuse? He seems unsteady on his feet, but he points again. He wants me to have his seat, so I make my way over. The carriage is airless, and the window is covered in smuts. Nobody seems to know what the problem on the line is. We inch along – there's a long wait at the signals, so the journey takes twice as long as usual.

We pull into Haydon Cross just after six o'clock. I grab my bag and squeeze back out of the carriage, thanking the man who gave up his seat for me. He looks exhausted and deathly grey but tips his hat like a much younger man. I wonder if Daddy looks like this – sick and tired but putting on a brave face in the face of a war that eats away at our patience.

*

I want to catch David outside the vicarage, like last week, but I've probably missed him. I walk slowly, enjoying the warm early evening air. A cuckoo is calling in the distance and rays of late sun cast shadows on the pavement. I love these golden moments – the streets of Haydon Cross are like the Garden of Eden after the frantic crush of Marylebone. I'm so lucky to be alive here and now. What did Wordsworth say? To be alive something, something, but to be young is very heaven?

'You're late.' His voice makes me jump. He's leaning against the wall. Was he waiting for me? A spike of pleasure slices through me. He'll know the Wordsworth quotation, but I won't ask him. He's exactly where I expected him to be, about half an hour ago – at the end of the vicarage road.

'It's been hell in the city this afternoon.' I breathe as evenly as I can. 'The train went on a countrywide detour. Anyway, what are you doing here? Helen will be annoyed if you miss the talk she's giving this evening.'

'My excuse is that I got immersed in my studies. I'm not risking life and limb, like you,' he replies, and I wonder if he's mocking me.

'I have to work, you know. I'd love to be studying in a quiet vicarage in a leafy avenue, in a sleepy town, like you.'

He flinches. 'I hoped I would see you.' My bare arms prickle. 'I wanted to arrange our evening in hell together.' Now I *know* that he's mocking me.

'If you're busy with your studies, it doesn't matter. It was a mad idea.' He mustn't know he's nettled me.

'Not at all. I've been looking forward to it all week. But if it's too difficult...' Goodness, his moods are so mercurial.

'As a matter of fact, there's a new Michael Redgrave film at The Ritz. You'd have to be there for six, though.' I hope I'm not speaking too fast. His face softens – he looks genuinely pleased.

'That'd be fabulous! Eva, you're a star. I don't study on Fridays, so I could come straight after the last lesson next week. I'll tell the vicar that I'm visiting mother – if he asks where I'm going, that is.'

'Why the lie? You'll be found out if Mummy talks to the vicar, and if I don't tell her I'm with you, when I'm late home she'll be worried sick.' I've hit a nerve.

'But the vicar might not like it,' he says, frowning.

'He's known me since I was a baby – he'll be *glad* that you're with me.' He is exasperating!

He looks down, as if he's thinking through some great conundrum. 'I could say I'm meeting you from work...'

'And the film?'

'I could say it'll help my history.' He's embarrassed. A million things go through my mind.

'It's up to you – what you say to the vicar, but I'll have to tell my mother where I am, who I'm with and what I'm doing. I'm not lying to cover up whatever your problem with Michael Redgrave is!'

He looks up at me, then down at the ground. He

mutters something but I can hardly hear what.

'Okay. I'll be there at six, outside the bank. I like to keep things private, that's all.'

'You'll make a good spy then. Anyway, I'm off home now. Can you tell Helen I'll see her later?' I'm upset, but I don't know why. 'It's Leicester Square, by the way.' I start walking away from him. 'The Ritz, Leicester Square, I wasn't sure you'd know it.'

'Of course I do. Can't wait!' he shouts up the road. Why am I wasting my time on him? He's a prig, but for some unearthly reason he intrigues me. I'll find out more about his family next time if it kills me. I'm sure he'll be an only child.

I stop instinctively, as I realise that this is the *exact* spot where I last saw Daddy nine years ago. I'm nearly twice as old as when I was on my way home from school, tracing the edge of the common and minding the cracks in the pavements. I remember his shape, across the road, slightly hidden by the trees. My fingertips were icy because I'd lost my gloves at school, and I was distracting myself by collecting bits and pieces from the side of the pavement. I saw him, but I don't think he saw me. I remember thinking that when he got home, I'd show him the treasure buried in my pocket. Then he didn't come, and the next day Mummy threw away the bits and pieces I'd collected.

I glance across to where he was standing that day, stupidly hopeful, but there's nothing and no one to see – it's just a dark, empty space under a tree. Perhaps it always was.

Chapter Twenty-One

ARTHUR

It had taken a while to accept that his days in grocery were over, but Arthur was out of Birmingham, at last. Whilst he tried to be enthusiastic about his new job, Agnes was suspicious. *Did Charlie have anything to do with it?* she asked him a week after he moved into her cottage and started travelling down to London. *I needed to move on from grocery*, was all he said. He saw her raise her eyebrows as she started to talk about her favourite thing – the cottage. *Her* cottage.

He had to admit, Wellesley Cottage was a tidy little place – she'd done well. The girls each had a room of their own and the downstairs was divided evenly into kitchen, dining room and sitting room. It was pleasingly set out and, best of all, reminded him of his parents' home all those years ago in Caversham. She made a point of saying that it was her name on the rent book, but she let him share her bed, and they were living together as a family again. Now, it was up to him to prove what he was made of, so they could make a new start – *another* new start, he reflected.

He started work after the Christmas rush. Charlie said Abe thought it'd give him time to get to know the business before things got busy again. *A new job for a new decade*, Charlie kept saying, as if newness ensured success. Arthur had to admit it wasn't a bad way to spend each day – in ale houses and restaurants, meeting other traders. London was much more like home than Birmingham and he didn't miss the shelf stocking and heaving flour sacks. Plus, it was good to look dapper for a change.

Most of his business was with men who sold necklaces, bracelets, pendants and earrings onto big London department stores. Everybody wanted gold – gold was money and money was gold and greed circled round every transaction. Each time a transaction was done, the value of the item increased, but because of the chain of salesmen, his share was minimal. He spent more time in pubs than he did anywhere else, so that cost a bit, too. But he wasn't going to tell Agnes that.

At the end of a particularly hectic Friday in early summer, he caught up with Charlie in the usual watering hole.

'Looking good, old man. Only a few months in but I can tell you're right for this.' Charlie looked good, too. As usual.

'It's not exactly what I'm used to, though, is it? And the mark-up isn't great.' Arthur fiddled with his beer mat as he spoke

'Come on, your head for numbers – your feel for the filthy lucre. If anyone can make money, it's you. And jewellery is the business right now.'

Why did his flattery always work, Arthur thought? 'Maybe you have a point there – jewellery is a player's game. If I made a few calculations and cut out a few of the other middlemen, it might improve the mark-up. The big boys wouldn't mind so long as they got their cut.' Charlie had switched a light on for him – got him thinking.

'I knew it. You're where you should be, doing what you should do, old man. Take my word.' Charlie raised his tankard to him, and Arthur did the same. He needed a prod sometimes – Charlie had his uses. He made him believe in himself.

Over the next few weeks, he learnt more about the pattern of the sales. He saw ways to shorten the chain and started to calculate which products and ways of selling gave him the best slice of the mark-up. If he made a profitable sale, he had an extra pint to celebrate before he got back on the train. And just for good measure, he dropped into the Black Bull in Haydon Cross, before he arrived back home.

Slowly but surely, he found his way back into family life – much like after his return from Salonika. It wasn't perfect, but this time there was Eva, who was always on his side. Every evening, after he got in, he put his head round her door and asked her what she was reading. Her smile made him glow inside, even if Agnes was a harder nut to crack. But sometimes, when they were all together, he did catch her smiling, too – it was a new smile, one he hadn't seen before – was it a smile of satisfaction? It suited her, he thought.

He had a wife, two girls and a job again. First thing in the morning when he applied brilliantine to his hair, the gleam reflected back his success. Life felt normal and months sped by. The new decade brought hardship to some, but not for them. For once, Arthur really *did* feel like one of the lucky ones.

*

It was over two years since he'd first decided to leave Birmingham and nearly a year since Haydon Cross had become 'home'. His time in Bournemouth now seemed like a flash in the pan – one that he'd rather forget altogether. One Tuesday in mid-November, he completed his rounds and went to meet Charlie at the usual pub. Sales had steadily increased and the system was working well. He pocketed a sensible share, then paid the rest which covered the cost of the stock into Abe's account. It meant he could concentrate on his buyers and build up the business, rather than spending time talking to a boss. He was making good progress and managing a steady income – the mark-up on jewellery was so high. Even Agnes looked at him with respect when he talked about the *gemstone business,* and he'd seen a delicate string of pearls just right for her Christmas present.

He sat at the bar and ordered. There was no sign of Charlie yet. The optics glared back as the barmaid pulled a pint of the dark bitter. He retired to a seat by the wall and noticed that the flock wallpaper was wearing thin in places and the chair rail needed repainting. What would it be like to manage a pub? Several of the men dotted about the room hung onto their tankards as if their lives depended on it. He picked up a beer mat and spun it between his fingers wondering what had kept him.

'Got one in already?' Charlie sounded nervy. Perhaps he'd come from a game that had turned sour on him.

'Just got here – end of a very long day. Only got an hour till the train,' Arthur said. He wanted to get back while Eva was still up. Charlie disappeared to the bar and then reappeared a few minutes later looking more sombre than usual. Arthur thought he must be getting a taste of his own medicine and losing money.

'Thing is, old man – well, it's awkward really. I know you're good for it but...' Charlie started.

Arthur put his tankard down firmly onto the beermat. His suspicions must be right. 'You know I would lend to you, but I don't have much spare, with Christmas round the corner.' Loans were a thing of the past and best avoided.

Charlie looked at him for a minute then continued, 'No, no – I'm fine in that department but the thing is,

I've been hearing that you're doing a bit *too* well for yourself lately – margins a bit on the fat side, if you follow my drift, and Abe's not too happy.'

Arthur stopped in the middle of taking a mouthful of beer. He put the tankard down and turned square on to him, 'I've been expanding the business that's all – no harm done, and everyone wins – including Abe.'

'That's not how the boss sees it, old man. He's put up with it for as long as he can. I said you were a hard worker and would graft. But I said a *worker*, Art, not a manager. Abe doesn't like that you've cut the chain. He needs those contacts, and you need to keep well down the pecking order. Some days you'll win, other days you might not – like the cards. Just like the cards.' Charlie leant back and surveyed him, as if he himself were the boss. 'I put in a good word for you, Art. Now you need to keep to the agreement.'

'And what agreement was that?' Arthur's collar felt tight and his face hot.

'At the end of the day, you're more of a carrier than a seller, I suppose.' The words stung. Arthur felt his temper rise. Charlie took a long swig from his tankard. 'It's take it or leave it – as it was, and before you started changing things. Abe wants to see the chain back and his share improve – or he'll find someone else to carry the stuff.' His voice had an ugly edge to it.

Arthur had heard enough. 'But he's getting *more* now because I'm getting him *more* business.'

Charlie looked up. He seemed amused.

Enough was enough – Arthur saw red. 'If he doesn't like it, *he* can find someone else.'

'Whoa, old man. Is that your final word? Shall I tell him to take his swag somewhere else, then?' Charlie finished his pint and started to get up.

'You can tell him to go to hell for all I care.' Arthur

wished he was on his feet like Charlie. '*You* can get lost, too, and don't bother me again.'

'I'd better deliver that back to Abe, then.' Charlie pointed to the black sample case.

'Take it.' Arthur grabbed the case and swung it towards him.

'Final word?'

'Final word!' he shouted back as Charlie tucked the case under his arm and started to leave. Arthur gave him a few minutes to disappear into the early evening crowd then he swiped his coat off the back of the seat. The pavement was like a blur under his feet and the cacophony of noise swirled around him. He might as well be on a battlefield. A car hooted at him as he narrowly missed its bumper.

What would he tell Agnes? By the time he arrived on the station platform, he knew for sure that he *couldn't* tell her anything. He'd have to find something else to do. But what? Another mistake to his name! He mounted the steps of the carriage feeling painfully empty-handed. Caseless, jobless – he might as well be homeless. Something in him had snapped.

Somehow he got back to Wellesley Cottage, opened the back door and crept in. Agnes and Helen's voices were a murmur in the sitting room. He listened – no Eva – she must be in bed. He put his coat on the back of a kitchen chair and went upstairs, making as little noise as possible.

'Why are you being so quiet, Daddy?' He could never hide anything from her.

'I wanted to read to you first, Bunny – not get talking about boring things to Mummy and Helen.' Her face was a question mark. On the bed cover, she had a large hard back book open called *Canadian Pictures* – it was one his mother had sent her last Christmas.

'Let's look at this for a bit, then I'll go down and surprise them.' He wanted to sound normal, even though his heart was like a rock in his chest. Eva shifted the heavy book around so he could see it. There was a picture of children tobogganing and another of a dog sledge.

'This is my favourite.' She turned the page and pointed to a line of men, snaking down a wooded slope with show shoes on their feet. 'Do you think tennis racquets would work the same? Can we try it when it snows here, or is their snow completely different?'

'Why don't we go there and find out for ourselves?' he said, forcing a jolliness he didn't feel.

'*Really?* Can we go soon?' Her eyes were alight.

'Why not?' Arthur knew his words sounded hollow – she wasn't a fool. 'I'd better let Mummy and Helen know I'm back.' He got up to go back downstairs before he could make her any more false promises. He could lie to Agnes and Helen but lying to Eva broke his heart.

Chapter Twenty-Two

The heavy ale fumes pinned him into the wooden snug in the Barley Mow. For a short while, he could forget. Finally, he heaved himself up and headed down Baker Street and past Sherlock Holmes's house. If only he could live a fictional life, rather than wander round the streets and pass hours in seedy pubs! But Agnes still didn't know, so he was trapped.

It was early December – cloudy with a penetrating damp cold. It would be better if there was lots of snow, like in Eva's book. The tall buildings and wide streets were even more bleak than usual. He turned around and retraced his steps. When he reached Marylebone Road, he swung right. He wasn't sure where he was going but needed to keep moving and see what he could find. Somewhere there must be a sign telling him what he should do next.

He came alongside a large square building with a billboard outside. Looking up, he realised he had arrived at the new Madame Tussauds building. 'Chamber of Horrors' was painted up in lurid lettering, styled to look as if blood was dripping from each letter. That's what my life feels like, he thought. But however bad things were, he was alive and well – down on his luck, true to say, but alive. Why *had* he survived when men he was at school with hadn't? It was like the teams that were picked for football, only these teams were teams of life and death and he'd been picked out at random to live. And even then, he couldn't seem to make a go of it!

He looked at the pictures showing pantomime villains and women chained up and a bolt of anger hit him. It was obscene that people wanted horrors for entertainment – horrors were all around and far too real! He turned away, anger turning to indignant fury. The men who came back from the front were humiliated and jobless while the public paid for ghoulish entertainment – what have we come to? Even the cinema was an insult – showing a 'comedy' about the Western Front. He turned away in frustration and disgust and pounded the pavements back to the station.

It was time to talk to Agnes – he had nothing left to lose. If she throws me out, I wouldn't blame her, he thought. He brooded all the way back on the train, as fury fuelled the shame that had burnt a hole in his heart. The truth was, he'd given up a job when there were men whose families were going hungry because their jobs had been taken from them.

'You're home early today.' She was unpacking her shopping basket.

'It was a quiet day and...'

'Hmm?' Agnes placed several items on the larder shelf. He watched her long straight back and arms reaching up to the top shelf. Every package and can was precious. She was always telling him how when she visited her family, she stood on the street for hours just to get hold of freshly baked bread.

She turned to face him. 'You were saying?'

'I was saying it was a quiet day. That's all'.

'Oh... Well, it'll be Christmas soon, so you'll be busier, and I'll have to think about the girls' presents and do the shopping.' He flinched and she looked up. 'Is everything all right?'

'Yes, of course. Why wouldn't it be – with Christmas round the corner?' He was sick to his stomach as he said it.

That evening, he hunched up by the fire and turned matters over. He was trying to forget that Christmas *was* round the corner, but now Agnes had cast a spell on him by mentioning it – it was almost as if she *knew*. He had one ten bob note in his pocket which he fished out and held out to Agnes as she came in.

'This should help a bit.' He tried to sound casual.

'We're going to need a bit more than that if you're thinking about Christmas. Sewing work is thin on the ground at the moment and won't even cover the rent. What's happened to that commission you were talking about a few weeks ago?' She narrowed her eyes at the crumpled note in Arthur's hand.

'There'll be more next week – like you said, it'll be busier.' He was astonished and appalled by the fluency of his lie.

'Next week is when the rent is due. I can manage to pay a bit of that, but the girls' presents need buying. I've had my eye on a few things – books mainly, but Eva keeps saying that she needs a new cardigan as well.'

She carried on but he wasn't listening. He fingered his watch as she talked – it might be worth something. That, and the cufflinks she had bought him when they married. He could always say he'd lost them – cufflinks were easy to lose.

'Are you listening?' Agnes was her usual insistent self.

'Yes, of course. Presents. Leave it with me.' He was weightless – worthless.

*

The next day, he left the house at the usual time, but instead of the station, he headed into the town. Someone might see him and report back to Agnes, but at least then there'd be an end to all the lies. The word 'dole' flitted in the back of his brain somewhere – but that was more shame; *deeply* humiliating. It was beyond a last resort – that's what she would think – but on this, he agreed.

The day was bitingly cold and bleak – the air, like a knife, sliced through him. Christmas decorations weren't up yet and there didn't seem to be an appetite for festivities. Perhaps it was just him, but the thought of Christmas seemed unbearably painful. He had no money for presents and no money for expensive food – nothing even for a train fare. He knew that Agnes had some savings put by, so could pay the rent if she had to, and she could just about manage to feed the girls from her sewing jobs. She was resourceful, whereas he was an abject failure. It was as if he was being kicked repeatedly – relentless blows flooring him with no way to get back onto his feet.

He sat among the young trees on the common for a while. At midday, he dragged himself to his feet and headed to the Black Bull to spend his last shilling on a pint.

The landlord looked him up and down as he launched himself onto a stool. 'Day off from the bright lights?' He turned to pull the pint.

'More like the rest of my life off from the bright lights. I'm looking to work locally. Need to be round here – support the family a bit more...' Arthur paused. 'I mean, for instance, if you need any barmen for the season.'

The landlord turned back with the brimming tankard and placed it neatly on a mat on the bar. 'Not really your line of work, I'd say. I've got plenty of experienced barmen who I can't fix up.'

'I was only thinking temporary like, while I get back on my feet in sales again. Just a long shot.' He tried to laugh but a strangled sound came out instead.

'It's tough getting through the winter with lean pickings, eh? I'd say better to jump into a bigger pool, if you get my drift. Family helped me out when I was down on my luck. What about brothers, uncles, that sort of thing?'

The man's kindness was too much for Arthur. He felt a metal bolt through the heart. Where family should be was a great big black hole. He had skirted round this hole for half his life. There was no getting away from it – family was a disaster – he was the one who *hadn't* made it. He turned swiftly away from the landlord and stumbled over to a seat where no one could see him and flopped down. He felt like a condemned man, partaking of his last ever pleasure.

He thought about the 'contacts' he could draw upon – the two Mr Woods, Ernest and Stanley, who had shown him nothing but kindness. If he went back to them now, their patience would have worn thin – they knew he was tainted. Then there was Albert Walters. He must think he was unreliable, leaving so soon. And perhaps Jessie had said something – she might even have said that he'd been ungentlemanly. No, he couldn't go back to Birmingham – that was also beyond a last resort.

Then, of course, there was good old Charlie. Enough said.

He racked his brains for someone – anyone – who could help him make a new start but there was no one left – he'd had his chances and Agnes's family would be shocked if they knew he had failed again. The sisters had always been sceptical of him, and supposing Agnes had told them about his forays into the gambling world? He couldn't be sure, but old Alfred had definitely cooled towards him when they last visited, and as for poor Alfie...

If, or rather, *when* Agnes found out that he was lying to her again, he would be forced to leave, so perhaps he should leave now – write her a note to say that he had gone to look for work – that the move to Haydon Cross hadn't worked out, after all? She thought nothing he did ever worked out, anyway.

His manhood lay at his feet in a sorry pile that couldn't be pieced together. There wasn't a single soul that could help him, least of all his wife.

*

Somehow, he got himself home that evening. He half hoped that the aching cold of alternately walking and sitting on the common had numbed his senses to the exposure of being found out. But nothing was said.

The next morning, Agnes turned to him after the girls left for school.

'Late again today? Or is it because there *isn't* any work?' He looked up at her briefly, then turned away and picked up his coat.

'Can't miss the train.' He bolted for the door, leaving her – he could picture it – with disdain written on her face. He turned away from the station and walked briskly onto the common once again.

He focused his mind on two things – lack of money and his daughters. There could be no more mornings like this one. Fate seemed to have made its own mind up, without a decision from him, and at last, he had some energy. He walked back and forth across the common, pacing the ground like an expectant father waiting for the cry to signal that all was well. Someone had probably told Agnes he was in the town yesterday. She'd never had faith in him, he thought bitterly. Otherwise, why did she keep her savings from him? If only she had trusted him, he would never have got into this mess, chopping and changing and finally falling. It was enough to break a man and now he didn't even have a shilling for a pint.

At half past three, as children had started to spill out of the school gates, he took up a position where he could look out for his daughters without being seen. Eva was old enough to walk home from school on her own now and Helen wouldn't be long after her, making her way up from the station and the train ride back from the High School. His daughters had done well, he reflected, and deep down, he knew that was because of Agnes. Especially with Helen, Agnes had led the way and formed her into a fully rounded capable being. He'd had very little to do with that, although every day he saw a look of his own mother in her. Maybe that was why he found Helen difficult to spend time with – she was a painful reminder of what he had lost.

Eva was a completely different case. Eva, Arthur dared to believe, had some of his own character. The deeply opposed halves that wanted safety and risk in equal measure. Seeing Eva gave him intense pleasure but also another sort of pain – the fear of a vulnerable personality. Eva would kill with her looks but *be* killed by her own lack of self-awareness. He caught a glimpse of her auburn curls as she walked along the edge of the common back towards home. Every so often she stopped to pick up bits off the ground – a scavenger, he thought – even if she makes mistakes, her intelligence will get her through in the end. If she knew he was going, she would want to come with him, so he would have to go without her knowing. He dug his hands in his pocket and clenched his fists. He couldn't face saying goodbye to her, anyway.

She turned the corner into their lane.

He was cold to his core now but still waited till he could see Helen approaching from the opposite direction, bulging satchel on her back, striding along the wide avenue at quite a pace. She was the rock of the family and Agnes relied on her – rightly so. She would keep the family together. He reckoned she would help him now, as well – and she'd help Eva, too, after he'd gone. As she disappeared from his sight, Arthur prepared to follow in her footsteps. The clouds in the early evening sky were a dark grey but elongated and innocuous; almost peaceful. Glad to be moving with more purpose again, he knew what he had to do – let Agnes know he was going and get Helen to help him to go.

It was as simple as that. Arthur felt – at last – a profound relief that he knew his next step. At a later date, he would make up for it all – perhaps take Eva and Helen to Canada to meet their grandmother before she died. And he'd pay Agnes back. She didn't believe in him, but one day he would show her again what she first saw in him. He would make up for everything.

PART THREE

EVA, 1941

—

There is a time in life when you expect the world to be always full of new things. And then comes a day when you realise that is not how it will be at all. You see that life will become a thing made of holes. Absences. Losses. Things that were there and are no longer. And you realise, too, that you have to grow around and between the gaps.

Helen Macdonald, *H is for Hawk*

Chapter Twenty-Three

This week has been bloody, that's for sure. The reality of war is sinking in, and excitement is turning to fear and worse. Last night, London was pounded by bombs, and this time St Paul's got it – I heard a wobble in the newscaster's voice as he described the scene. And now, it's a bright spring morning which seems all wrong. Helen is rushing to get to work and we're both trying to get the milk out of the fridge.

'My evacuees will be so worried about their parents. They hear people talking about bombs and fires and so on and think it's their mums or their dads caught up in it.' Helen's commitment to her class is impressive.

'Poor mites – if even St Paul's gets it, it shows that God can't protect anything, doesn't it?'

'God *intervened* – St Paul's survived.' Helen's fixing me with her teacher's eye.

'God mustn't like reading, then. What about the publishers in Paternoster Square who lost millions of books?' I'm being provocative but she isn't shaken – I knew she wouldn't be.

'He's protected us, so far, Eva, remember that – and especially you – he's protecting you.' She's generous to a fault. One thing I *do* know is that my sister loves me.

She flies out the door and I walk briskly to the station, as befits a Bank of England employee. At the other end, I walk into the City, not really thinking about St Paul's, though I should be. I'm thinking about David's latest letter, and the wreckage he's missing – not the notable places like St Paul's but the ordinary places – sheer unscalable walls like cliffs, rising out of the beds of dusty rubble left over from bombed buildings, and still smoking in the spring sunshine. I can't explain to him why we walk past as if these sights are normal – but they *are* normal because they've been absorbed into the patchwork of daily life that we carry around with us. I wish David could see that the battle-ravaged stone of the City is as heroic as the college buildings that he marvels at, but he'd rather write about Keats than bombs. He says there are poets who could teach us a thing or two about the current situation we're in – so that's me told. The bombsites in front of me are as unreal to him as his college lawn is to me.

He says that I can visit him after exams, but I can't get the thought out of my head – if he really liked me, surely he'd want me to visit him sooner? Does he even worry about me walking through a bombsite every day? Eastern coasts freeze in the spring wind, he says, and I can't get a vision of an icy sea out of my head as I spy the battered dome of St Paul's on the horizon. Freezing winds or not, I wonder if he knows how much I'd give to sit on that college lawn right now? The sun has turned to heavy rain as I turn the last corner to the bank.

*

We've been herded down the stone steps towards the vaults. We could be down here for several hours while they check the registers, and I'm still damp from dodging through the rain. Why do I always forget how unstable spring weather is?

'Don't look so miserable, you lot. We're moving the canteen down to the vault soon, so you'll be able to eat in peace.' Mr Wells is patrolling the lines of staff, trying to cheer us up. He doesn't realise that it's not misery, or even fear, a lot of us feel now – it's anticipation – even excitement. How can I be excited whilst real people are dying? But I am, and it makes me feel inhuman. This morning, at the entrance to the underground, I saw a family with a trail of children climbing up the steps, clutching soiled eiderdowns. One boy, about fourteen, was pulling along his little brother with a spare hand. The little boy's hair was tangled, and he was crying loudly. Their mother was struggling to keep up and hugging a large wicker basket with both arms. She looked harassed and I wanted to help her carry her things, but my fellow passengers jostled past her, so I carried on, too, heading for the City with the others – to our own fate.

I look up and see Brenda threading her way round some of the other girls. 'What a bore,' she says, pouting and pulling the corners of her mouth down. 'The Jerries are dropping the bombs at night, everyone knows that, so I don't see why we have all these drills in the morning. It's pointless – too late. Don't suppose a drill would have made the slightest difference if that crater at the tube station had been a few feet to the right...'

'God certainly does have a soft spot for the money lenders,' I say, thinking about my exchanges with Helen this morning. 'He protects a stack of bullion but everyone else has to take their chances.' The gloomy grey vault seems to add a certain gravitas to my words.

'Anyway, forget about bombs – that's not why I've found you.' Brenda brushes the sides of her head to check her hair is in place. 'I had to ask you first, Eva – especially with your film star credentials...' Brenda does a good turn at dramatic statements, so I know not to interrupt. 'It's my birthday on Saturday and I want a few of the girls on our floor to come with me and Bill to the matinée of *Gone with the Wind* at The Ritz. You've not been yet, have you? I don't suppose your chap could come too, could he?' She clasps her hands together as if in prayer.

The thought of David taking time away from Keats for an American film in London makes me smile. I remember how he analysed every shred of the last film we saw at The Ritz. *And* what a fuss he made about going in the first place. I try and look enthusiastic and regretful at the same time. 'That's a wonderful idea, Brenda, but David's revising for his exams. I'll try and talk my mother round. She can be a bit funny about me coming into town on a Saturday.'

Brenda looks amused.

'I would *love* to come, of course. But you know what mothers are like. They worry so,' I say quickly.

'You're old enough to make your own decisions, surely. Bill would be fed up if my mother interfered in my life.' There's an edge to her voice.

I shiver – the damp finally seeping through to my skin. What does Brenda know about my life? On one side of her desk is a photo of Bill and on the other side is a photo of an older couple holding hands. Brenda, as she keeps telling us, is one of four daughters who all adore their sensible parents. Us office girls regularly soak up stories of birthdays and anniversaries in her happy, healthy family. I, on the other hand, rarely say anything about Mummy and Helen – and I absolutely, never, ever mention Daddy. She has no idea.

'My father had to go away, so Mummy needs me to be around – it's hard for her,' I say as curtly as I can manage.

'Oh, I see – I didn't mean...' I see her hesitate, wondering whether to ask more, but then she looks away and adjusts her hair again. 'Well, never mind. Just try and come along. You'll love it – and I'd like you to be there.' She starts to take off her cardigan. 'Here, it looks like you need another layer on.'

'Thanks, but I'll be fine – really.' I force a smile.

Brenda can be kind and she's right, of course – I *will* love the film. I've read so much about it and it's here to raise morale. Surely Mummy will see that I *should* see it.

'Come on now. Back to work – the holiday is over!' It's Mr Wells struggling to be heard over all the chat that has broken out. We shuffle back to the stairs, and I climb briskly, trying to get my blood circulating again.

*

Mummy agreed straight away, when I said it was Brenda – she likes the stories I pass on which confirm that Brenda's family is respectable. Of course, I don't tell her *all* the stories Brenda comes out with. I'm glad to get permission to go but being on the train on a Saturday feels tedious. The smell of wet wool fills the carriage. Cigarette smoke hangs like a veil, and the people in the carriage are crumpled and damp. The man next to me looks up from his newspaper as I settle down, then buries his head again. The train labours into the capital. How exhausted everyone is, even on a Saturday! The sense of weariness is sharper than on a weekday. I can't help but think I must be mad coming into the eye of the storm when I don't have to.

Once out of the station, I take my usual route down Baker Street and onto Oxford Street. It's hard to believe this was once the most fashionable street in the country. The ruins of John Lewis look like pictures of classical Greece and rubble litters the side of the pavements. I can hardly bear to look at Selfridges – its beautiful restaurant obliterated. In my early days at the bank, I was amazed I could stroll into Selfridges and see palm trees bathed in light, leaning over starched white tablecloths. I want to remember exactly how it was but worry that my memory will combust like so much else around me.

Peter Robinson is still open for business with boarded-up windows. It's extraordinary. The bomb site dust catches the back of my throat, but I breathe it in, glad that this street hasn't been defeated and commerce goes on. I'm gladder to be here than anywhere I know in Haydon Cross – Mummy and Helen simply don't understand how grateful I am to be at the heart of the storm rather than clinging onto its ragged edges, like they are. I smile at every stranger who passes me by, and they smile back – it's wonderful.

'What's put a smile on your face then?' says Brenda when I catch up with her and the others at Leicester Square.

'Nothing really. Happy birthday.' I take a small package wrapped in tissue out of my bag. It's a hanky that Mummy has crocheted a lacy edge onto.

'Thanks – I'll open it later.' Brenda tucks it into her bag beside another large green package. She sees me looking. 'Oh, that's from Bill – an item of jewellery, I'm led to believe.' She winks.

We take our seats. I'm next to Joan who has brought along her young man, Archie. He makes sure she's seated before he sits down himself. She leans in and whispers, 'Do you think Bill has proposed?'

'Under pressure,' I whisper back, and we giggle.

'You all right up that end?' shouts Brenda from the other end of the row.

'Lovely, thanks – this is a real treat,' shouts Joan which sets us off again. The lights go down and I settle back to enjoy what definitely *is* a very big treat for us office girls.

*

When we file back out onto the street, it's still drizzling.

'Don't think much of this birthday weather.' Brenda tries to be jolly. Vera is still dabbing her face with a hanky and Joan is leaning against Archie. Bill has his hands in his pockets. Nobody wants to talk about the film. What would David have made of it, I wonder? He'd probably make a cutting remark, but I still have Rhett Butler in my mind's eye, even though the damp evening light cancels out the dusty sun of Georgia and there's not a cotton plantation in sight – just rubble and holes where buildings once were. Brenda looks round at us. 'Who's coming to the Lyons Corner House on Tottenham Court Road for afternoon tea, then?'

Frankly, it's a miracle we've escaped our worries in the cinema and avoided a bombing, so I don't think we should push our luck any further. 'It's been a wonderful afternoon out, Bren, but I promised my mother I wouldn't stay any longer than needed.'

Joan and Vera follow my lead and make their excuses.

Brenda's jollity takes on a warning edge. 'We should be showing the Jerries that we're not changing our lives because of them. A birthday is a birthday, and I promised *my* Mum that I'd have fun.' She looks directly at me. 'Besides, I need to open my presents.'

'I'm sorry, Bren – I want you to have a marvellous time, but we can't pretend that everything is normal. It'll be nicer to open your presents when you're safely home.'

'It's like Eva says, we have to get home in good time.' Joan takes the pressure off me and releases herself from Archie.

'We can have a damn good try at normality, so that's what *we're* doing,' Brenda does up every button of her coat then grabs Bill's arm, while we wait. I know she wants to open Bill's present in front of us all. Suddenly, I wonder if she has a point. After all, if we all just scurry away when she's paid for us to see the film, it's a bit rude.

'Perhaps we could walk to Piccadilly Circus and see the billboards before we go home. That'd be a fitting end to a lovely afternoon out,' I say. Everyone except Brenda looks relieved.

'If it's all the same to you, me and Bill will go to the Lyons in Tottenham Court Road – Piccadilly Circus isn't the same without the lights and who knows where we'll be for my next birthday?' She's still hurt. 'It's all right, Eva. You get back home, if you have to.'

'If you're absolutely sure... It was a wonderful film, Bren. Just what we all needed.' My words have cheered her a bit.

'I'll let you know how it went on Monday,' she says, widening her eyes with a half-smile on her face.

'I'll look forward to that.' I try to imitate her expression then kiss her goodbye and walk off briskly, leaving Joan and Vera stranded. Never mind – they have their young men to make decisions for them. I head for Piccadilly Circus thinking about Scarlett O'Hara. How possible is it for a woman to be independent? Supposing I was the one studying in Cambridge, rather than David? Would he come and see me? Bert in invoices is always joking that he'd go to the ends of the earth for me, yet David keeps me at bay. Brenda is right to try and have fun – after all, will we even still be alive next year?

I aim for Coventry Street and catch sight of the ruins of the Café de Paris opposite the Lyons Corner House. People are crowding in but the Café and the Rialto above it are just a dirty mound. We heard that the club was packed when it was bombed because people thought they were safe underground. I try to imagine the scene – people, like Brenda, determined to have a good time despite the bombs above, thinking, why should it be me when there are so many others who might die tonight? But it *was* their turn this time – Snakehips himself was killed as he sang. Brenda was full of it the next day. She went on about how some people washed wounds down with champagne and ripped up evening gowns to use as tourniquets. Some of them even brushed themselves down and went off to find another place to have a good time! That's how much bodies and twisted wreckage have become an everyday, or every evening, occurrence. I stop and stare at the space where it used to be.

'Shocking, wasn't it? That no one came to save them.' A small man, about sixtyish, with his raincoat collar buttoned and turned up, stands beside me, hands in his pockets, looking into the same space. He shakes his head. 'Could have been us – could have been anywhere.'

'It all seems so random,' I reply. I think of Brenda, sitting in Lyons in Tottenham Court Road, complaining about how lily-livered her friends have become. What's to stop a direct hit on her now – the birthday surprise to end all birthday surprises?

'We always think these things happen to other people,' he says, as if reading my thoughts. I turn my collar up against the invading drizzle and face him. 'It's my friend's birthday and I was just thinking about how awful it would be if she got hit today of all days.'

'And how you got away scot-free just in time?' he replies.

'Something like that.' I'm surprised at how freely I can talk to this man I hardly know.

'You, young miss, are what we need. Nurses who'll come out when they're called, no matter what – heroism on our own soil! You probably think that it's your father, or your boyfriend who has to serve their country but it's not just them – it's people like you and me, too.' He sounds as if he *does* know me.

'Take me – I'm too old to be called up. Even if I wanted to, they wouldn't take me. But I can drive an ambulance – that I can, and that, I do...' His defiance peters out and he catches my eye. 'I came here that night, you know, and it was a mess – a real mess. We didn't get the call till too late and there weren't enough nurses on hand to help out.'

A chill runs through me – what on earth can I say? 'That must have been terrible for you, really *awful*, but I'm sure you did what you could. I would help out, of course, if I could, but I'm not a nurse – I work in a bank.'

The man shifts his weight and looks down again. 'It doesn't matter a jot where you work during the day, miss. It's what you do *after* work that matters. You'd get enough training as a volunteer.' The thought of Mummy agreeing to me staying in London a minute more than I need to almost makes me laugh out loud but the sombre mood that the man has created lingers.

'I'll think about it,' I say.

'Tell your father from me, he won't be any prouder of you for doing anything else, if you do your bit here and now. You tell him.' He tips his hat and walks off. I stand in shock for a few minutes. He has no idea what a gaping wound he's left behind. It's as if the tourniquet on my emotions has been released and blood is flowing freely. I walk the rest of the damp streets to Marylebone with tears streaming down my face.

Chapter Twenty-Four

The heavy rain overnight has turned the dust and dirt into a grey sludge. It stopped the bombing, at least, and people now bless rain as holy protection from the ravages of fire. It's Friday but I'm thinking about last Saturday's encounter outside the Café de Paris. I love my job, but when it comes to the war effort, it's hard to be proud that I'm typing up invoices in the most heavily fortified building in London.

Halfway through the first letter, the ribbon on my typewriter starts to ink up.

Brenda looks up as I tear the half-finished invoice out of the typewriter and screw it up. 'I don't know why you're bothered about that. Hitler won't care about the odd smudge when he takes over.'

'It's about doing the job properly.' I don't mean to sound sharp, but she's been annoying me this morning. Before we started typing, she gave us a blow-by-blow account of a row she had with Bill and how he thought she'd 'stood him up' because she'd had to stay late at work to re-do a letter. Brenda does herself no favours the way she rushes her work and then goes on about marrying Bill before he gets called up, even though he has yet to propose to her. She's right about the smudges, though. They're the least of our worries and I only care about them because I've nothing else to care about and haven't got a boyfriend at home to row with. I spend several minutes wiping ink off the ribbon with the tissue from my pocket.

'Where will the bombs fall this weekend, I wonder?' says Joan on my left.

'Who knows? Hitler doesn't like to be predictable, does he?' I reply.

'Hmm. Hard to lead a normal life, isn't it?'

We bend our heads as if in prayer and start to type again. The keys clatter and I wonder what a 'normal' life is. I can just about remember when it was normal to live above a shop and hear the muffled sound of a doorbell jangling. Then I remember the cramped attic we lived in when I shared a room with Helen and had to be quiet so I didn't disturb the old lady who wore a cream blouse. But now, when it should feel normal and I go home to a mother and sister and a hot meal in our own cottage, it feels as if I'm waiting for something else to happen. Is it just the war which has upset everything? The feeling that I should be doing something more is starting to choke me. I knuckle down and concentrate on my typing.

By lunchtime, I've typed five invoices which by anyone's standard is good going. Mr Wells has a pin stripe suit on today. He grabs a hanky which is tucked into his top pocket and waves it around like a white flag.

'Eva, you're a marvel. I surrender to your speed and efficiency.' I'm embarrassed for him, as well as for me. Brenda isn't happy about it either. We break for lunch and traipse down to the new canteen. Looking at the fortified walls and ceiling, it's impossible to see how they could be destroyed. Some of the girls say that the vault makes them feel claustrophobic, but I feel safer than I've ever felt before – there's something solid and almost primaeval about it – I can't imagine coming to any harm down here, which is the point, after all.

I queue up, noticing that Brenda is talking to Joan and avoiding looking my way. Queues have become a way of life. The pile of mashed potatoes is huge but there's not much to go with it and some of the clerks from the Trade Department are pushing in to get served.

'Oi, you lot. Wait in line like the rest of us!' shouts a young man just behind me. I've seen him a few times down here and noticed his brogues – a beautiful tan leather. Not many of the men wear brogues like that in the City. He must travel in from the country, like me.

'We've all got work to do,' he leans forward and confides in me. 'I don't know why Trade think they're so important.' I nod encouragingly, and see Brenda looking, then shaking her head and turning away again.

'The bangers are running out. They want to get there first,' I say. He looks nice.

'Johnny,' he says, offering me his hand. 'International Department.' I'm impressed.

'It must be complicated at the moment in that department. I'm Eva, by the way.' I shake his hand. 'Who are you dealing with?'

'South America mainly. Trying to keep imports coming in.' He's tall with light brown hair and high cheekbones which makes his face quite beautiful. He seems nervous and I wonder if he's got a university background. He reminds me a bit of David but taller, which I like. We're stuck in this queue now, so there's nothing for it but to keep talking.

'South America sounds so exotic,' I say. 'Which countries are you working on?'

'Bolivia, mainly. Do you know how much tin we get from there? It's staggering.' He clearly doesn't expect me to answer this question. Out of the corner of my eye, I see that Brenda has taken the last seat at a crowded table. She looks my way, probably curious about my conversation with a new young man, but despite a stiff wave, she turns away.

'A friend?' he says with an enquiring tone.

'Yes – Brenda – she sits next to me in Accounts. Don't suppose it's as exciting as International. Nobody would miss us if we didn't turn up for work. The biggest excitement is finding out what time Brenda's meeting her young man after work.' I'm conspiratorial now.

He laughs – the corners of his mouth turn up comically and it makes me smile, too. 'And do you meet a young man after work, too?' I'm surprised that he's being so forward and feel embarrassed. I've already said too much and have no idea what to say next. 'Sorry, I didn't mean to – I mean, of course, that's your business.' We stand awkwardly looking at the diminishing pile of mashed potatoes. 'The thing is, Eva – is it all right for me to call you Eva?' He carries on anyway, 'If you *did* have any spare time after work...' I'm even more surprised at his persistence and glance longingly at the pile of mash which doesn't seem to be getting any closer. 'Let me start again. You see my father is a consultant at St Barts and one of my jobs here is looking for female colleagues who might be suitable to train as VADs. Everyone's taking on extra and I just wondered – if you're looking for something more to do, that is, if you'd consider it?'

I'm relieved and confused, but also oddly disappointed that his charm is a recruitment drive. I'm flattered, as well. 'Don't you need training?' Why does he think I can jump into being a nurse? He's only just met me in a queue. 'I'd have to ask my mother...'

'Of course – and if she agrees, you can do the training on a Tuesday afternoon – they're setting up something in the next vault. I could ask your manager to release you. Some of the girls in International are fire guards but we don't have enough nurses, in case – well, you know – just in case.'

I wish I could tell him that I'm already working as a fire guard, or a warden, or driving an ambulance. I think of the old man at the Café de Paris – how his words made me cry. I can't keep coming into London and just going home as if all this is normal. The sausages have run out because the clerks from Trade got the last few, but it seems churlish to talk about that now. The queue is moving along, and everyone is getting a plate of mash and gravy. I can't believe that I was bored when I came down here this morning – the cavernous vault seems to breathe amidst the underground suffocation, and I feel a guilty excitement.

'I would like to do something to help out, if I can, Johnny. Is it all right to call you Johnny?' He laughs. I've found a friend.

'Tell me who your manager is, and I'll send a memo to say you need to be released on Tuesday afternoons. You might be late home, but it depends on which first-aid post you're stationed at. You'll make a great VAD, I just know.' I blush.

I can't imagine Mr Wells taking a memo from Johnny in International very seriously, but then again, he does take his warden duties *very* seriously, so you never know. The war is like that. It opens things up – people talk to strangers and things happen – even to a girl from Haydon Cross.

*

I tell Helen first. We're sitting at the kitchen table, and Mummy has closed the door to the sitting room, to sew in peace. Helen hasn't changed out of the navy skirt and wool jumper she wears for work, and she's looking about for a clean apron so that she can clear the table and wash up. I recount my conversation with Johnny as she pulls open several drawers. I leave out the details about his nice smile and lankiness.

Eventually, she turns to face me, apron in hand. 'Here, take this and I'll get another one. These clothes have got to last another day.'

'And? What do you think?'

'I don't know, Eva – Mummy expects you back here at a sensible time every evening. She worries sick about the bombing and if you're not in by six, she doesn't settle to anything. I can't always be here – with the youth club and Sunday school to run. Last week when I got in, she was standing on the table with a broom in her hand because she'd seen a mouse. She'd been there at least an hour.'

I wonder why I didn't hear about this incident. I imagine Mummy swinging the broom round and whimpering. I can't help but laugh.

'It's not funny, Eva. She needs us here to help.'

'But other people need so much *more* help. I can't just walk past people in London and get on the train as if nothing's happening – they don't even have a table to stand on and they've seen bodies pulled out of rubble – Helen, *bodies*. You and Mummy don't see it. For goodness sake, some of them are living in the tube stations.'

'I do hear about it, you know. I just don't go on about it. My children have enough on their plates without me talking to them about bodies.' She thinks I'm exaggerating; I can tell.

'I know children need to feel safe and so on, but I'm a grown-up for goodness sake – I should be doing something to help. I mean even the princesses are doing their bit, comforting the evacuees!' I can talk Helen round sometimes.

'Mummy thinks you're safe at the bank – if you make her think you're in danger, she won't let you go to work at all. Then where will we be? Really Eva, you're so dramatic.' She looks riled rather than persuaded.

I keep quiet and help her stack the plates. She'll be trying to think about things from my point of view, if I know her as well as I think I do. Clattering fills the kitchen as steam rises from the sink of water. She snatches up the dishcloth and sets to work. I grab the tea towel from the wooden peg by the sink and shake it out. We work companionably at washing and drying for a few minutes.

'Well, if you *are* going to ask her, just make sure I'm not here.' She looks into the sink. It's not often she lets me talk to Mummy. Usually, she sorts everything out.

I flap the tea towel in her face. 'As you wish, my dear.'

Despite herself, she smiles back. Suddenly I see how hard it must be for her and how wonderfully she helps us. Over the years, she's become the man of the house. I make a mental note to do something nice for her at the weekend.

*

The training room and makeshift hospital are hidden away beyond the canteen, in a side vault that I'd never noticed. The massive door is propped open, and the interior has chunks of plaster missing. The walls are reinforced with metal girders, and it looks more in need of renovation than patients.

When I slipped out of the office earlier, Brenda shouted after me so everyone could hear *Why can't you do fireguard duty like the rest of us, Eva? You can see the whole of London from the roof and it's every bit as important as first aid. It's just like you to be different.* I had to placate her by saying that I'd tell her everything about it. She's not stopped asking me about Johnny, but there's not much to tell her. She thinks my clever boyfriend might not be impressed by another man taking an interest in me. I'm not sure David would care when there's exams to study for.

The air in the training room is cooler than in the office and there's none of the comforting steaminess of the canteen. I'm glad I've worn my cardigan, even though the sun is blazing down outside. A few girls have arrived ahead of me, and we're being directed to a table which has a list of names on it. I tick the list against my name and then wait till more people arrive. By three o'clock, there are ten of us, but no one I recognise, and any anticipation I had is draining away fast.

We sit down in two rows of wooden chairs at the far end of the room with only a weak bare bulb to pierce the gloom. I can't imagine anything less like the scrubbed cottage hospital ward in Haydon Cross. The nurse who was at the table, strides onto a platform, then turns to face us and introduces herself as the Matron. Following her is a tall thin man, in his fifties, I would say. I wonder if he's Johnny's father.

'Don't be fooled by what you see around you. We have all the beds and equipment that we need next door. We're using the best room as an operating theatre, but you'll be stationed at the first-aid post to begin with, so we can see how you handle the range of challenges you come across.' She's an angular-looking woman, but her voice is pleasant and calm.

She turns to the tall thin man. 'This is Mr Dexter, we're very lucky to have him on our team. He's one of the best orthopaedic surgeons in London.' He shakes his head and looks embarrassed. He seems genuinely modest and I'm sure must be Johnny's father – there's the same lankiness and wide mouth. He gets to his feet and scans the room. He has the kind of eyes that seem to look right at you, even when he probably isn't. His pinstripe suit is more suitable for an employee of the bank, than a surgeon.

He spreads his arms out and looks down. 'Don't worry everyone – I'll soon be putting on my white coat and getting down to business. First, I must welcome all of you brave young women and say that the training you'll get from Matron here is absolutely first class.' She looks embarrassed now. Johnny is lucky to have a father like that – or even just a father, I think to myself.

He sits down and a second nurse climbs onto the makeshift stage – her sleeves are rolled up and fastened with an elastic cuff. 'I'm the sister on the main ward here. Before we get started, I want to introduce you to a few basic principles that form the bedrock of nursing practice. When you're in the ward, always remember to wash your hands – and do it properly, *always* up to your elbows. Florence Nightingale's principles hold fast today – soap, water and ventilation. It sounds simple and it is. Cross infection is the enemy.'

I gaze at her reddened arms in admiration. Her apron is starched and spotlessly white. The light flickers above her.

'Don't be concerned about that.' She points to the lamp. 'We've generators to make sure there are adequate lights in the theatre.' I imagine huge lamps glaring down onto an operating table, as Mr Dexter fights to save yet another life.

We file out to an adjoining room to collect our uniforms and a strong smell of chlorine hits me. We must be near the surgical area. I swallow hard and try to concentrate on standing up straight, but the movement is making the room swim in front of me. I'm nearly at the front of the queue but blood is draining from my head. Someone taps me on my shoulder, and I'm forced to turn around. The walls close in as Mr Dexter smiles down at me.

'You must be the young lady that John hand-picked to join us. I want you to know – Eva, isn't it? You'll be doing *very* special work here and I hardly need to tell you just how important it is, whatever role you take. But make sure you listen to everything the nurses tell you. They're marvellous – we couldn't manage without them.' His words boom out at me. I attempt to smile and grab a package of uniform from the table at the same time. I concentrate on reaching the door and rest my back against one of the cold metal girders to steady myself. What must Mr Dexter think? I can't black out here – it would be too awful. How can I be a nurse if I faint all the time?

'Are you all right?' It's the nurse with the red arms.

'I'll be fine – just skipped lunch, that's all.' I force another smile. 'Can't wait to help out.' The words sound strangled, but they must reassure her because she turns away to talk to another girl.

As I move towards a seat, she looks over her shoulder and says, 'We have to make sacrifices if we want to help out, you know. Chin up!'

*

When I get home, I tell Mummy about Mr Dexter – I know she'll like the sound of him.

'Eva – what a marvellous man he must be, helping out like that – and so brave... And you're sure that you'll be in the bank all the time?' Nothing escapes her. It's all right for other people, especially men, to be brave, but I have to be completely safe. She once told me that the time I went missing out of the garden and she couldn't find me nearly killed her, even though Daddy had me and I was safe.

'Yes – that's where the first-aid post is. I'll probably just be sticking plasters onto cut fingers, to begin with.' I'd say the same if I'd been asked to stand in the path of a bomb. No point worrying her.

She sets about altering the hem on the skirt of my new nurse's uniform. When she's finished, I slip it on, along with the cape, and go upstairs to the mirror on the landing, so I can check how I look. The large ornate mirror once belonged to Daddy's family so it's a miracle we've still got it, but despite its provenance, Mummy lets it hang there. I pose sideways and for a split second think I can see Daddy behind me – shaking his head, a bit like Mr Dexter did when the matron was introducing him. But Daddy's shake of the head isn't a sign of modesty – it's admiration. He's admiring me, as I'm admiring myself. The uniform suits me, I think. Johnny might have been the one to choose me, but perhaps he saw something in me that was waiting to be discovered. Daddy sees it too. I smile at him, and myself, in the mirror.

When Helen comes in, I'm still wearing my uniform. 'Is it what you expected?' she says.

'Matron's going to show us bandaging and how to dress shrapnel wounds. She said she'd never seen any injuries as bad as when the Bank station was bombed.'

'So, you'll be in the thick of it, then?'

'Oh no, not really. Just first aid in the bank. It'll probably be boring – if the bombing continues to die down, that is.'

She raises an eyebrow, as only she can. 'Well, we must hope so. You don't *want* people to be injured, surely?'

'No, of course not. It's just, well, I'll need to practise.'

'Patience, not practice – that's what you need,' she says, not for the first time. 'Things happen – or don't happen – for a reason. It just takes time to see what the pattern is.'

'Umm. Maybe.' I take off my cape and hang it up. She's right, of course. She often is right. I used to agree with everything she said without question. Now, I think about it first and sense that she likes me to have an opinion, even if she doesn't always agree. I'm so lucky to have her. I don't tell Helen about nearly fainting during the training, but what she says makes me think about David and his quiet life in Cambridge. Is he part of 'the pattern' I need to see? I'd almost forgotten that he matters, I've been so caught up with life in London. Maybe it's time I visited Cambridge.

Chapter Twenty-Five

Helen comes into my bedroom as I'm reading David's letter. 'How are things going for him? He must have had his exams by now. Any results?' she says.

'Don't know about that – he doesn't say, except that he's had his head in a book all spring.' I scan through the last paragraph. I'm a bit put out that it's such a short letter and that she's interrupted me reading it. Then I see the bit I've been waiting for. 'Ah, he says it'd be a good time to visit him and see the college buildings, so his exams must be over now.'

'Just visit the buildings? Do you think he might be the one, Eva? I mean you're still so young...' Helen is six years older than me and, as far as I know, hasn't got anywhere near to marriage yet. I don't want to hurt her feelings, but it's not so much that I'm too young to marry, as she is too old to.

'At least with his brains he won't be cannon fodder,' I say.

'Hmm.' We're both thinking about Billy Collins, a boy who was in my year at primary school whose mother is constantly saying to our mother how blessed Mummy is to have two girls.

'The one or not, I *would* like to see him again.' I steer our thoughts back to David. 'And Cambridge – I've always longed to see what it's like to be a student there.'

'Well, David is lucky, as well as clever. Most boys of his generation don't have a choice between university and the army.'

'You don't think,' I venture. 'I mean – could Daddy have joined up?' She gives me a warning look.

'Why do you have to think about him all the time? He was my father too, you know. We had our times together. It wasn't always about you.' I shrink backwards, with the force of her vehemence. But at least she's talking about him.

'I know, I know. It's just so odd that you and Mummy don't seem to care.' It's close to the bone. She's flushed and looks as if she might cry, which alarms me. Her cheeks almost match her wool cardigan – every inch the teacher these days. She looks up to the ceiling, as if searching for inspiration, then turns to look directly at me. She's in control again and I sense something important. Suddenly, I'm the one close to tears.

'There are things you don't know, Eva. Things that it's *better* that you don't know. We need to keep it that way. Daddy will be fine, whatever he chooses to do. Get on with your own life. Go and see David. Have a lovely time away from the war and London and Mummy and me. We'll be all right.'

I'm sick with fear. What does she mean? What can she possibly know that I don't? My flowery wallpaper looks lurid. I am caged in by it – and her, standing over me.

Her face softens. 'Look, Pixie, there's no need to be alarmed. I'm just saying you're doing so well – at work – with boys – in every way that you *can* do with a war on. Don't spoil it all with worrying about something you can't change.'

'So, you think it's a good idea to go to Cambridge, then?'

She sits down beside me, and my fear drains away. She looks thoughtful. 'Well ... I would say yes – if you really think David's important to you. Mummy will be pleased that he's asked you – and, of course, she'll need to know that you've got somewhere decent to stay while you're there. But, yes, why not? He's quite a catch. You lucky old thing.' She pokes me in the ribs, playful now. I smile, of course. It's what I wanted – a seal of approval, so why do I still feel close to tears? It's probably the war; the nursing; the office – it's probably me, getting things wrong.

She pulls her cardigan together and springs up. 'Now, what would you do with a class of eight-year-olds? A few of them have seen things they should never have set eyes on – and their mummies and daddies are still stuck in the East End, getting bombed. I mean how do you explain that to them?' I don't have an answer. Helen lives in her school world whilst I walk past children and know that someone else is looking after them. She's halfway into the darkened hallway.

'A nature walk?' I shout after her, as I hear her step deliberately down onto each stair.

*

Mummy is making me a picnic lunch. Mesmerised by the summer sun slanting through the kitchen window, I watch her spread the sliced bread with dripping, press on a top layer and then cut off the crusts precisely, so every slab is the same size. What a waste, I think. War hasn't affected her pride.

'Mind you don't eat them too early, Eva. You might not have your dinner till late tonight. Are you sure David knows where to meet you?' Her concern touches me, even though I'm irritated. What does she think I do every day? On second thought, it's better she doesn't know – and doesn't ask, either.

'He says he'll be outside the station. Oh, and he sends you his best regards, too. Did I say that?' I know I've told her, but she glows with pleasure all over again.

'Such a nice boy, and *so* clever...' she muses. Cambridge is like Shangri-La, as far as she's concerned – a magical land where only good things happen. You wouldn't think it's only thirty miles from London – and hasn't escaped the bombs.

I pack my lunch, say my goodbyes, and walk briskly to the station. I'm more excited than I can ever remember. I can't wait to see Cambridge. Blood pumps round my body faster than usual. The journey is a hindrance – London an obstacle. I just want to *be* there. I've waited to see David, but I've waited even longer to see Cambridge. The train rumbles into the city and familiarity slowly settles me.

Walking through London is less tense now. Hitler has moved north, and Manchester is getting it. But with the ease of tension has come a sick feeling of being in limbo – not quite knowing when London will be targeted again. Have we won or lost? We're less scared, but more confused, and in some ways, it's a worse state to be in. I feel a fraud at my first-aid post with nothing to do whilst the real nurses are a different breed altogether – they've always got something to do.

Miraculously, the train is on time. As it clears the wreckage of the east end, fields flatten and spread out on the horizon. Sunlight filters through the smuts on the window and speckles the carriage floor. It's as if I've escaped to another country – sparse and open, yet vulnerable. Suddenly, I understand the need to defend the east coast. We've been hiding behind the bulk of London in Haydon Cross but here, there's only the thin wedge of sea to stop Hitler.

By the time we approach Cambridge, I've eaten my sandwich, pocketed the folded greaseproof paper, and restyled and pinned back my hair. The man sitting opposite looks up from his paper, so I tell him that my boyfriend is meeting me at the station.

'Hope he appreciates it then, love,' he says, as the train pulls into the station, and I go red from head to toe. I'm so flustered that I nearly forget to pull down my case from the rack but at least I get to it before he offers to help. I step onto the platform and lug the case down the steps. There's a chill wind, but I steady myself and try to stay calm. I can just about make out the still, slight figure waiting for me by the ticket office. Thinner, paler but still that crooked smile. I wanted to stay cool but instead am nervous and flushed. He kisses me, lightly, on the cheek and I smile back. I can't stop smiling and my heart is beating all over the place.

'You've caught me at a good time, Eva – you really have. I've just heard that I've got a first in my first year! The results were pinned up today – and you're the first to hear the news!' His smile is now a broad grin.

'That's marvellous, you clever old thing.' His results take the shine off my arrival. I so want to tell him about London, the journey, Mummy, Helen, but in his world, my worries seem petty.

'Anyway, I expect you want to see the sights while you're here, not hear about my results.' He must sense my disappointment. Why am I disappointed? I do want to see the sights and I *do* want to hear about the results and know what it's like to study here. But I want David to be as pleased to see me as I am to see him. Things have got off on the wrong foot. 'Come on, let's show you to your room. Then we can go for a quick walk before dinner. Did you have a bite to eat on the way?' He examines me like a concerned parent.

'Mummy did me a sandwich.' I feel childish and tearful. I don't have good results or interesting books to talk about and my case is suddenly too big and too heavy.

He grabs it from me and heads off at a brisk pace. I look back at the station entrance as we walk away from it and think about getting back on a train to London. But he has my case and is about twenty yards ahead of me, so I've no choice but to follow.

After we've all but run down two streets, he slows down, and I start to look up at the buildings. The stone has a lightness and honeyed colour which reminds me of somewhere we went when I was little – before we came to Haydon Cross. We pass a gate to a college, and I peer through to the world on the other side.

'You won't want to see another college when you've seen Kings.' He chivvies me. 'Peterhouse is all right but … well, you'll see.'

He's right. Once we are through the impressive portcullis and into the grounds of Kings, I am staggered by the austere space encased by the quadrangle of college buildings. It's imposing in its emptiness. I shake as I stand and spin round to get a 360-degree impression.

'It's, it's – well, I couldn't have imagined what it would be like, just from the pictures.' I stutter as he turns to check on my reaction. He lets me catch him up for the first time since we've left the station.

'I knew you'd like it. It's not like anything you'd see in Haydon Cross, or even London. It's so – *important*.' I know what he means. That's the thing – I just know; he doesn't have to explain.

'You're so lucky to be here – the tradition, the learning, everything. I want to see it all. And I want to know what it's like to be here as a student.'

I surprise myself with such a long and passionate speech. David knew the effect Kings would have on me – that's why he was rushing to get me here. I see it now – he was excited, and he's got the reaction from me that he was expecting. Suddenly, everything is wonderful.

We look at each other and don't need to say any more. He holds out his spare hand and I take it.

'Your room awaits, Madam. This way,' he says.

*

I'm staying in a wing mainly reserved for military personnel, but also a few visitors. The rooms are sparse, but I don't mind it – in fact, I love it. There's a threadbare sofa in the corner and a single metal bedstead with a lumpy mattress and faded eiderdown. I've been told, under no circumstance, to use the gas fire, but it's so warm there's no need. Just as well – David says that the rooms under the eaves leak when it rains. I've propped my novel up on the bookshelf to pretend that I'm a student. It's a luxury, even to pretend.

The next morning, David gives me some of his powdered egg and sausage and we find a place to squeeze in beside some airmen. The breakfasts in the college canteen are strictly rationed and food is shared with the RAF soldiers billeted here.

'You've got to see all the things that make Cambridge the place it is – punting on the Cam; visiting the Fitzwilliam; walking on the lawn at King's.' He's fervent, so we eat quickly and clear out of the canteen to escape pressure from the military.

The sun is blazing as we sit between the tropical plants that line the ancient walls, then move on a few yards to lie by the river. Time slows. David recites bits of poetry, and the willows bend their long fingers into the river. I am in heaven – and maybe, in love, too. Neither of us wants to move onto sightseeing, even though I've only got two days to see everything. The glaring light makes everything transparent and unreal. I might as well be in a different country to London, or even Haydon Cross

– everything is so fresh and new. I can't decide if it's seeing him or seeing Cambridge that's making me feel like this.

In the afternoon, we stray to the famous chapel. The beautiful windows have been replaced with grey tar-papered boards which he says rattle menacingly when it's windy, but the west window has remained – its beauty translucent against the almost pitch-black interior. We stand underneath it and look up. He pulls me to him, then kisses me gently on the lips, and I can hear his breathing change. It makes me want to kiss him back, but the chapel is so austere, it feels wrong. I shudder and pull away.

He takes my hand and looks straight at me. 'Let's save the best till last. We'll go to evensong tomorrow, as it's your last night.' I'm not sure what to say back. It's so romantic, I feel as if I'm in a film or on a boat – the ground under me isn't quite solid. We shade our eyes when we reach the outside again. He leads me by the hand and I follow, temporarily blinded.

*

The punt has had a few knocks. In some places, the wood is splintered and most of the dark red band of paint is peeling. I step on, gracefully enough, and spread out on the bench seat, waiting for David to get us moving. He bends down to take up the pole. After the kiss in the chapel yesterday, today feels a bit awkward. The sun has retreated, and he keeps looking at his watch.

'I want to see the backs of all the colleges so I can tell Mummy and Helen what it's like to be a student here.' It's the first time I've even mentioned them.

'I'll do my best to give you a guided tour then,' he says. I peer up to see if it's going to rain – probably not,

I think, and we set off. I close my eyes for a second to hold the moment. Daddy floats into my mind – has he been here, I wonder? I want to tell him about Cambridge, and I want him to meet David.

'I'm glad you've got a chance to see what it's like here because there's a good chance I can stay on after I graduate, now that I've done so well in my first year. Once this war gets sorted out, they'll need academics, and studying for a doctorate is the next step.' It's an announcement and David sounds nervous – unusual for him. I sit up straight. I know he's clever, but I never imagined him as a professor. I thought he might end up in London, where his parents live, or perhaps in the bank, like me. International Department – obviously high up, *not* like me. But not here forever.

'I was just thinking about Daddy.' I don't know where my voice has come from. 'Did you ever wonder about my father? You've never really asked about him.' I sound churlish, but I can't help it. He raises his eyebrows.

'I'm talking about my *future*, Eva. I know you miss your father – I can sense it, even when you don't mention him, he's there in the background, but let's try and think ahead, not back.' He sounds annoyed that I've changed the subject, and something feels odd and dangerously auspicious as we glide past the ivy-covered walls of Trinity. I keep quiet. He lifts the pole out of the water and we both watch the drips ruffle the smooth surface of the river. 'I'm sorry about your father. I hate to see you upset but – well – we could have something together instead.'

I look up at him and hold my breath. 'Instead of what? Of having a father? And what's *something*?' I hardly dare imagine what he's got in mind.

The punt is carefully poised between us, and we both freeze like a tableau.

'It's just that – well – we like each other. And you like Cambridge, don't you? I thought perhaps that if I stayed on, you might – well – perhaps you could join me here.' His voice is cold when it should be warm. I look up at his lean silhouette against the sky and shield my eyes. I want to spring up – but can't – I'm pinned to this seat.

'But what about Mummy and the bank? And what about the beastly old war! You sound as if it's easy... What about money?' I sound brusque, but he doesn't seem to understand my life at all

'I'm saying we could get married, Eva, and I'd look after you here. I thought that's what you wanted...' Suddenly, it comes to me that he's planned this moment and thought I'd be grateful – and perhaps I *should* be grateful.

'It'd be different if I was a student, too.' The Wren library appears on our right. 'After all, I do love reading!' I still sound churlish, but I don't know why.

'Yes, you're bright, and *if* the world was different, maybe you *could* have studied in your own right. But we have to be realistic, and you'd be such a big help to me – you helped me get here, after all. All those long discussions we had – they made me see the point of it all.'

He's right – *me* studying is fantasy and I see that he's made me a good offer. After all, what's so great about my life as it is? 'Let's get back and onto dry ground, then I might say something sensible – I think I'm river-sick.' I try to make it sound comical. I think he's relieved not to argue anymore. He nods and we proceed back in silence.

*

David takes my hand as we walk into the chapel, and I let him. The rain is holding off – all but a few spits – the air is heavy.

'We'll talk afterwards,' he says, as we file into a pew together. We've barely exchanged any words since we got back from the punt. It's my turn to nod and the drama and gloom of the music sweep over me. I crane my neck up to see if I can make out the famous fan vault ceiling, but it's sunk into blackness. I look down at my feet instead, as the soprano solos hit a high note. Evensong is everything I wanted it to be.

I think back over the past couple of days. Helen would be dancing in the next pew if she knew what David said this afternoon. She'd say I'd be mad to turn him down when he's more or less declared himself. I've been taken by surprise, that's all. I smile to myself, thinking about Helen lecturing me on marriage – pragmatic as ever.

After the service, I whisper to him that I want to explore a bit on my own and he lets me go. I spy several nooks and crannies and wander into a side chapel where I find myself face to face with the Virgin Mary. It's odd – a female figure and child in a dark cavity, filled with and built by men. I look her in the eye and am captivated.

'Eva?' David is behind me. He swings me round to face him. 'So, Eva Mary...' He repeats my name in a jokey voice. Then he kneels before me. 'What do you say?'

'Do you mean...?' I smile at him kneeling.

'Yes, *that*.' He's all good humour now – the boy I first met. Wise and funny – and very, *very* clever.

'Well, then, I say *yes*, of course... What else can I say?' It's a strange way to accept a proposal. He folds me in his arms, like we're on a film set, and kisses me properly, there and then under Mary's watchful gaze. The fractious afternoon seems a long time ago now, and I've just agreed to get married.

Chapter Twenty-Six

Mummy comes and stands in the doorway. Helen and I are sitting in the armchairs on either side of the fireplace trying not to shiver. The evening has turned chilly, but we can't light a fire till the summer's over. I've been back for several hours but haven't told them about the proposal.

'Are you ready to tell us more about Cambridge? Fancy David getting a first.' Mummy never normally asks about him and hardly ever asks me about my day at work or first-aid shifts. Cambridge excites her.

'Well, it's grand and stately and we did lots.'

'That's marvellous, dear. And what was the college like?'

'There was something about the stone which reminded me of somewhere we lived when I was little. When we lived in a shop by the sea ... or did I imagine that?' I catch Helen and Mummy looking at each other. Mummy comes over, picks up her sewing, and settles on one of the dining chairs.

'I'm sure Cambridge is nothing like Bournemouth. That was a wild goose chase we went on with your father. You were very small and – thank goodness – we came back.'

'I remember the sea – and, I think, a chair with a brown cover. I remember Helen teaching me to read! Do you remember that?'

Helen stares at her book and Mummy sews as I try to picture the room with a sea view and a stained brown armchair – it's like searching for a vital piece in a difficult jigsaw puzzle.

'And now, we have this lovely home here, in Haydon Cross,' Helen butts in. 'And what about David? How was he?'

'Fine.'

'Did you see all the sights?'

'We did.'

'And is it all as magnificent as you hear?' asks Mummy.

'Yes, I suppose.' I bristle with frustration. I want to talk about before. I don't want to be a tour guide. I want a bomb to fall – something to get their attention. 'Well, if you must know – David and I are going to get married!' Helen looks up. Mummy goes pale and stops sewing. 'Isn't that what you wanted to hear?' I want to punish her for being more interested in Cambridge than she is in me.

'Not just yet! Really, Eva – you've barely seen him in the past few months. He's a nice boy, but it's a bit soon for that. Did you put him under pressure?' That cuts me.

'You mean he couldn't possibly *want* to marry me!'

'Yes, of course, in good time – but not with a war on. You have to save up to get married.'

'I don't think *you're* in a position to tell me about marriage, do you?' I say. It comes out in a high-pitched, clipped voice. It doesn't sound like me at all. Helen gasps.

Mummy puts down the sewing. She looks at it for a long time, as if it might hold the answer to an age-old conundrum. I'm scared.

'You do know that he left me with nothing, don't you? I hope to God that you never have to go through what I did with Arthur.' Her voice is strangled, but at last she says his name. She carries on. 'If I'm cautious about marriage, it's because when you marry, you have to follow your husband. Think very carefully about that. It's not always – how can I put it – for the right reasons. It wasn't with your father. Hopefully, you'll be luckier than me, and David will get a good job near here.' She pauses and looks down.

'Why does everything always come down to jobs and money?'

'Because it does,' she says looking up and straight at me.

My eyes fill up. I wish I could tell her I was marrying for love, but in truth I'm not sure.

'Well, congratulations, you silly thing – and cheer up everyone!' says Helen. Mummy and I both jump.

'It won't be like with you and Daddy...' I say, but I don't know what I'm talking about. I don't know anything. Mummy sighs and goes back to her sewing.

'We'd better start saving up, then,' she says.

'Why don't I take you for a walk on the common to celebrate, before it gets dark?' Helen says. I nod. She's determined to lighten the mood. 'Blackout in half an hour – we'll have to be quick,' she says. I follow her and get my coat. I can't help feeling there's not much to celebrate any more.

*

Brenda splays out her fingers to show off her new nail polish. 'Isn't it a bit soon? I mean Bill and I are going to wait – you know, for things to settle down. There's still a chance he'll be called up – and, well, who wants to be a war bride, left all alone?'

'David's got his academic career.' I say.

'Oh, I see – all la-di-da, then, are we?'

'No, it's just that it's different for him, isn't it?' I feel uncomfortably hot. Mr Wells gives us a pointed look and we start to type.

Three hours and several invoices later we're in the canteen eating lunch.

'Eva won't be with us much longer – she's got a boyfriend with an *academic career* who wants to marry her,' Brenda says to everyone at our table. I sink into my chair. All eyes are on me. Luckily Pat and Jean aren't in Brenda's usual circle, so don't pick up her disdain.

'That's wonderful news,' Pat says. 'Who'd want to stay in this dirty old city if you can go somewhere that isn't a bombsite?'

'Good for you, Eva. Quite a catch this mysterious David, by all accounts. I wouldn't work if my husband had a good career.' Jean's quiet and doesn't seem to have much of a life outside work.

'And if you had a husband!' Brenda says, and we laugh.

'Yes, of course. But Eva's such a stunner – the rest of us have to work much harder to get our man.' Jean looks down at her meagre lunch.

'You'd think an academic might want another academic for a wife,' muses Pat. 'I mean you hear about professors who are husband and wife at the same university, don't you? That's usually how they meet. Do you think you're clever enough for him, Eva?' My stomach churns.

'She can always type up his articles,' Brenda says, not unkindly. I feel bound to say something.

'I help David think things through, as well.' My knees shake under the table.

'Hmm. How does that work, then?' Brenda asks.

'Well... that's what he says sometimes...' I pick up my plate and scrape back my seat, before they say any more or even, God forbid, ask about the 'Big Day'.

'Nursing shift tomorrow. What about you girls?' I say, my voice bright as a tin lid. The clatter in the canteen seems especially loud.

'Oh, the fireguard stuff is scaling back at the moment. Everyone's relaxing more – if you can call it relaxing; living in bombed-out houses, wondering what Hitler's next move will be,' Brenda shouts back. I've deflected talk of my impending marriage onto impending doom. Funny how much more comfortable I am with that subject.

*

I'm on the stairs going up to the first-aid post when I see Matron coming towards me. Her crisp figure glides down the steps. She stops, so I stop, too.

'How are things going, Eva? Are you getting enough experience?

'Well, it's interesting... but sometimes it can be too quiet.' Matron looks at me as if I've become her rival. I wonder if I've said something out of turn.

'Well, I don't hear *that* often. Most of our volunteer nurses find it challenging.' I wilt under the piercing gaze.

'It is,' I manage to gasp out. 'I just thought it'd be more – dramatic, I suppose.'

'Surely, it's a *good* thing that the bombs have tailed off? But if you're finding it quiet, we'd better make sure you have more excitement.' I think she might be making fun of me. Her eyes are a very pale blue – they look right through me. I look down and notice a large chip on the stone step.

'We could get you more training. That is unless you want to be typing when the war finishes.' The idea of life after the war is new. Not many people talk as if the future is certain – as if the war can be over and that there will be an afterwards that we recognise.

'Nothing lasts forever.' Matron has read my thoughts. She shifts her feet and seems to grow even taller. Then she looks at her fob watch and back at me. I wait awkwardly with one leg bent.

'Right you are – we'll cancel your *quiet* first-aid shift and make a start with some very sick patients on the ward, this afternoon. I can't promise drama but it's vital work, nevertheless.'

'That'd be marvellous,' I clench my hands in embarrassment – rooted to the spot and confused as to what to do next. Matron raises one eyebrow and points to where I've just come from. I turn around, relieved to get away but wondering what I've just gone and done. She follows me down.

The stench of Dettol in the ward is overpowering and the floor looks like a skating rink, but this *is* the image I had in my head when Johnny first mentioned volunteer nursing. It beats the first-aid post by a mile. The beds are lined up evenly along the walls and the starched sheets are turned back with precision. I try to control my breathing to avoid another fainting incident. Mind over matter.

'Nurse Borton – we need another pair of hands. Get an apron on and come and help me turn Mr Bell.' The Sister on duty calls me over. She's a sturdy woman with tight curls showing under her cap. 'I hope you're up to this. Matron has just said that you need experience, but I need hard work and someone who knows what they're doing!' She has nothing of Matron's firm elegance. I wonder for a minute if I should have stuck to the first-aid post. But then a bolt of energy fizzes through me and the nausea goes. I grab the apron.

She points to the last bed in the corner. We make our way over and pass three men – one who is asleep on his back and snoring loudly; one who is hunched up with his hands over his ears; and another who is sitting up and appears to be reading. He looks up as we pass by.

On the final bed, there is a man who looks to be in his early fifties. He's pale and awake. His sandy hair is receding, his nose is long and thin, and his mouth is set in a grimace. He smiles wanly as I squeeze round the far side of the bed.

'Morning, miss. You've brightened my day.' I smile back. Sister draws the curtains round the bed.

'Follow me with the movements,' she says. I watch her closely as we heave Mr Bell onto his side. She tucks the sheets in and in one fluid movement whips back the curtain. I take note. 'Mr Bell will need to be moved again in two hours.' She moves briskly back down the middle of the ward. 'We have to be vigilant when it comes to bed sores and patients who are bed-bound.' I jog to keep up with her. 'I need you to do all of Mr Bell's observations this afternoon. You can call me over if you need help, but I've five other patients in the next ward to see to, so only call me if you really need to. I'll be back to help with the lifting.'

'Yes, Sister,' I say. Her decisiveness cuts through the ward – I wouldn't dare to die on her watch. She flips up her fob watch and checks the time. Her curls bob very slightly as she turns to me.

'Be aware that Mr Bell can get easily upset. He's in pain, mentally, as well as physically. His wife and daughter didn't get to the shelter in time...' She gives me a meaningful look. 'He goes over and over it – well, you can understand. So many poor souls like him...' She heads off and I imagine the trail of emotional and physical, wreckage she is going to.

There's a clipboard hanging by the desk. I grab it and check the list against the occupied beds. Then I return it to the hook and smooth down my apron, adjust the safety pin on the bib and glance at my watch. Perhaps I could get a fob like Sister has. The ward is peaceful for the next few minutes. I hear some muffled groans, but they soon peter out and are replaced by snuffling snoring sounds. When we were training, Matron said that the patients hardest to manage are the well ones. *Don't disturb them unless you have to*, she said. It's strangely serene and a world away from the frenetic clatter of typewriters.

Half an hour later, I make my way over to Mr Bell's bed, armed with the blood pressure cuff. He's lying on his side, exactly where we left him, staring into space.

'Hello again, miss.' The ghostly smile once more.

'Sorry to disturb you, but I need to take your blood pressure, Mr Bell – as soon as you're ready.' I try to sound like Sister.

'You're welcome to my blood pressure, miss. Good practice. My Joanie wanted to be a nurse and I wouldn't let her. Thought it was too dangerous, can you believe it? More dangerous staying at home, as it turned out...' He looks away.

I wonder what to say, then he looks right at me. 'About your age, too. Not as tall, but a good girl, a really good girl...' He stops and his head sinks back onto the pillow. The cuff dangles from my hand and I'm not sure whether to carry on or wait a bit.

'Was Joanie your daughter, Mr Bell?' The words come.

'My daughter – aye, yes – my daughter. Only one. Beautiful girl.'

I grasp the cuff and steady my voice. 'Can I have your right arm, please?' He lifts his arm slowly, some old wounds beginning to form scars. 'It must be hard.' I push up his pyjama sleeve and fasten the cuff tightly round his upper arm. He doesn't speak again and the silence while I calculate his pressure is awkward. 'Very good.' I unfasten the cuff. He still doesn't speak. I've let him down, and it makes me want to leave the ward and go home – but I won't. I place his arm back under the cover, roll the cuff up and turn to walk back to the nurse's station.

'You take care, miss,' he says to my back. 'You take care.'

*

'You look wrung out,' Mummy says, after dinner. 'Is this nursing getting too much for you? What does David think about it?' She's trying to mend bridges, but I can't get Mr Bell's words out of my head. My skull is like an echo chamber which I can't switch off. I haven't thought about David for at least twenty-four hours.

I look blankly at her and let her words sift into my mind. 'He wants me to help him with his work when we're married.'

'Good – well he'll have a good job, no doubt. I am pleased for you, dear. I'm sorry if...'

'It's all right.'

'Good. An early night, for you now, by the looks of things. Off you go.' I feel like a child, but it's a good feeling. I head upstairs. What will it be like to be a married woman – to wake up without Mummy and Helen? I burrow under the covers.

Sleep doesn't come. There's something said or unsaid that I can't get hold of – something important. Daddy's presence is here. I switch on the light. Helen is moving about next door. She'll be tidying her schoolbooks and laying her clothes out for the morning. Then she'll say her prayers. I wish I was more like Helen, but it feels hopeless. I've never been as serious about my work as she is, and soon I'll have a husband. Not Mummy, or patients, or typing letters for the bank.

Just David.

Chapter Twenty-Seven

It couldn't be more perfect. Saturday morning and the smell of bacon. Mummy is standing by the cooker, busy frying. She smiles at me as I enter. I slide my bag off my shoulder and plonk it down on the floor. Inside is my attempt at a wedding list. I got up early and headed to my favourite bench on the common to try and clear my head and make a plan, but so far, all that's on the list in impeccably neat handwriting is *Dress!*

'Feel better for a walk?' she says.

'It was beautiful. I can't believe how everything keeps growing, despite the war.'

'Even the war can't stop that!' she says brightly.

'I was thinking about the tiny neatly stitched darts you sewed on my first school uniform – the one of Helen's that you altered.'

'And why was that?' She shakes the frying pan firmly.

'The wedding dress – I wondered if...'

'Of course, dear. I wouldn't expect not to. Have you heard from David?'

'Not yet... but he's always working. I mean – we've both got a lot to do at the moment.'

'Planning a wedding must be top of the list though?' The bacon is spitting.

'Well, yes, that's why I've made a start.' I sound churlish but the silence from David is worrying. 'The bacon smells divine!' I say, changing the subject.

'Mr Evans let me have three rashers yesterday – back, not streaky. The queue was out the door, but I got there early. Queuing is so tiresome!' She turns around and looks straight at me. 'When I remember *our* shops and the way we treated customers, it was completely different.' Ah, at last she's telling me something important.

'Helen says that she used to help you behind the counter and that you sat me on your knee to put the customers in a good mood,' I say, trying to get more out of her.

She carries on frying but shakes her head slightly. 'We knew how to treat people, even your father did ... but it wasn't a good time, Eva. You do what you have to do to make things right, and that brought us to Haydon Cross.'

'We're lucky to have you, Mummy,' I say, out of the blue – relieved that she's talking so freely. She switches the gas flame off and shakes the pan.

'Well, that's a nice thing to say, Eva – thank you. I won't say it's always been easy, but we've managed, haven't we?' She grabs some tongs and lifts the rashers onto a plate next to a slice of bread and dripping.

'So, can we talk about – the *wedding?*' I use a deliberately dramatic tone. She laughs at the stagey voice.

'I'm all ears, dear.' She passes me the plate and we sit down together. I want to eat but I want to talk too. She sits opposite, watching me, her hands folded in her lap, as elegant as ever. Head down, I start to saw at the bread and dripping.

'I don't know – I'm not sure what to do first – I mean we haven't actually set a date.' I stop sawing and look straight back at her. 'Do you remember? I mean, I just wondered ... what it was like when you and Daddy...' I trail off. Her smile has drained away.

'It's *your* wedding we're talking about, dear, not mine. Wartime isn't the best time to get married, but I expect you and David have thought about all that.'

I'm not sure what she means by *all that*. I cast my

mind back to Cambridge, but can't remember talking about the war, except in general. He could be in London with his parents now, for all I know – the parents I've yet to meet. I cut my rasher into tiny squares, so I can savour every mouthful, but Mummy reads my mind.

'We don't know much about David's people, do we? Except the poor souls have had to put up with bombs. They must be clever, though, with him doing so well...' she tails off and I sense that she has something else on her mind. The uneaten tiny squares of rasher are starting to congeal and suddenly seem less appealing. This conversation isn't heading in the direction I was hoping. 'It must be difficult for poor David, working hard to better himself and then not knowing what's happening to them.'

'I think they just want him to do well...' I say, but I have no idea what they think – David says so little about them.

'You'd think they might have moved out of London to a better area, like *I* did when I had to,' she says, but why *hasn't* David taken me to meet his parents? The frustration of everything overwhelms me – her voice – her pride – his secrecy – like glaring lights suddenly blinding me, out of nowhere.

'At least he knows *where* his parents are!' I say and bang my knife and fork down. They clatter onto the plate, but the sound is quite distant, as if I've entered a tunnel with the rest of the room outside it.

'What on earth do you mean by that, dear?' she says, eyes widening. I can see her, but the sound of her talking is quite muted. I don't know what's happening, but her face is drawn and worried. Her hands have moved from her lap.

'You've never actually told me *where* Daddy is – *or* why he went.' I gasp out. 'I've spent the last ten years wondering and not knowing, and just – well, just *worried sick*.' I'm on my feet, but so is Mummy. Her hands are on my shoulders and she's pushing me back down. I haven't got the energy to resist, so I flop back down. We sit breathless side by side for a few seconds. There are tears running down my face, but I have one more question – the question that's been in the background bothering me. 'And ... without Daddy ... who's going ... to ... give me away?' It's weak and silly and comes out between sobs.

There's a sharp intake of breath. 'For goodness sake, listen to me, Eva! You're better off without him. *He* agreed with us, Eva. Look at me – *he* agreed!' This makes no sense at all. It's a line from a different play than the one we're in. I start to shake. Her face is luminous and ghostly. I'm sure I'm going to faint.

'Eva, *Eva*,' she's saying, over and over. 'Shall I get Helen?' All at once, I know who the *us* is – and there can only be one *he* – Mummy and Helen must have seen him! But where was I? My bruised mind searches the past but can't find an answer. The scrubbed kitchen table looks darker than before and the floor tiles underneath dirtier. The familiar bones of the kitchen are spiked and dangerous. My world which was shiny this morning is falling apart.

*

Helen's holding a blanket. Mummy sets down a hot mug of tea. Faintness washes over me in waves and turns into sickness. My legs are heavy and cold, but the blanket brings them back to life.

'Come on, Bunny – big breaths, now.' Helen's using *his* name for me at this moment! It's hard to believe she could do this. I look back into her concerned face and finally manage to speak.

'You know where he is, don't you?'

'No, I – we don't know – not now. It's not that simple.' Mummy hovers behind.

'Is he all right – is he even alive?'

'Don't be dramatic, of course he's alive – well, probably. It was just before the war started when he turned up out of the blue. We told him how you were doing, but he could see it would upset you, after so long, if he waited...' She's jabbering.

'Where was I, when...?' His presence folds into the air.

'He was staying in London.' Mummy is speaking now. 'You were at work and Helen was here, so we told him you'd got a good job, and he went away. There was no point in him waiting till you got home. You weren't supposed to find out like this...'

'No point?' I try to think if there was a day when I knew, just *knew* he'd been here.

'He didn't want to get in the way – said he might try and get to Canada and see Grandma and the rest of them. He was fine, Eva – probably got out before the war started – lucky him. Imagine how it would have looked if he'd stuck around or even written to us. It was better this way.' It's Helen speaking again.

'Better for whom?' Even anger is too difficult to feel – I'm totally flattened.

She ignores the question and carries on. 'Honestly, he said he'd be fine – had his own plans – that's why we didn't tell you.'

The thought that I might have seen him, or that he might have seen me in London without me even knowing, breaks my heart. I might have been looking the wrong way – have missed him on Oxford Street by five minutes. Anything. It's too much. I push the blanket aside and get up. The chair scrapes on the floor and nearly topples over as I head for the stairs and the comfort of my own room.

*

I wake up in half-light and switch on the bedside lamp. It's just after four o'clock – still too early to get up, but ... *tomorrow is another day*. Helen tried to talk to me through the door late yesterday afternoon, but I told her to go away, and she did. I sneaked out to the bathroom when I was sure that they were both downstairs and then managed to sleep for a bit when the light dimmed. The thought of trailing to church today with Mummy and Helen is unthinkable. I need to write to David. Perhaps we could marry straight away?

I think again about that last evening. Not yesterday, but *the* last evening when I was nine-years-old. I picture this bedroom in the late afternoon, just *before* that evening and before Helen gave me the book and I started to read. If I close my eyes and think really hard, I remember that there was someone downstairs talking to Mummy. I heard her voice, but not the other person's which made me curious, so when the person had gone, I went downstairs and asked her who she'd been speaking to. She told me that it was Mr Burton, delivering the bread that she'd left on the counter by mistake. *Silly me,* she said, and was flustered and a bit tearful. I did wonder why she was upset and thought – yes, I did think it, I'm sure – she *never* forgets things like that.

My head splits in two with the effort of remembering so far back. The bed is jelly-like under me. Of course, it's obvious – I see it now! She must have been talking to Daddy and she must have *known* he was going, even then. In fact, she probably *told* him to go but didn't tell me. Then, when he finally came back, she still didn't tell me! And what does Helen know? I can't bear it any longer – I pile the covers on top of me but can't stop shivering, thinking about the missed years and lost opportunities. I bury my head in the pillow and wail.

After a while – my stomach empty and my head heavy – I heave back the covers. The fancy lettering of an old book on the shelf hits a raw spot. Here he is – this very book in hand, with a young girl leaning into him. There's a picture with piles of snow near the middle which we – that girl, now me, and him – used to look at. A photo that made us dream. I haven't looked at this book since he went. Summer dawn strains through the curtains as I pull the book out from the pile and let it fall open. If I look at it hard enough, perhaps I'll know where he is. But it's just a game and the pages open at the list of contents.

Mummy and Helen have sent him away again. He could be anywhere.

Chapter Twenty-Eight

Helen pushed it under the door late last night, a white oblong on the olive green carpet, with his scrawling writing – *Miss Eva M. Borton*. Only David uses the initial of my middle name. He wants to meet in London and suggests a long lunch. I shudder with relief – maybe I'll even meet his parents at long last. He's suggested next Friday at Lyons Corner House on the Strand. If only it were sooner, but it's a sign – to have a letter from him.

It's nearly midday by the time I venture downstairs. Mummy and Helen will be worried that I missed church, but I have to face them sooner or later.

'How are you feeling now, Eva?' Mummy says. I turn away.

'The vicar asked where you were,' says Helen. Provocative.

'So, did you tell him that you sent my father away and didn't tell me?' I say. Churlish.

'Don't be silly – and we didn't send him away.' Helen's irritated.

'Well, you definitely didn't tell me he'd come back.' They have no answer to that.

'*Maybe* we should have told you. I can see that now. We were looking after you as best as we could.' I can hear it in Mummy's voice – I've given her a scare.

'With the war and all the suffering, we thought you'd be glad that he was out of the way.' Helen again.

'But you don't *actually* know where he is – it's just a guess.'

'We'd be told if he was – you know – well, if he was deceased.' I can't believe that Helen can be so cold.

'*Deceased!* He's our father. Well, mine, anyway.'

She looks upset now. 'He's mine, too, you know – you're not the only one with regrets.' She goes into the sitting room and slams the door. Very un-Helen-like. *Regrets* – a strange word to use.

I look at Mummy. She stands with her head bowed, leaning against the sink. It's her thinking pose. She looks up.

'I'm sorry, Eva.' She doesn't move. 'I should have told you, but you were so young. And then…' she trails off. 'But he'll be safe. I'm sure of it, and after the war you'll be able to see him.'

'If I can find him!' She's given me the nearest thing to an apology I've ever had, and I want to forgive her, but the house is like a warzone all of its own. 'I'm going to meet David, this week, to make plans. You probably won't like them, but if he wants to marry straight away, then I will.'

She's drained of her usual fervour. 'Yes, dear. You must do what's best for him. It's uncertain times for us all, but at least I've still got Helen.' That sends the blood rushing to my face again. Oh, yes, she's *always* got Helen. Perhaps she doesn't care about me leaving at all? Like she didn't care about him going!

It's exhausting. I don't want to follow Helen into the sitting room, so I turn to go upstairs instead.

*

Brenda is full of the week's news. 'Bill says that we need to watch out if they bring in conscription for women. They might not think that we're useful here and then where would we have to go? There's a good reason to get married, if ever there was one.' She looks pointedly at me.

'Is Bill going to propose, then?' I try to deflect attention away from my situation. All the girls think Bill is prevaricating, and that Brenda won't admit that, really, she'd like a wartime wedding.

'We don't want to rush things.' She looks at me with something like defiance. 'A wartime wedding isn't ideal, but nobody knows how long it'll last. Now Churchill has gone swanning off to Canada to talk to the Yanks. I really don't see why we should help them out with the Japs, if they don't help us with the Jerries, do you?'

The mention of Canada nearly topples me. It's bad enough having to talk about marriage, but Brenda's idea of world politics is limited, and I happen to know that Newfoundland, where Churchill's been, *isn't* part of Canada. And I don't want to talk about Canada – full stop.

'Umm – we don't really know what's going on behind the scenes, though, do we?' I try to steer the talk onto a more general footing. 'And we'd better get this pile of work done so we can go for lunch.' I haven't told her that I'm taking the afternoon off. She can interrogate me about that next week.

A few hours of the incessant clatter of the typewriter keys has a calming effect. I focus my attention solely on the invoice in front of me. I'm safe in this position – legs rammed under my desk, ankles firmly in position, as we've been taught to do – I feel much better than I did an hour ago. I look up at the office clock and see that it's midday. Brenda's biting her lip in concentration and Joan has turned to chat to the girl behind her. I unreel the last invoice and place it in the out tray, reach for my jacket on the back of my chair and pull my arms through the sleeves.

Brenda looks at me with raised eyebrows. 'You're not

coming to the canteen, then?'

'I'm going to take a walk.' She'll be mad when she realises that I'm not coming back.

'Well, don't take too long over it,' I hear her call out. I smile to myself, imagining her fury that I haven't told her where I'm going.

*

It's a fair distance from the bank. The streets, as usual, are dusty. Rubble clearing has been done over the past few months, but the scars are all around. The dome of St Paul's appears – more imposing now that the buildings around it have been razed to the ground. Helen is right to consider it a miracle. There's some damage, but you'd never know at a distance. It still reigns over us, so to speak – battered but resilient.

The build-up to this meeting has renewed my anger with Mummy and Helen and I'm frightened of what I might say or do if I talk to them. I need to see David and feel his calming influence – he'll know what to do and say for the best.

As I approach the Strand, I try to make him out and finally spy him, unmistakable, hands in pockets, waiting outside. My stomach lurches and I'm not sure whether to wave or not. He hasn't seen me yet and he's on his own – no mother or father with him, so I was wrong about that. Perhaps they're already inside? I won't let on that I suspect it. He sees me and waves in my direction. He's the first to speak.

'There you are – it's wonderful to see you.' He kisses me on the cheek. I'm so happy to see him, I can't wait to get the pleasantries out of the way.

'If only you knew…' I start, as he ushers me through the door.

'Let's wait till we're inside,' he says firmly. We wait to be shown to a table. It's busy and noisy, but there's just the two of us which is better – it would be difficult to speak frankly with his parents here. Strains of music surface through the chatter. I sneak a look at him as he takes his jacket off. To think that I almost turned him down.

'How are you, Eva? You're looking well – and as beautiful as ever, of course.'

'I'm fine, but there's so much to tell you and a lot to sort out. I don't know where to start.' I'm gabbling.

'Let's order, and then we can swap news.' He's right. I want him to be shocked at the way that Mummy and Helen have treated me, but I must be calm. We take the menus from the waitress. The words are a blur. The last thing I feel like is eating, but I'm in a Lyons Corner House on The Strand for goodness sake!

'I'll have a cold drink and an egg and cress sandwich.'

David looks at me and raises an eyebrow. 'I hope you're looking after yourself.'

'Like I say, there's a lot to tell you.' I'm bursting to tell him. The waitress takes an age to come back, but at last, we give our order.

I lean forward across the table. 'David – it's been awful, but I want us to get married as soon as we can. I know I might have seemed a bit taken aback when you first proposed, but it was a shock – a wonderful shock of course – and now, it's so right...' He's leaning back in his seat, barely looking at me. 'I'm trying to tell you, you were right – you're always right, of course.'

'I'm glad you want to marry me. I want to marry you, too.' He's stony-faced and I sense a 'but'. He looks around, then back at me. He leans forward. 'Things have changed a bit,' he says.

'They've changed for me, too. Daddy came to see us.' It sounds dramatic, but then it *is*. He looks surprised, but not as surprised as I expected.

'Oh, I see – good, I suppose.' He grabs my hand across the table. 'The thing is, Eva. Things have changed for *me*'. I want to tell him what Mummy and Helen have told me, but he has an intent look on his face which stops me. The food arrives and the waitress fusses with the plates and finally backs away.

'What do you mean – changed for you?' I feel something like an icy stab in my chest. I'm not sure what's happening at all. He looks so grave. 'Has someone died?'

'No, it's nothing like that.'

'Well, what is it then?' I glance at my plate which is truly pretty.

'I've just been to the war office. That's why I'm here.' He's speaking so quietly I can hardly hear what he's saying. 'I'm *needed*, Eva. I can't say more than that. Just that, as we both know, there are sacrifices to be made while the war's still on.' My sandwich is cut into two perfect white triangles. It's lovely but I've suddenly lost my appetite. I clutch the edges of the tablecloth.

'We're getting married though, like you said?' I look deep into his eyes. He doesn't say anything. Then he takes my hand again.

'Of course, we're getting married.' I feel a huge wave of relief. 'Just not *yet*.'

'Why ever not? I need to marry soon. Today even!' My voice is like a screech and pairs of eyes turn to look at me. He squeezes my hand hard like a vice.

'Eva, calm down – it's embarrassing. You know I love you, but there's a war on and I have to help out. That's all I can say. Believe me, I'd tell you more if I could.' He takes a breath. 'The important thing is that we *will* get married.' I nod, despite myself. Then he says the words I really, *really* don't want to hear. 'So, we can wait as long as we need to, can't we?' It's not a question.

I stand up. The plate rocks on the table and I grab my jacket off the back of the chair.

'Sit down, Eva.'

'I *can't* wait any longer.' I spit out. 'I've been *waiting* all my life. I *won't wait!*' I stuff my jacket under my arm and look for the door. I glimpse the perfect white triangles of sandwiches and regret leaving them there, but if I stay, I'll be sick, and even more people will turn and look at me. I have to leave.

On the other side of the door, I stop for a second and see David through the window, getting his own coat on and grabbing my bag which I've left behind. I wait for him to catch me up. We stand by the window, breathless.

'That was quite a performance,' he says. He's a blur.

'Daddy came and I didn't see him. And now he's gone – and you're going too and won't tell me why. I thought you needed me and were going to be a professor.' I sound like a stupid child.

'I will be,' he says. 'Eventually.'

'I need you to be one soon. There's no point otherwise.' I'm looking at my feet. My shoes look so neat.

'But who knows what will happen tomorrow even?'

'That's why we need to be happy now,' I wail. '*Now!* Why did you ask me to marry you if you thought that?'

'Let's walk to the station. You'll feel better then.' He grabs my arm. Something has closed in him – he's not the quirky boy I used to walk to the youth club with – or even the young man trying to steer the punt on the Cam. He's on a mission.

'Leave me alone.' I pull my arm away and start to walk. I want to be as far away from him as possible.

*

The streets flash past me – I barely know where I am or where I'm heading. I can't go home, and I can't go back to work. The broken buildings lining the streets are my only friends – their bare bricks fragile yet defiant, the worst of the rubble cleared. How quickly we want everything to be normal and how quickly is it destroyed again! I'm not really thinking these thoughts – they're raw emotions. I can't even cry. I feel destroyed, like the buildings – my dear friends.

I'm on a bridge with water churning below. There's a woman with a small child pointing and smiling. I ache for that child – she knows nothing yet – how many holes there are in the fabric of life. David's voice was thin and reedy as I strode away – I thought he was a poet, not an insistent whiner! I clutch my bag and make my way down the cracked steps to the riverbank. There's a war on but still a bench and a river and a few shillings in my purse. Marriage is so strange – setting up home with a relative stranger – no wonder I was wrong-footed when David proposed! And now, he thinks he can ask me to wait in good faith, while he does who knows what, who knows where.

I tip the shillings into my hand. I should understand money – I work in a bank for goodness sake. What did Mummy say? Something like, *love is all well and good, but money is what really matters*. I must talk to her – I need to understand what she means. I stand up and start walking – glad to be alone. Away from David, away from Brenda. On my own two feet, heading home.

Chapter Twenty-Nine

No one is in. She must be out shopping. I fill the kettle and place it on the lighted hob, then get out my favourite red cup and tea caddy from the cupboard. Everything is in slow motion – I'll grind to a standstill if I don't keep moving. If only she would come back. She should be here when I need her – isn't that what mothers are for?

The kettle rattles on the stove, starting to boil, so I grab the teapot and measure out two rounded teaspoons of tea. The oily aroma fills my nostrils. I should be able to make a pot of tea and pour it out, but every action feels alien. Mummy or Helen usually do this while I sit and wait. Why didn't I see before how different their lives are from mine? I'm just the baby.

The pot is filled, the lid on. I find the knitted cosy in the drawer and a covered jug of milk in the larder. See, I can do this. I can make a home, even without a husband. Being a wife is a fantasy! I leave the pot to brew under the cosy and drift into the sitting room, pull out the drawer and start looking for the photo which I know is there somewhere. It's the photo that defines me – a baby in the sunlight – adored, adorable. It's why, even though I work in a bank, I still don't understand money, or struggle, or, as Helen would say, the need to *do as I'm told*.

The drawer is full of papers and envelopes. There are brown envelopes that look like bills that are neatly bundled up with Mummy's firm writing on the outside of each one – 'Paid' – and then a date. Underneath them, right at the bottom of the drawer, is a large brown envelope, labelled 'DOCUMENTS' along the top edge. So where is the photo? I was sure this was where it was kept. A pale blue envelope pokes out from the large brown envelope, so I put my hand under all the piles, lever them up and pull it out to look at. It's addressed to Mrs Agnes Borton – and it's been opened. The writing is spiky – familiar. I pull it to the surface and lift it out.

'What are you doing? Why aren't you at work?' I turn just as I remember the writing on the envelope is the same that addressed the letters to my grandparents in Canada. It's *his*. 'Those are personal things in that drawer. They don't concern you.' Mummy comes up behind me and stops when she sees the blue envelope in my hand. 'I was saving that,' she says. I look down at it. There's a rough tear along the top where it's been opened.

'Saving it for what?'

'For your twenty-first, if you must know.' I have no idea what she's talking about.

'My twenty-first what?'

'Birthday, of course!' I sit down, still clutching the letter.

'My twenty-first?' I'm like a stuck record. I can't work out where this letter fits in with the other things I've uncovered in the last fortnight.

'Let's sit down in the kitchen and I'll explain,' Mummy says. She holds out her hand and I need her to be kind, so I take it and let her lead me into the kitchen. We sit down opposite each other, and she pours the tea into the red cup. The steam floats up into my face. The letter is on the table between us. We're avoiding it.

'Why aren't you at work, dear?'

I look at her through the steam. 'Afternoon off – it doesn't matter now. I wanted to see you,' I say. She looks surprised. 'I wanted to talk about money.' She looks even more surprised. 'Money – and why things are as they are with us.' My voice drifts off. 'But it doesn't matter now.' I look down at the letter. 'It's from him, isn't it – and if it's meant for me, why haven't I seen it before?'

'It *is* from your father, Eva, but it wasn't time to give it to you yet. Otherwise, I would have told you the other day when – well, when it all came out about the visit and so on.'

'But it's got your name on the envelope and you've opened it.' I'm even more confused now.

'As I said a minute ago, it was meant to be given on your twenty-first. That was what *he* wanted – that was what we all agreed when he visited, and you weren't here.' She's fixing me with her eye.

'What else haven't you told me?' All this agreement without my involvement and I have no idea why, or where, *I* fit into the plot. 'Does Helen know?' I spit out. Her hesitation tells me everything. 'So, to be clear...' Anger electrifies me. 'You made sure he didn't wait to see me, then agreed that he could send me a letter to read nearly three years later?'

'We all wanted you to live a normal life. We were protecting you.' She looks at my face which feels hot and prickly. She starts again, 'Anyway, there it is – you know now, and you can make of it what you want.' She's almost brisk – as if this is all in a day's work. I want to do something – tear the pale blue envelope to shreds. It might as well have *You've been had!* written under the address. She looks away. 'And now you're getting married, perhaps all this won't matter so much.'

I bury my head into my hands so she can't see my face. 'All this?' I shake my head, lost for words. Then I drag myself up from the chair and tidy away my cup. I haven't even bothered to move the envelope. It just stays, like a vial of pale blue poison, on the table where I put it. We are circling round it.

She speaks to my back with a sigh. 'Well, I suppose there's no point waiting another two years till your twenty-first now, especially with the war on. War wasn't even declared when he sent it.' She's trying to be careful, but I'm still speechless – a dangerous cauldron. She carries on, 'I nearly gave it to you the other day when you found out ... but then, the moment passed and you were upstairs and so upset.'

'But it would have been the *right* thing to do,' I say with contempt.

'Well, anyway, there it is now.' She shrugs but sounds hurt.

'I'm waiting because I want to know why you opened it, if it was meant for me.'

'You don't miss much,' she says, which is ironic, given the extent of things that I *have* missed.

'Well?' I say with Helen's teacher voice.

'There was something in it for me – but I didn't read your letter.'

'So, what *was* the something?' I know this is hard for her. She looks at the door. She's willing Helen to come in and save her but she's not due home for another few hours.

She sighs. 'You might remember that we used to have a grey ceramic pot – it was an old tobacco jar of my father's.'

'In the corner? The one with the mouse on top? What on earth has that got to do with it?'

'Ugh, the mouse – yes, that's the one. Anyway, at first, I just kept spare change in it, but when it mounted up, I decided to start saving properly – just in case. I kept it from your father – he wasn't good with money – and I never touched it, *never*. It was my rainy-day fund – and when you have a rainy-day fund, Eva, you try and make sure that there's never a rainy day, if you follow me.'

'So, has this got something to do with why he left?' I'm confused, as well as angry now.

'Yes and no. You won't know this, but your father was a gambler. That was bad enough, but he must have guessed what was in the pot and when I wasn't looking, he emptied it – *stole* every last penny – the night he left, and then – *then*...' She looks at the ceiling. 'Left us – his wife and daughters – with *nothing*. Do you understand, Eva? *He left us with nothing.*' Silence envelops the kitchen. I swallow hard. This can't be the whole story and despite the drama she's created, my mind is clear.

'But you still haven't said – what did he send you?'

She looks up and blinks. 'In the envelope, you mean?' She shudders and looks straight into my eyes. 'It was the money he stole. When he visited, he said he'd always meant to repay it, but the damage was done on that evening in 1931 – so it was several years too late!' She finishes with a snort of derision.

Relief floods through me with the possibility that he *is* the father I thought he was, after all. 'Surely it's a good thing he repaid you? Can't you try and forgive him, after all this time?'

'Well, what would you have done, Eva – what would you have done, if it had been David?' Her words cut through the air and slice into me, and with a jolt, I remember David and what he *has* done to me. Oddly, it makes me feel more certain that she's wrong about Daddy.

'Why he did what he did, I'm not sure, but I think you should be glad that he kept his word and sent the money back – even all these years later.' There's another heavy silence but I can't wait for her to answer. 'And, by the way, there is no David anymore!' I swipe the letter off the table, shove it in my pocket, and make my exit.

*

The bench is partly in shade. Before David – before it was *our* tree – it was *my* tree, my place. Even though it's my nineteenth birthday in just over a week and I'm not a child, it's still where I feel safest. If I'm going to read this letter, this is the place to read it.

I put my hand into the pocket and feel the rough top edge where it was opened – it's as if it was torn open in anger. Inside are the sharp edges of a single sheet of thick paper. Should I save it for my birthday? Nineteenth, not twenty-first, but it'd be partly what he wanted. No, it's stupid to use a birthday as an excuse to tell the truth, let alone a twenty-first! But supposing what I already know is the tip of a very large iceberg? How much more pain can I take in one day? I lean back on the bench like a tragic heroine.

The sun disappears behind a cloud, and it looks like rain. My work clothes are flimsy, so I button up my cream cardigan and cross my legs. My stomach is in a knot. It's hard to believe I saw David only three hours ago. If I keep saying to myself, *he's not important*, perhaps it will become true. I've managed without a father for ten years, after all, and Helen always says life goes on, even after bad things happen. She's the one that people look to in a crisis – not people like David. He only ever thinks about himself. I clench my hands into fists. Why am I still thinking about David, when what I've waited for nearly all my life, is in my pocket?

I look up and catch sight of the vicar's wife, lugging a shopping basket across the common back to the vicarage. She's so careful not to embarrass us with donations of food and clothes, it reminds me that I wanted to talk to Mummy about all the years of hardship when we were younger. Suppose Daddy really did steal from her

– can I believe that?

There's only one way to find out – I pull out the envelope. It's got a crease where I've been clutching it, so I have to tug firmly to get out the sheet of paper inside. There's acid burning my throat. Sucking in air between my gritted teeth, I unfold it and start to read.

London
August 1939

Dear Eva

Happy Birthday, my dear girl! I can't believe that you are grown up, but I know you will be a marvellous young woman!

You're probably wondering why I'm writing to you now after all this time – why not before? The answer is that I didn't want you to make the same mistake that I did. When I was 17, I let my parents and brother and sister leave. I stood by and waved them off from Liverpool docks and ever since then I haven't lived a proper life. I did try, my dear – I want you to know that I tried to be a good husband and father but, in the end, I knew that if I left, <u>you would have a better life</u>. I brought trouble to your mother because I was half a person after my own family left, but the truth is that I should have gone with them. I made a mistake. But then the great war happened and did its own damage.

But, if I had gone in 1911, you wouldn't be here today and I'm so glad you are. I loved reading and talking to you. You were such a clever child – everyone admired you and I was proud to be called your 'Daddy'. It was hard to go when you were still so young, but I know your mother and sister have given you a good life since I went. Your mother is a marvellous woman and your sister a tower of strength, so <u>you must stick with them.</u>

You might be clever, but you need an anchor. I lost mine when I was 17.

I've waited all this time to write, so that you don't think that you have to come and find me – it's been hard being near, yet staying away, but I had to prove to your mother that I could pay her back for the trouble I've caused her. I wouldn't like you to have seen the places I've lived in, but I've managed somehow. And now, I'm going to do what I should have done when I was 17 – I'm going to Canada to see your grandparents before they die. You can't imagine how much I would love to take you with me, but your place is with your mother. She needs you. A young lady I worked with once told me I was kind, but I haven't been kind enough, as your mother knows full well.

Now you're 21, you might have a husband of your own. I hope he will be right for you and look after you better than I looked after your mother. You might still be working in London – I knew you would make a good life for yourself. I'm sorry I have to go so far away but there's another war on the horizon, so I must see them while I still can. War changes everything – thank goodness I had daughters! Maybe, one day in the future, you'll come and see your family in Canada, but I wouldn't blame you if you thought I was best left alone!

By the time you read this letter, my hope is that I'll be back with the family where I belong – the one I should never have let go. I'll be fine and so must you be. I remember your strong spirit with so much affection.

Forgive me.
Your loving father

P.S. I enclose a photo so you can see what your old father looks like. If you have children one day, who knows, you might see me in their faces!

I hardly notice the tears until they drip onto the pale blue sheet and stain it with dark patches. I want to scream. Why? Why? Why? How could he think he was doing the right thing? Weren't we his family – me, Mummy and Helen? Why care about the ones who chose to go? Even if they were his parents?

And the underlined words – so mistaken, so misguided. *Forgive me* catches my eye and I bury my head in my arms – too much sadness. I'm almost nineteen, not that much older than he was when he was deserted. The scalloped edges of a small, faded snap rests on the bench beside me where it fell. I don't want to look at it yet – not until I've decided what to do. I slide it, unexamined, back into the envelope and then into my pocket. There's only one person I need to see now – Helen.

Chapter Thirty

My plan is to ambush her on the Common Strand. I look at my watch – I must look like a madwoman, pacing up and down, rubbing my arms and clutching a blue envelope as if my life depended on it. As I'm about to give up, she comes round the corner carrying two large bags. I wave but she looks through me. Her face is contorted with the effort of carrying the bags.

'What on earth have you got in those?' I shout.

'Eva! What are *you* doing here? Why aren't you at work?'

'I took the afternoon off.'

She stops in her tracks, drops the bags and shakes her arms. 'Marking in that one – and veg in the other.' She nods at the handmade sacking bags which sprawl on the pavement. 'A woman's work is never done, but never mind – my dear sister has arrived at just the right moment to help me.' Strands of her hair fly about, and she smiles.

'I thought Mummy did all the veg shopping on Wednesdays.' Delaying tactics.

'She does but there were bargains at the market. Too good to miss. 'Anyway, you must tell me why you've come to help, like a guardian angel.' She looks at me, her face a question mark. She knows me too well.

I shake under her scrutiny. 'Can we go and sit down? I want to ask you something.'

'Sounds serious.' Her mouth turns down at the corners.

I feel sick thinking about all the times I've tried – no, not just tried, but desperately *wanted* to ask her about him. All the times I've convinced myself that it wasn't the right time to do so. We head towards 'the battered bench'. The landmark, so apt, is a bench that no one cares for. There's a plaque on it to a local boy who died on the Somme, and Helen and I make up stories about why the parents don't ever come here. She hands me one of the bags.

It only takes a couple of minutes to get to the bench. We dump the bags and sit down. She turns and looks at me, eyebrows raised. 'So what's on your mind? We'd better not be long – Mummy will be expecting us.'

It's now or never. I *have* to say it. 'It's just that I know about the letter *and* I've read it.' I wave the blue envelope at her.

'What letter?' She looks genuinely confused.

'The one from him.'

Her eyes shift from puzzled to worried. 'You mean the letter Mummy was saving for your twenty-first?'

'I can't believe that you thought it was a good idea to keep this from me.' The release of tension is like a powerful drug. Heat pounds me in waves – I want to be in control but I'm already a decibel below a shout.

'Ah...' is all she says. She's almost nonchalant. 'So, you've heard from him. Can we go now?' she says. My boiling transforms into wordless rage.

'*No*, we can't. Mummy told me about the money. If you'd explained before, I would have understood. I mean how could he do that to her? Even if he did pay it back. If I'd known, I would have seen why you were both so *against* him – it would have helped me to be on your side. Do you see that?'

'I'm not sure what you mean by *side*. It's not about sides, Eva.'

'Then what is it about?' She draws back from me, as if she's wilting before my heat – as if she's curling up in the face of righteous anger. And I just know there's more. I'm *sure* she knows something more.

She looks down, then up. She bites her lip. 'You seem to think that I wasn't upset when he went – that it was just you. That *I* didn't lie awake wondering where he was. But I did. I just decided that what is done is done, and Mummy needed our help. The missing money was the final straw for her, so I had to make up for that somehow. I wish now...' She looks down at her knees on which goose bumps have appeared.

'What do you wish and why did *you* need to make up for the money?' I sense something unexpected. My desire to know is all there is now. She looks at me as directly as she ever has done in our whole lives. *This is it*, she's saying. The bags are slumped at our feet and the battered bench is our prop. *Tell me*, I want to yell. Then she speaks.

'He didn't take the money. Mummy thought he must have done, but it was me. I knew where she kept it and I took it because I wanted to help him. I saw him on my way home that night – they'd had an argument and he was looking so desperate that I took every last penny from that horrible jar and gave it to him. He said he'd repay it as soon as he could, and I told him there was still some money left for us and that we'd be fine. I didn't realise she'd take it so badly.'

It takes me a while to absorb what she has just told me. My mouth gapes open.

'Well, there you are,' She looks at me with fear. 'No one knows that – and certainly not Mummy and you mustn't tell her. Imagine how I feel, knowing how she reacted and thinking it was him that took it.' Helen looks smaller than I've ever seen her. I put my arm round her.

'He did tell you he'd pay it back – and you were just being kind, I suppose.' I say.

Her eyes slant downwards with relief. 'He was set on going and kept saying something about a pattern of leaving and how he didn't belong here. I couldn't stop him from going, Eva – really, I couldn't. All I did was help him to do what he was *going* to do anyway. I knew where she kept her savings, and it seemed better not to tell her I'd given them to him. That's all. It really was for the best. But I didn't think she'd hold it against him for so long, even when he came back and said he'd repay her. *And* he never told her it was me, so you mustn't either.'

We sit there saying nothing. I feel wretched but I'm also happy now that I know things that I've needed to know for a long time. 'I won't tell her, I promise – and he *has* repaid her now, so you mustn't think any more about it.'

'Yes, she told me. Can we go now?' she says. The escaped strands of her hair look straggly.

'Let's go and get dinner cooked. We can do it together.' For the first time ever, I feel as if I'm the older sister.

'But you haven't told me what he said to you – in the letter.' Her voice is sad.

'Oh, I'll tell you later – he was just wishing me well really, because he never said goodbye.'

'Ah, I seem to have done nothing *but* say goodbye.' We stand and stretch.

'Let me carry one of those. You've done enough for today.' She nods. I'll tell her about David later. He's a speck in the distance – my sister needs me now.

*

There's a moaning sound. Helen drops her bag on the table and goes straight through to the sitting room. I hear her gasp.

'What on earth's the matter? Whatever happened?' I rush to the doorway and see Mummy, lying askew on the floor her yellow skirt crumpled, one shoe on and one off. Helen is bending over her as she speaks.

'It's nothing. Just this silly old leg that won't move. I tried to pull myself up but thought I'd better wait for one of you to come back.' She's wedged between the dining room chairs and underneath the window. I survey the scene. Helen is trying to pull her up.

'No, no – you shouldn't move her. You'll do more harm than good. I grab a couple of cushions. 'Now, let me see...' I ease her head onto one of the cushions and place the other under her arm. 'Helen, get the plaid blanket. She's cold.' I feel for her pulse and start counting. It's jumpy but still beating. 'You'll live. Where does it hurt?'

She looks up at me. 'It's my leg. This one.' She points. I don't think anything else is wrong. 'Do you think it might be broken?'

'Could be, but what on earth were you doing? Why are the chairs here?' Helen has arrived with two blankets. We cover her, so her head is poking out. 'We're going to need an ambulance. You shouldn't be moved until we've checked where the damage is.'

'I'm sorry for causing so much trouble. When you left, I had to do something, so I tried to get the curtains down to wash them, then the chair slipped and then I thought Helen would be back soon.' She purses her lips in pain.

'I should have been, but Eva waylaid me on my way back,' Helen says, stricken.

'Well, we're here now.' I'm firm but am not going to apologise – I didn't make her climb on the chair to get the curtains. I look down at her and see how grey her face is. The shock of the accident is taking its toll.

There's saliva at the edge of her mouth and her eyes are watery. She's fading. 'Get the smelling salts, Helen.' She hears the urgency in my voice and springs up. I try to remember what I've seen Sister do when patients are brought in with shock. She reappears with the small bottle and throws it over to me.

'I'm off to fetch the ambulance now. Keep up the good work!'

I grab the bottle, unscrew the top and bring it close to Mummy's nostrils till they flare out. She gasps back into life.

'Thank you, dear.' She clasps one of my hands, as I support her back with the other. 'Thank you.' She looks up at me and I see gratitude in her eyes – and something else. Pride? 'You'll make a marvellous nurse. To think that a daughter of mine could be so – *commanding*.'

'It's all part of the training. Helen will be back with help soon.' I hold her hand and she gives it the lightest squeeze in return. 'Matron says that people need you to be firm – need to feel that you're with them, walking alongside.'

She smiles up at me – yes, she's proud of *me*.

*

Helen's giggling and keeps setting me off. 'You should have seen Mr McBride's face when he and Mr Judd were trying to lift Mummy into the ambulance. You were getting her overnight bag and they were absolutely terrified of her.' That starts Helen off again and so I start again, too.

'But, really, we're lucky that she had no choice but to go. You know what she's like. I'm sure she'd be cooking dinner with a broken leg if she could get away with it.' We're laughing with relief as much as anything. I look around the kitchen. The bags we brought in are still lying on the table where we dropped them. A few onions and a sole carrot have strayed out.

'It's not really funny, though. When I saw her lying there, I thought the worst – with what we'd been talking about, it just seemed like – well, like *retribution*.' Helen sounds strangled.

'You've done nothing wrong. *Ever* – from what I can remember,' I say, catching her eye.

She shrugs. 'She looked so helpless, that's all. Not like her at all.'

'And it's not like *you* to be dramatic! You've looked after her *and* me, and you looked after Daddy when he needed it, too. Don't ever talk about retribution again.'

'Thanks,' she forces a smile. 'Really, Eva – *thank you*. I suppose we should be grateful it wasn't more serious. How would we ever afford the hospital, if she had to stay in for more than a few days?'

'It's so strange when she's not here. But now I'm hungry – thank goodness you did the shopping. Even if it did mean she was on the floor longer.'

'At least we got to her before any more damage was done but she was obviously scared...' Helen's voice starts to waver again. We look down, each with our own thoughts of guilt and love.

'She'll survive and maybe it'll make her more careful in future.' Some hope, I think privately.

Helen puts her hand on my arm. 'You were competent, Eva. That nurse – first-aid training, or whatever you've done, has paid off. It really helped. Perhaps...?'

'Perhaps what?' I don't want any more surprises today.

'Well, it made me think you might take your VAD training further – that's all. Do the full nurse training, perhaps. You could do more with your life than work in a bank, even if it is *The Bank*. Helen says this in Mummy's voice which sets us off giggling again. But she has a point. I never imagined I'd end up a typist when I got my county scholarship. I imagined something more dramatic. I didn't know exactly what, but I did think I was going to be important.

'I'm too tired to think about it,' I say, even though I *am* thinking about it. We curl down into our chairs, and I carry on thinking. After a bit, I decide to say something. 'I will do more, Helen, because everything that's happened to us – having no money, Daddy leaving, and now the war – makes me realise that it's good to be needed. Daddy didn't feel needed enough, or he wouldn't have left us. And whatever she says, Mummy likes it that we needed her more after he left. And you like it that I need you, too. So, perhaps now, it's *my* turn to be needed.'

Helen gets up. 'Quite a speech. But that's what I've been saying. It's time to go your own way, Eva. Find a job that's worthy of you.' Her face is soft with kindness. She's pure Helen – completely herself again, after her revelation on the battered bench which was only a few hours ago. 'But first, help me with the dinner. It'll have to be a simple beef stew – without the beef. But there's Bovril to make it taste beefy. Let's make it together then you can tell me what's happened today to make you so wise. You haven't told me everything, have you?' She arches one eyebrow.

'I can't believe that one day can be so weighty. Life's funny. Nothing happens for years, then in just one day everything clicks into place.'

'It's called growing up. Tell me about it while you chop the onions. Then you can cry as much as you like.'

The thought of crying couldn't be further from my mind. I sense that a huge burden of sadness has started to evaporate with the exposure of secrets finally told. But there's still the meeting with David to tell her about. It's raw and hard to explain, so I grab an onion and take a deep breath.

Chapter Thirty-One

Brenda glances at me, as I get ready to take a pile of letters to Mr Wells. 'Going to ask for another afternoon off?' She's annoyed with me for not telling her I was leaving early on Friday, but she doesn't want to ask me where I went. I'd rather not talk about it – the lunch with David has been filed away in my mind as still too painful to dwell on.

'It was a one-off, not to be repeated,' I reply. She looks confused.

'Joan thought you might be meeting your beau.' I smile at her choice of words, so un-David-like. I don't want to be stand-offish with the other girls, but I can't talk about it yet.

'I was – but it's all hush-hush.' I cup my hand to look like a spy. Little does she know how true it is – I have no idea what David's up to. Her eyes light up with the eagerness of finally learning my secret. I bet she'll have traded it with Joan by the time I get back from delivering this typing.

I can't explain what is happening to me and I wonder if the accident is a sign. When I told Helen about the disastrous meeting with David, she said that perhaps I'd been relying on him too much and had rushed into marriage. It made me realise that my pride is hurt more by being rejected than my heart is hurt by losing him. I'm not sure now whether I was ever really in love with him.

Matron switched my shift this week to the orthopaedic ward, because Mr Dexter is drowning in fracture cases. I could tell her that *we're* drowning in a fracture case at home, too, and how much I'm learning because of it. It makes me wonder if Mr Dexter would support my application to do nurse training, but I haven't told Mr Wells that I want to leave the bank yet, so first things first. Mr Wells is at his desk. I cough and stand politely waiting for him to look up.

'Yes, Eva – is it important?'

'It's about the war effort, so I do think it's important, sir.' Unaccustomed assertion from me.

'Ah, well yes, then. What can be more important?' He puts down his fountain pen.

I place the pile of letters in his in tray and stand to attention. 'Thank you, sir. You may remember that when I first trained to be a VAD it was because John Dexter encouraged me to do so and contacted you to that effect.'

'Indeed, I do remember that a young man in International intervened...'

'Well, I wish to progress a bit further with my training and think that, with his contacts, he may be able to help me. His father is an orthopaedic surgeon and it's an area that interests me.'

He looks at me long and hard. I stand there determined not to flounder. 'I see. And what is it that you want me to do, exactly?'

I thought I'd made it plain, but I make it plainer still. 'I want to train to be a nurse.' His face is a picture of surprise.

'So, if I understand what you're telling me correctly – you want to progress further?' He sounds annoyed as well as surprised.

'Yes, that's it.' I say.

'But Eva, your work here is highly valued, so you must be careful not to overdo your voluntary effort.' I wring my hands together behind my back.

'Typing isn't the only job I can do, though.'

He raises his eyebrows in surprise and wrinkles his nose. His neat moustache twitches just a shade. 'Well, no, indeed. In time, wife and mother, no doubt.' I think about the names that the girls call him behind his back. Brenda is right to say that he's a fool – *a silly old fool*, I think she said. I've always defended him but now I want to call him names too – *stupid*, for one. I take a deep breath as he turns away. He thinks the conversation is over.

'But, sir, I could help the war effort *even* more as a trained nurse – and that would mean leaving the bank.'

He looks up again, his forehead creased in shock. It's as if I've told him I'm going to lead the war cabinet. 'I'm not sure that...' he starts.

'If I'm accepted for the training course, I'll have to hand in my notice – I'm afraid there's no alternative – if I'm to serve my country, that is.'

He looks at my typing and sighs. 'Well, if you have a *vocation*, I suppose I can't stop you – and the war effort has to take priority, of course. You are one of my best typists, though.'

'Thank you, sir,' I say. After all, a compliment is a compliment. I smile – now he's agreed, at least I can try and restore his world order.

*

I glance at my watch nervously. Johnny suggested that we meet in the training room because it was quieter than the canteen. Perhaps we should have arranged to meet somewhere busier, but I can't stand the thought of Brenda giving me the eye. I'm sitting in the corner, feeling very conspicuous, as it is.

Five minutes late he appears. 'You were very cloak

and dagger in the canteen yesterday. The other chaps thought you must be an undercover agent.' It's a joke but I don't laugh.

'I'm not one,' David's air of secrecy when I last saw him comes to mind, 'and I'm sorry if I embarrassed you yesterday, but it *was* you who got me into all this.'

He pulls over another chair and sits opposite me. 'I wasn't embarrassed, just curious. What did I get you into, other than the VAD? You look very serious.'

'I want to leave the bank,' I say, conscious I sound dramatic.

'Oh – and why's that?'

'Because I think nursing is more important at the moment, and I've realised I might be good at it.'

'Well, that's marvellous, old thing. Well done – I picked out a good candidate that day.' He beams at me and I notice how his eyes slant down when he smiles. I smile back.

'It's nice that you think I'm up to it. Mr Wells says that I should get married and have children instead – when I've finished doing his typing, that is!'

'Nursing isn't an easy option, of course, but if you're fired up to do it, you absolutely should give it a try. Our manager says that Wells is stuffy, so don't mind him.' He crosses his legs and waves a leather brogue around.

'Nice shoes, by the way,' I say.

'Thank you. Best war issue. So, tell me how I can help with your application.'

He's so relaxed that I feel completely relaxed with him. I've never come across someone *so* relaxed. I like it. 'I was wondering what your father would think about me training to be a nurse in an orthopaedic ward. I mean, obviously, I'd have to do training in all areas, but I'd like to specialise in that area. Do you think he'd support my application?'

He doesn't hesitate. 'I should say so. Dad says they're desperate to train up new medical and nursing staff in his area, and with the VAD training you've already done, I'm sure he'd give you a reference. But, did you know that St Barts have moved their nurse training north of London? If I remember rightly, your mother likes you to stay at home.'

'I've heard about the move, but my sister thinks I should do it, so she'll smooth the way for me. I haven't told my mother yet, but if your father would give me a reference, I'm sure she'll come round. I wanted to talk it over with you first.'

'Me?' Johnny sits back. 'Well, I'm honoured, of course, but isn't there someone else special you might want to talk it over with?' I blush – annoyingly.

'Special people are complicated, and after all, it was you that pushed me in this direction. Call it fate, or whatever, but I'd probably be a fireguard like most of the other girls if I hadn't bumped into you that day. And your father was so kind and encouraging when he spoke to me.' *Shut up, Eva*, I tell myself.

'Yes, he is. Everyone loves my father. But don't be fooled – he spends so much time with his patients, he's not around much for his own family. What about with your father? Is it the same?'

Here we go again. 'Well, there's a story there which I don't tell many people. It's a long one, but it might have an ending soon.'

'Sounds interesting. Is it a long enough story to tell over lunch sometime?' He looks at me in a certain way.

'Too long, probably. But I'd like that, especially if you tell me how you get shoes of that quality in war time,' I reply, glad that I'm not blushing any more.

He laughs and his laugh is even better than his smile. 'Well, that really *is* classified information... How about

Lyons on Friday, after I've spoken to Dad?'

'Marvellous.' The power to ask and receive is making me bold. I think about my father and Johnny's father and wonder if they're really so different – they've both gone their own way in life. Thinking about fathers means that I don't even notice that I've just agreed to another Friday lunch at a Lyons house. I hope it won't be like the last one, but it doesn't help to be superstitious. I smile to think what Brenda will make of it.

*

'I don't understand why you'd want such a complete change of direction, dear.' Mummy twists round to try and reach her sewing on the dining room table. Aunt Kate jumps up to help out. Two weeks of convalescence is getting on our nerves and Helen's escaped for an evening walk.

'Really, Aggie. *Leave* the girl alone – and for goodness sake ask us when something needs fetching!' Aunt Kate says, but she won't leave it.

'You've got a good job, Eva – and nursing is dangerous. It'll be a constant worry, and have you thought about how we're going to manage without your wage coming in?'

Aunt Kate answers again. 'She's grown up and at a time like this, young people have to go where they're needed – even young women. You can't expect Eva to support you forever.'

'But she's barely started at the bank – it's a well-paid job for a girl like her. She was about to get married five minutes ago, but that doesn't seem to have worked out, so why should this?'

'I am here, you know,' I say. 'Aunt Kate is right – the war effort affects us all, and I've explained that David is too busy to think about marriage.' I'd rather not have to talk about David, but she knows there's more to it and keeps trying to find out.

'Think what a fuss mother made when Alfie decided to join up. But she realised he had to go in the end.' Aunt Kate is using everything to help me.

'It still broke her heart – and he was a boy, anyway.' Mummy and Kate are locked in their own world now.

'Women are doing a lot more in this war, Ag. Eva knows what she's doing and she's older than Alfie was when he left home.' My aunt's tenacity in the face of my mother's obstacles, impresses me. *Uncle Alfie was born to suffer*, Mummy always says, though I won't remind her of that now.

'Well, Kate – and I'd rather you didn't call me Ag – nursing is *much* messier than typing and the only reason I've considered agreeing at all, is because Mr Dexter has been *very* persuasive. It's not often that one's daughter is selected by an *orth-o-paedic* surgeon.' It looks as if Mummy has played up her reluctance to let me go, so she can show off to Kate. Ever since I received the reference from Johnny's father, it's been *Mr Dexter* this and *Mr Dexter* that. She even called him *Edward* once which made both Helen and I share a raised eyebrow.

'Aunt Kate is right – I *do* know what I'm doing. Mr Wells has said that I can always go back to my job at the bank, so long as the war's on. Anyway, it's not as if I'm going to be *that* far from home, is it? Well, not to start with…'

Mummy looks down, shifts her plaster cast and fiddles with her ring – her wedding ring, I note. 'You talk about the war as if it's not a terrible thing, Eva. But it *is*. The last one changed all our lives. It wasn't just poor Alfie. When your father came back, he was a different person. Kate will tell you that.'

'We're not talking about Arthur, though, are we? That was a complicated situation,' Aunt Kate says.

'What do you mean by complicated?' My curiosity is well and truly piqued.

'War does funny things to people, that's all I'm saying. If you intend to nurse at the front line – God forbid – you'll see things you won't be able to forget. Sometimes it's more important to stay at home with your family!' Mummy waves her hands around.

'Helen will be here for you.' I'm careful – her eyes have panic written in them – what with talk of Alfie *and* Daddy.

She looks up at me – it's more of a stare really. 'You always were your father's daughter.'

'Come on,' Aunt Kate intervenes. 'Arthur wasn't a bad man, and anyway, isn't it better to be an honestly bad person than a deceitfully good one? Eva *isn't* Arthur. In fact, the truth is, I see a lot of *you* in her, Agnes. That intolerable stubbornness for a start... You were hard on Arthur – don't make the same mistake and push Eva away.'

I can't believe what I'm hearing. And neither, it seems, can Mummy. 'For your information, Kate, Arthur might not have been *all* bad, but he let me down when it mattered. The situation he got himself into was shameful. And I don't think Eva should be hearing all this.'

I open my mouth to speak but Aunt Kate beats me to it. 'Maybe you never *let* Arthur help you and maybe it's about time Eva *did* hear this.' I sense that Mummy would jump up and leave the room if she could. But she's trapped here with a thick plaster cast on her leg. 'Isn't it time you forgave Arthur for the sake of a few lost shillings?' Kate is relentless – so much so that I want to cheer her on. 'Forgive him for Helen and Eva's sakes. Then Eva *will* come back home because she'll know what a marvellous mother she's got.' She's speaking quietly, but with utter authority.

Mummy looks up at me – her face has softened. I go over and perch awkwardly on the arm of her chair and take her hand. 'You are,' I say. 'You absolutely are the best mother I could have had.'

She covers her face with her free hand. 'I have tried, Eva. I really have. I'm sorry that your father left. He was weak but no, you're right, Kate, he wasn't all bad – maybe empty in some ways, but not bad, and I can't say that I was always easy. I tried to make our marriage work when he came back from the war, but in the end it came down to money – I've tried to tell you that before, Eva – the shame of it all was too much for me to bear.' The air in the room suddenly feels fresh and I take a deep breath. But she hasn't finished. 'If you do track him down, Eva, you can tell him that I'm sorry things turned out as they did – but Kate, it was a bit more than a *few* shillings – it was several pounds, and it was all we had in the world, so it's hard to forget what he put us through.'

That's as near to forgiveness as she's going to get. Aunt Kate is unimpressed, but I see my chance. 'If you're *really* sorry, then you should let me go where nursing takes me.'

She hesitates, then nods. She knows that this is the right way forward. 'And there's one more thing I need from you,' I say.

'What's that, dear?' She looks up at me like a child.

'I need my grandparents' address in Canada. They might know where he is, and he needs to know that I've forgiven him.'

'At least one of you has, then,' says Kate.

Chapter Thirty-Two

David's standing there, a foot back from the front doorstep, wet through. Despite everything, my heart lurches, but my head says to be wary, so I freeze.

'This is a surprise – are you here to see the vicar?' I finally say.

'Don't be stupid. I've come to see you, of course,' he replies.

'Oh, I see. Well, you're very wet.'

'Can I come in?' He shuffles through the door and drips on the door mat.

'I suppose I'd better get something to dry you off.'

'Yes, that'd be good.' He drips a bit more and I go off in search of a towel.

'It's a bit threadbare – sorry.'

'It'll do the job. Are you going to let me sit down?'

'The kitchen's probably best – with the wet...' I lead him through into the kitchen and he sits at the table. It's a shock seeing him here like this.

'Where's your mother and sister?' he says.

'Oh, they're at the Doctor's. They'll be back soon.'

'Nothing too serious, I hope.'

'Just a check-up after an accident, but it could have been worse. How are you?'

'Oh, fine – well, you know... And you?'

'Fine.' I sit down on the other side of the table, then jump up again. 'Do you want a cup of tea to help you warm up?'

'That'd be nice.'

I set about filling the kettle. 'It'll take a little while to boil.'

'I can wait for it.'

I twist the faucet and the water splashes into the kettle. This is ridiculous – why is he here? When I turn round, he's staring at me.

'You know, Eva – I wanted to say, after I last saw you – well, I'm sorry it wasn't what you wanted to hear, and I want you to know that I do love you.' He must have practised this, but it's coming out all stiff and wrong.

'I *thought* I loved you, too,' I say, much more smoothly.

'And now?' he says. I look in the cupboard for the tea pot and try and work out how to reply to this. Something is broken – the spell of first love has lifted. 'I'm sorry that...' he carries on.

I yank the tea pot out of the cupboard and put it in front of him. 'Sorry that what? That you won't tell me what's going on?'

'I *can't* tell you.' Firm and distant.

I sit down, the shiny tea pot a beacon between us. 'It seemed right for us to marry when you asked me, but now – well, the timing is all wrong – and I simply can't *abide* secrets.' He flinches – I've never challenged him like this.

'But I'm here – that must mean something. And I couldn't leave when you were so upset. I thought that maybe, it's just a thought – but what if we married *before* I went? Would that make a difference to you?'

It takes a while for his words to sink in. 'You mean get married and *then* you disappear? I'm not stupid – I know you're doing something for the war effort and if you can't tell me what, I don't think I could stand it.'

'I simply can't say – it's too important, Eva. But they need people who can, you know, work out codes – that sort of thing. Several of the chaps at Kings have been approached – it's not just me. And I'd send you money. You'd be looked after.' His heart is set on something, and he thinks he can convince me. The kettle starts to whistle, and I automatically get up and turn it off, then swivel round to face him. Suddenly, things are clear.

'Can't you see? I don't *want* to marry you anymore – not if I have to wait around with no idea where you are. I don't care if you're breaking codes or whatever. I'm not even sure if I *love* you now.'

'But can't we start again? It'd be romantic to marry before I go.'

His words are like a red rag. 'Waiting for someone to come back is *not* romantic – take it from me.'

'You mean your father, I suppose – but this would be different…' A sullen tone.

'How would it be different? The last war changed my father. I don't know exactly how but it ruined our family. It took my father's pride and he had to leave us because my mother was so humiliated by him. And as for me – well, *every day* I still wait for him to come back. So go, if you have to, but don't expect me to wait for you!' I don't attempt to make the tea now – my feelings for him have crystallised into anger because he simply won't believe what I'm saying.

'But you loved Cambridge – and they'll keep a post open for me, they said…'

'I did love Cambridge, yes. And I'd have loved to study there, too. If only…'

'If only what?'

'Well, obviously places like that aren't for people like me, are they?'

He doesn't try and contradict me. He can't change my mind, and it scares him. 'But you could be my *wife* – and help me to study. And I can send you money if you need it.'

I'm completely cool now. My anger and his desperation have settled the score. I sound steely. 'Don't give me money, David – I might not be able to pay it back, and in my experience that causes problems.'

His head is down. I almost feel sorry for him. 'But what will you do?'

'Don't worry, I've got my own plans – my *own* war effort.' He looks up. I can see this isn't what he was expecting.

'But what we have, Eva – surely we shouldn't just abandon it.' It's his final fling.

'*You're* the one who's abandoned it. And you're not even interested in what my plans are.' He winces. I think it's the first time he's heard me speak. Really *heard* me.

'Well, even if *you* don't wait – I *will* – I'll wait for you.'

I feel embarrassed for him. Everything has changed and he doesn't realise, even though it was him that started the change. I catch sight of his foot tapping on the floor. Why didn't I see before how small his feet are?

'Your mind will be on other things,' I say. I grip my fingers till they go white. I want him to leave me alone – there's nothing more to say. Shuffling footsteps make the back door rattle suddenly. Outside, Mummy and Helen are shaking the rain off their umbrellas.

'It's better if you go now. It'll be less awkward if you don't have to explain things to them.' I nod towards the door. David's face drops – his eyes narrow for a second. His hair is still wet and sticking up where he rubbed it.

'Well, I...' He stands up and puts the chair neatly back under the table. 'I came a long way to see you today, Eva. Doesn't that mean anything?' He's pleading or annoyed. Or both. The handle on the door goes down, as he disappears into the hallway. I follow him out of the kitchen, as Mummy and Helen step inside laughing and talking.

I unlatch the front door and we stand on the step.

'Good luck with whatever...' I say. 'It does mean something – you coming. Thank you.'

'Well, I'll come again, after...' He sees me recoil and doubt flits across his face. I look at the afternoon sun which has suddenly appeared from behind the rain clouds and see, as clearly as the day he walks out into, that marriage was an illusion for both of us.

'I hope you find what you're looking for Eva,' he says quietly. It might be the nicest thing he's ever said to me – and the truest.

'Look after yourself,' I say, and I mean it. He walks down the path and I close the door, strangely relieved that he didn't ask about my plans for the war effort or, in the end, tell me his.

*

'They might be dead by now, of course...'

'They might, but it's worth a try. Did you ever write to them, you know, after...?'

'No,' is all Mummy says, and her look warns me. 'And if they hadn't left your father in the first place, things could have been different.

'What do you mean?' I say. I've become used to asking more questions this week.

'Since our talk with Kate the other day and because you and David – well, it didn't work – I've thought a lot about your father – why he was the way he was. I've wondered if it wasn't only his fault that our marriage was a mistake – yes, he was weak with money, but the problem was there before that.'

'Are you saying that it was his parents' fault – that he left?'

'No, not exactly, but he *was* stranded, and I didn't

realise it – I was too caught up with getting married and having my own house and then my own family. Perhaps I should have understood your father better, but can you ever see the world through another person's eyes, Eva? Maybe it was the same for you and David.' I can't believe what I'm hearing.

'What I'm trying to tell you is that I never saw your father *clearly* because there was no background to show up his outlines. Did he see me? Maybe he did – but maybe that's also why he ran away. *My* background gave me an edge that cut him...' She pauses and turns to look at me full in the face. 'That's the cut you're trying to heal, Eva, but it's deep and I can't help you – I want to, but it's impossible for me, like Kate says. You're on your own, like he was.' I want to cry, and I can't say a word, so I just open my arms and hug her. She feels more solid than I can ever remember.

After I've let her go and she's discreetly wiped her eyes, she goes to the drawer, picks up her address book and turns to the back cover. My Canadian grandparents' address is written in tiny letters there. She must have hoped that they would be indecipherable, but now I watch as she writes the street name and number out in large letters on a piece of torn cardboard and hands it to me. My stomach clenches. Supposing they're dead? When the books stopped coming at Christmas, we thought it was because of Daddy, but maybe something bad had happened to them in that vast snowy country with wolves and moose.

I'm still clutching the address after she's leaves, and Helen comes in. She sees me sitting on the settee, head down, shredding the edges of the cardboard. She must sense my fear.

'Are some things best left undisturbed? It's your birthday tomorrow.' She eyes the cardboard in my hand.

'I've got to write back. He won't know that I've read his letter otherwise.'

'First of all, he won't expect you to have read it yet, and secondly, your letter might never get there. Have you thought about what it will feel like if you don't get a reply?' Helen's logic is always self-preservation, never risk.

'I've learnt lately that it pays to be brave.' I stop shredding and start tapping instead. 'And bravery is hard.'

'Spoken like a true soldier. And while we're talking about how brave you are – are you sure you were right to send David packing? I mean suitors don't come along every day.'

'It was a lucky escape. I would have had to devote myself to his career forever. And, Helen – suitors! For goodness sake, what century are you living in?' We both laugh. Helen plumps the cushion on the settee and sits down next to me. Working in a primary school where the only men are a married headmaster and a caretaker hasn't helped her own marriage prospects, so I feel for her.

She shifts to face me. 'I do think you're right about something, though. You need your own career. You know, Eva – you should have stayed at school. I let Mummy persuade you to leave but we'd have managed somehow. I'm sorry about that.'

I'm completely taken aback. A stuffy classroom at Wellesley flashes into my mind.

'Everyone seems to be saying sorry to me, this week. I mean, I loved English – and art, of course – but I was never going to be a teacher like you. I had to leave to find out what it was I wanted to do. I've never been as sensible as you.'

'You have to be sensible to be a nurse, though.'

'I suppose so, but thanks to the war and the bank

I've had the chance to grow up. And thanks to you, of course.'

She looks unconvinced. 'It shouldn't have taken a war, or the bank, to complete your education. Some women go to university, and we should have found a way, so you didn't have to work – money isn't everything.'

'No, it isn't, but also it *is*. I do understand, Helen.' I pause – we're both thinking about the same thing – the pound notes in the tobacco jar.

'You were right not to tell her. It wouldn't help her to know now, either. Perhaps we should both write this letter to Daddy. Have you thought about that?' I wave the address at her. 'As you once told me, he was your father as well as mine.'

She shakes her head. 'No, Eva. I did my bit. It's your turn now – that is, if you're *sure* you want to. But give him my love, you'll do that, won't you? And use my fountain pen – nothing impresses more than nice handwriting.'

I look at her to see if she's joking, but no. She was born to teach.

*

'Nurse Borton?'

I put my hand up.

'Higher, please. I can't see you.' I elevate my hand further.

'There you are. You'll be doing medical for the first rotation.'

This room reminds me so much of the Wellesley School Hall with its heavy smell of lilac polish. There are about ten lines of young women in clean new uniforms each with her own reason to be here sitting on an uncomfortable wooden chair with the King looking down on her. Our starched caps and white aprons crossed over our backs make us important.

I said goodbye to the bank last week. Even Brenda wished me luck. She was in a good mood because Bill had finally proposed, just in time for a Christmas wedding. She was worried that it'd upset me because of my *break up*, as she calls it. I told her not to worry. She doesn't know that Johnny insisted on taking me out to lunch last week. He says he wants to see me again which is nice. He's taller than me – unlike David – and I like that.

As Johnny made sure to point out, nurse training is a full-time commitment, so there's no going home yet. Home is the nurse's home and I share my room with Doreen who reminds me of Gwen, my old school friend – red hair in a single plait down her back and the air of burdens from a young age. I'm a child beside her – she even reminds me to fold my uniform each night. I make her laugh which she says is just what she needs to keep going.

It's the last day before we start on the wards with three-month rotations. Doreen is sitting next to me. 'Children's ward will be home from home for me,' she whispers.

I stifle a laugh. I've heard about her nine younger brothers and sisters. 'Psychiatric ward will be home from home for me.'

Doreen digs me in the ribs with her elbow. 'Don't be silly – your mother and sister sound *lovely* to me.'

'Sometimes...'

Sister is looking our way. She's talking about what we can do after we've finished training – she's already mentioned midwifery, health visitor and district nurse. 'Nursing is war work, girls – but war work with a *future*.' Then she pauses and scans the room. Her dramatic monologue is well timed. All our attention is on her as she starts to speak again. 'For a few of you, if you enlist in the QAs, the war will be even closer at hand.' We've heard about the QAs, the Queen Alexandra Corps. They're practically a branch of the armed forces. Some of them have been awarded medals.

'If you think you could travel overseas and withstand difficult conditions, it's a path you could consider.' She pauses again. This woman could easily have been on the stage. 'But the QAs will only recruit the very best newly qualified nurses, so you'll have to work hard, if that's your vocation.' She shakes her head slightly, as if we'd be lucky to make the grade. 'If you *are* accepted, you might be sent anywhere – and that includes fighting on the front line.'

There's a respectful silence. I sit up straighter. The wooden slats have made my back ache but now I feel a cord of excitement flow through my whole body – I'm ready to spring to my feet. I love that word – *vocation* – it sounds so vital. Every nerve in my body buzzes in time to the rhythm of her talk about *fitness* and *fortitude*. After dinner, there'll be a visit to the wards where we'll work for the next three months. We've learnt about hygiene, sanitation and bed baths, so I'm ready for excitement now.

Next to me, Doreen fiddles with a hair grip. 'I'm already qualified to be a midwife.' She smiles grimly. She more or less delivered her youngest three siblings. 'I think District Nurse sounds the most exciting, don't you? If there really is a future, that is... I suppose you'll go for fracture work.'

'Well, I did think that, but now I've changed my mind.' We file out and I wait a few seconds till she looks back at me.

'What do you want to do now then?'

'I want to join the QAs.' I curtsey and she laughs.

'Yes, I can see you doing that. But what about your boyfriend?' Her eyebrows crinkle with concern.

'He says that when there's a war on, you've got to do your bit to help. Anyway, it's not up to him, is it?'

'That's a very modern view.' She has a tinge of envy in her voice. For a second, I think of the bank and Brenda who finally got married to Bill last week, just before he left for his army training.

*

A reply comes when I've given up expecting it. I've got a week off between my first and second rotations and I'm at home. The letterbox clicks and Helen appears. She holds out a heavily postmarked envelope. 'Well, who would have thought? The postal service must have risked heaven and earth for this!'

I take off my coat and hang it back on the hook. 'For me, I take it?'

'Good news, I hope, but if not, you'll come and tell me?' She holds onto it until I nod, then she hands it to me. 'Good luck.'

'I'll be in my room.' I try not to shake as I climb the stairs holding the manila oblong between my thumb and forefinger like a delicate flower. It's a paper miracle. I shut the bedroom door firmly behind me.

I finally looked at the photo Daddy sent me on the afternoon I last saw David. It's true that his hair was thinner than I remembered and his nose more prominent, a bit like Helen's. But his smile was still warm, and his eyes had the mischievous spark that used to make me laugh. I propped it up on my bookshelf. That's where he looks down at me from, as I hold this new letter. It's so slim and light, yet it's here, against the odds.

I place it carefully onto the bedside table, my patterned paperweight holding it down while I get into bed. I swing my legs up and drag the eiderdown over them. Then I adjust the pillows. Everything is very deliberate – almost rehearsed, but it must be right. I release the letter from the paperweight and peer at the scrawl on the envelope – characteristically spiky. My throat is dry, and the room feels muffled, so I get up to open the window. The air has the mushroomy scent of moist leaves which I breathe in deeply. This is it.

My dear Eva it begins. My eyes dart ahead. *I've no idea if you will receive this or not.* Who's this? *I've heard so much about you.* I turn over the second sheet feeling crushed with disappointment that it's not him. It's signed *Uncle Harold*. I remember the edge in Daddy's voice when he talked about Harold. And now, here he is, writing to me. But why? I grip the paper tightly – fear creeping over me – and scan the page for mention of Daddy – anything. Why isn't he the one writing?

I can't tell you how delighted we were when Arthur turned up. My stomach unclenches with relief. Thank God – he's there. *And your grandparents were overjoyed that you had at last written...* I turn over. At last – his name again. *Arthur settled with us for several months but missed home. He felt compelled to join the Active Veterans Guard. It's what you call the Home Guard in England.* Ah, I see ... I should have realised he'd miss England and then wouldn't be able to get back. So, he did something for the war effort over there. Despite his age – and however mad he thought the last war was, he stepped up, like I want to. And he's alive.

I read on. *I've sent your letter onto Arthur in Newfoundland.* Newfoundland! *To hear from you will keep him going. We're all very proud of him and I'm sure in time he'll write to you himself...* Then the last lines:

When all this is over, your family in Canada hope you and your sister will visit us. We pray the day will come when we'll be together. Your grandmother wept with joy when we got your letter. Sending you all our love...
I let the news sink in. A huge wave of joy seeps into me. If they're proud of him, then so am I. He's helping out – and he's safe.

I hear Helen and Mummy downstairs. I'll tell them soon, but just for now I sit quietly letting Harold's warm words wash through me. They're all there – my family in Canada, waiting for me! I look up at the photo again and smile.

You've done it now, Bunny – you really have, he says, smiling back at me.